D0291377

Rich GIRLS

A NOVEL BY:

KENDALL BANKS

Life Changing Books in conjunction with
Power Play Media
Published by Life Changing Books
P.O. Box 423 Brandywine, MD 20613

This novel is a work of fiction. Any references to real people, events, establishments, or locales are intended only to give the fiction a sense of reality and authenticity. Other names, characters, and incidents occurring in the work are either the product of the author's imagination or are used fictitiously, as are those fictionalized events and incidents that involve real persons. Any character that happens to share the name of a person who is an acquaintance of the author, past or present, is purely coincidental and is no way intended to be an actual accountant involving that person.

Library of Congress Cataloging-in-Publication Data;

www.lifechangingbooks.net

ISBN- (10) 1-934230820 (13) 978-1934230824
Copyright ® 2008

All rights reserved, including the rights to reproduce this book or portions therof in any form whatsoever.

Dedication

This book is dedicated to all the haters out there who never wanted me to succeed as a Rich Girl...

Acknowledgements

I would like to first thank my family and friends, whose support has made this book possible. There are way too many of you to name, but I thank each and every one of you from the bottom of my heart. A special, special thanks goes out to the professional team who made it all possible: Azarel, my publisher, thanks for believing in me and seeing my project through. Leslie Allen, thanks for all the late nights. I couldn't have done this project without you. To the rest of the LCB staff, Tasha Simpson, Kathleen Jackson and Nakea Murray, thanks for keeping me on point. Kevin Carr, your graphics are top notch. Thanks for the hot cover.

Now, thanks to my new LCB family. Danette Majette (I Shoulda' Seen It Comin and Deep) Tonya Ridley (The Take Over and Talk of the Town) Capone (Marked) J. Tremble (Secrets of a Housewife, More Secrets More Lies, Naughty Little Angel) Chantel Jolie (In Those Jeans) Ericka Williams (All That Glitters) Tiphani (Millionaire Mistress and Still A Mistress) Nissa Showell (Reign of a Hustler) Mike Warren (A Private Affair) and anyone else I failed to mention. Thanks for welcoming the new kid with open arms. I know I'm with the best team in the industry.

I especially want to thank all of the distributors who have sold copies of Rich Girls all around the world; Nati and Andy at African World Books, Hakim and Tyson at Black and Noble, and to the many other independent booksellers across the country. Also I thank all the African-American bookstores for pumping this book. Last but not least, whether you've given technical, moral, or emotional support during this project, I thank you.

If you get a moment, stop by the LCB website and post a comment@ www.lifechangingbooks.net. Let me know what you think of my debut novel.

Peace,

Kendall Banks

Rich Girls For Life!

Here's What People Have To Say...

"Rich Girls will take you on a drama filled journey with realistic characters that you'll either laugh with, cry for, or want to slap some sense into!"

-Darren Coleman, Essence Magazine Bestselling Author of Don't Ever Wonder and Do or Die

"Rich Girls is a sizzling tale filled with shock it to me drama. What more could a reader ask for?"

-Three Chicks on Lit

"Once a woman gets addicted to the good life there's hell to pay when the money runs low. The streets won't be able to resist what this novel has to offer."

-Azarel, Essence Magazine Best-selling Author of Daddy's House and Bruised

1

Nadia

The moment my professor looked at the clock on the wall, I closed my pink tablet, ready to jet out of class and meet up with my girls. After making his last statement, everyone hopped up and placed yesterday's assignment, as he instructed on the right hand corner of the desk.

I made my move toward the door with a dumbfounded look on my face. Shid… I'd forgotten all about the assignment and my final due to my fucked up work schedule and my late night rendezvous with my man, Day-Day.

Day-Day had bread, plus it was the legal kind, so I was gonna force myself to stay in love. I stopped and laughed at myself, thinking, *love- huh! Why should I keep trying to fool myself*. Day-Day was simply a partial paycheck- needed to help me pay last month's rent. It was already the first week of May, and I hadn't even paid for April. Sadly, it seemed to be the story of my life. I had to make some moves before I got kicked out.

Just as my slight depression crept up on me, the ringing of my cell snapped me back to reality. "Yeah," I answered, knowing it was Jewell's impatient-ass.

"Where the hell you at? We were supposed to meet at three o'clock."

"Listen, chick, I know you have nothing else to do but go to the spa, shop, and spend money all day. But on the real, I wasn't born with your last name." I switched my raggedy-ass phone to my other ear so I could push the button on the elevator to the parking garage. "I was in school, damn it! Try'na have a career someday. Some of us need a job."

"Don't get mad at me because I don't have to work. Now how long before you get here?"

It was one of those days where I needed to get my words across. "Look here, Jewell, everybody wasn't born with a silver spoon in their mouth like youuuuuuuu." I put emphasis on the word you, so she'd get my point. "I'm getting in the car now. Be there in twenty. Bye."

I hung up thinking about what I'd said. It was true. I did need to keep a job, and grind out my school work, so I'd become a CPA. I had one hundred and two credits, and needed twenty-eight more to get my undergraduate degree. It seemed like I'd been in school nearly twenty years. This part-time shit wasn't really getting it, but what else could I do. My parents had given up on me. Disgusted is what they called it.

Both my parents were former educators, with thirty years plus in the game. Of course they were distraught three years ago when I dropped out of UNLV to hang out and party with Jewell. Or let me say, before I was put on probation for too many low grades. Either way, it was the worst mistake of my life. Here I am, twenty-two years old, on my way to being a part-time student for the next five years, and working at the MGM Casino for ten dollars an hour. *Great life*, I thought, as I turned onto Paradise Road.

Oddly, the Vegas strip seemed to be more crowded than usual for a Thursday afternoon. The streets buzzed with black limo trucks and high dollar cars. All of which put my old-ass Nissan 240SX to shame. It was pitiful how I'd driven the same beat-up car for the last five years, while Jewell was on her third Benz. This month, her father had upgraded his baby girl to a SL63 AMG. Ugh! The thought of spending $140,000 on a car made my stomach tighten. Not to mention, she rarely even brought her Porsche Cayman out the garage.

My thoughts must've had me oozing with envy, cuz somehow I ran the light, and almost passed the restaurant. I looked up at Manchelli's before turning the corner and zipped into the parking lot. I couldn't help but shake my head. Jewell was so booshie. I'd be willing to bet the entire forty dollars in my pocket, that she, not Tori, chose Manchelli's, a place where we'd spend at least seventy bucks a piece just for lunch. No matter what, I vowed that I'd get up on Jewell's tab today.

Before I knew it, I'd parked and walked into the restaurant, where some guy was eyeing me down as I strutted toward Tori's waving hand. She was standing up at the booth, waving like I couldn't see her, or her new set of tits. I swatted my hand her way, motioning my girl to take a seat. That shit was embarrassing; especially since the lettering on her t-shirt, CAN'T HANDLE THIS seemed a bit over the top for the type of restaurant we were in. It was bad enough the guy was still following me, trying to get my attention, and my face wasn't even in order. For starters, I wasn't glossed up, nor did I even have on eyeliner. That was a big no-no, when hanging out with two fly broads.

"Excuse me, beautiful…"

"Uh huh." I stopped abruptly to ask, "Yeah?"

"You seem to be in a rush. Got a minute?" the dark-skinned gentleman asked. He stood with his hands tucked inside his pockets.

"Depends," I responded.

I looked over at my girls, to see if they were giving up any facial expressions. As the youngest of the crew, their opinion always mattered to me. Besides, Tori could spot a nigga with money on contact, so I really wanted her to give me a sign.

Before I knew it, my stalker's cell rang, so he handed me his business card and mouthed, *call me*. I nodded back and stepped further toward Tori's embrace.

She used her favorite term of endearment. "Bitch, trash

'dat card," she roared, and snatched it from me like I'd stolen something. "He ain't 'bout shit…and ain't drivin' shit. I saw 'dat nigga when he pulled up. Huh! Chrysler!" She frowned. "'Dat mufucka even walk broke."

"Oh." My expression sorta apologized for being so ignorant.

"What's up, baby girl?" Tori shouted real hood-like. It seemed as if her negative attitude switched immediately. "You ain't been hangin' and you certainly ain't checked on a mufucka." As usual, she smacked in between each word. "C'mere…lemme look at you."

Tori grabbed me by the wrist, and stared me down like a new product in a clothing store. She twirled my petite body and ended with a firm stare at my short, trendy hair-do, which framed my miniature face perfectly.

"Now you know we gotta rep to uphold in Sin City. Fly hair is a must. Especially when you rockin' short shit." She patted her twelve hundred dollar lace front wig, and did a sexy dance, eventually bumping into our cute bald-headed waiter in the process.

We all laughed and sat down, ready to order, before starting our weekly get money chatter. As usual, by the time we finished ordering, you woulda thought three big football players were sitting at the table, instead of three chicks trying to keep our figures. For me, I was a buck twenty, and fit perfectly into my size twenty-seven Rock and Republic Jeans.

For Tori, she always ordered loads of fattening pasta, in hopes of thickening up a little. In her line of work, the fatter her thighs, the more loot came her way. Jewell, that broad was another story. She ordered all kinds of unnecessary shit off the menu just cuz she could. Her money was right, while mine was tight- real tight. But as usual, I acted as if money was no big deal, and ordered just as much as the other girls.

I ended with my favorite, "Ciroc on the rocks, please."

"I'll have another Belvedere and orange juice." Jewell raised her glass for a toast toward the waiter, complimented by a crazed grin.

He frowned slightly, but kept it professional. "Anything else?"

Our sexy waiter seemed extra polite, so I figured commenting him on his bulging bi-ceps was a no-no. He was sorta cute, but obviously broke. A waiter, "Nah," I said to myself. That was the last thing I needed, a broke nigga. *I can do bad all by my damn self*, I thought. Suddenly, Jewell broke my train of thought.

"So Nadia, what took you so long to get here?"

"Girl…traffic. That shit was thick."

"Yeah, I know. But what did you expect. The fight is Saturday night. So you know all the ballers started rolling in today. Just wait until tomorrow. We bound to meet somedamn body worthwhile this weekend." Jewell stopped, opened her make-up case, and powdered her cheeks. "I don't give a fuck if it's Mayweather, Allen Iverson, or Sweet Dick Willie. I just wanna fly out in somebody's G-5 by Sunday."

"Is Kenny gonna be the mufuckin' pilot?" Tori joked. "'Cause the last time I checked, you had a man, and he surely don't own a jet!"

"Fuck Kenny! I'm taking care of his ass, so I call the damn shots. And I do need some extravagant shit in my life right now, like a G-5. Besides, my father's jet isn't always available," Jewell replied.

"Bitch, if you wanna ride in a G-5, you gotta get you a pair of these," Tori commented, plopping her Double D's on the table. She'd only had them about five weeks, but they looked gooooood. Little did she know, I wanted some too, but didn't have the money to get any.

"Nadia, I thought you said you were gonna make yo' consultation appointment," Tori asked me.

"I will," I lied. "Your insurance covered the bill?"

"Bitch what insurance. I ain't got 'dat shit. Plus I heard you gotta have back problems or somethin' for 'dat. Get 'dat nigga you layin' up wit' to drop some cash. Tell 'em you need a new set of tits for him to suck on."

I didn't have the guts to tell her Day-Day wasn't dishing out the dough like she thought, and that I hadn't snagged anybody else with money the way she and Jewell could. Tori was my cousin from Watts, a district in L.A., so she was way more exposed, and dealt with all kinds of lying-ass dudes. Although only a year older than me, she'd seen the evils of the world, and had the answers to most relationship issues, so I looked up to her.

"On the real though, I'm gonna upgrade and get me some of those," I said, pointing to her breasts.

"Girl, I'm tellin' you these tits are a investment," Tori repeated. "And, I'm gettin' a tummy tuck in September as soon as the summer is over. Hell, a bitch is in heat right now, and can't miss all the action 'dats 'bout to go down over the next couple of months." She then stood up. "Oh, and before I forget, let me show y'all bitches my new tattoo." She lifted up her shirt and turned around, showing us a tattoo that said the words '*Paper Chase*' going across her lower back.

"See when niggas read 'dat shit, they gon' know what time it is," Tori said, sitting back down.

We laughed, then turned our attention to Jewell, who banged her fist on the white linen table cloth.

"Okay, listen to this," she uttered, typing into her Blackberry. "I already told Kenny I was helping Tori move this weekend, because I can't be locked down with all these fine men coming to town. Plus…I got us VIP passes to the hottest party in town!" She waved the exclusive passes in the air as if we weren't allowed to touch the treat.

"Who's party?" I asked anxiously.

"Mr. Sean Carter himself. Who else?" Jewell asked.

"Dammmmmmm. How'd you pull that off?"

Jewell ignored me and kept punching the keys on her Blackberry with a vengeance.

"I bet you had to get yo' knees dirty," Tori joked.

"Nope," Jewell replied, scrutinizing her perfectly polished nails.

"Then how?" I asked again.

"My little secret." Jewell smiled.

I wanted to say, yeah right, Jewell. We all know how well off your daddy is, and that he'd probably pulled some strings to get you the tickets. He was the CEO of Givens Music Group or better known as GMG, and knew every celebrity in the music business. Mr. Givens made millions, and had no problem with giving his baby girl, Jewell, the best that life had to offer.

I decided against preaching to my girl, when all of a sudden three females from the kitchen staff showed up at our table to assist our waiter. They bombarded us with all the great smelling dishes, and fresh breads. Tori and I moved all the unnecessary table fixtures around, trying to make room for the plates, while Jewell dialed Kenny's number and left a nasty message right in front of everybody.

"You got exactly five minutes to call me back, damn it!" she shouted, causing a scene. "And bring me another damn drink," she instructed a waiter from another table.

The waiter's eyes widened. "S-u-u-u-r-e."

Tori and I laughed at how she was requesting service from any and everybody in the restaurant. She had even started snapping her fingers at numerous service workers. It soon became obvious, Jewell had really lost her cool. That was her thing…she was known to throw temper tantrums at the drop of a dime. I just watched as Tori watched Jewell. We both thought she was crazy, and knew her spat with Kenny would escalate as it always did. I decided to dig into my food, just in case Day-Day didn't lace my pockets for the weekend, and I ended up eating Ramen noodles and biscuits for breakfast, lunch, and dinner. At least Jewell had this bill, so I dug in.

If I didn't know better, I woulda thought Tori had a bun in the oven by the way she was stuffing food in her mouth. It was hard to believe her father and my father were actually brothers. We were born from the same genes, but totally different worlds. I watched her closely as she slurped up the pasta like a scavenger. Huh, no class! Then I looked over at Ms. High Sadity Jewell, who cut her food like she was in an etiquette class. I laughed though…cuz I loved being with my girls.

Twenty-five minutes into our meal, Jewell picked up the phone and called Kenny again. This time, all hell broke loose.

"Who's the bitch in the background, Kenny!"She paused while he spoke into the phone. "Yeah right, muthufucka! I heard a female's voice!" Jewell stood up and shouted, attracting the attention of anyone in a five yard radius. "Who's the bitch! Who's the bitch!" she repeated. "I will fuck you up, Kenny! Where are you?"

Her face boiled with anger as I moved my hand back and forth, trying to motion her to lower her tone. It was a loss cause cuz she had already flipped. I hated when Jewell's spoiled personality showed. She was used to getting her way, and didn't care who watched, listened or commented.

Before I knew it, she'd thrown her linen napkin onto the table, and hollered for Tori to take her to the pool hall. She said she knew that's where Kenny would end up, and wanted to be there when he got there. I stood up too, requesting the bill, so Jewell could pay before we all left. Unfortunately, she hit me with five words that hurt me to my heart.

"You got the bill, right?"

Her defying look told me I'd better say yes. She was heated. Besides, I didn't have the guts to tell her I was broke, and couldn't afford the bill. For all she knew, I was getting money just like they were.

"I got it," I said softly. "Why you gotta go, Tori?"

It took Tori a few seconds to respond. She stood bent over the table, trying to stuff more fettucini into her mouth.

"'Cause 'dat bitch got her license taken last night for drivin' drunk again. But I'm sure her pops will pay somebody off by tomorrow. So she'll get it back. Go home and rest up for tomorrow night," she told me.

"I can't. Day-Day is taking me shopping." I lied, hoping she'd be proud of me.

"Oh, well I'll call you later. Lemme get 'dis drunk bitch outta here."

Tori grabbed a piece of garlic bread for the road, and gave Jewell the let's go thumb. Jewell threw on her Christian Dior shades and barged her way in between tables, headed toward the front door like a mad woman, while Tori followed, fixing her short mini which showed off her firm butt cheeks. I on the other hand, sat with a lump formed in my throat thinking about the $370.00 bill which had just been handed to me.

With only $40.00 cash in my pocket, there were only two options. Get up and leave, or use my Visa, which I estimated having about $350.00 left in credit. It was the same available credit I'd planned on using to clear up my balance at school. Like a pussy, I took the easy road.

I handed the guy my Visa and slammed my head onto the table thinking about my life. There had to be a better way. Maybe Vegas wasn't for me? Maybe school wasn't for me? Then again, maybe Tori and Jewell weren't for me? I contemplated hard for nearly three minutes.

"Miss…" the young waiter finally interrupted.

"Yeah," I answered, never even raising my head.

"Your card was denied."

I looked up and nearly cried inside. "Oh, give me a sec," I said with confidence. "I'll give you another card."

My options swirled around in my head. *Call Day-Day, or make a run for it?* I contemplated hard cuz my parents had taught me better. So really there were no other choices. Respect and honesty were their golden rules.

Sigh after sigh, I wondered how to explain things to the waiter once he came back. He'd given me my space with the expectation that I was going to be able to pay. I mean who would come to Manchelli's and not manage to handle the bill?

A few seconds passed while I watched him shuffle his way carelessly around the restaurant. It was at that moment, I became convinced. I looked to my left, then my right. I hated going against my upbringing.

Suddenly, I lifted my body from my seat, took a deep breath, and pretended to search for something inside my purse. With a quick scan of the room, I realized there weren't any eyes on me. Like Marion Jones, I jetted from the table, knocking over a chair in the process. At once, four yards away, my waiter's eyes met mine at the same time.

That was it! How would I explain to my father that I'd gotten locked up for skipping out on a bill? At the thought of my father, my feet shuffled even faster, knowing I had to make a clean getaway. I glanced back one more time, just in time to see the waiter waving and running behind me.

My heart raced, but my speed was perfect. I dashed out the front door, down the spiral staircase, and straight out onto the street. With each increased huff, my reflexes caused me to continuously look behind me. Luckily, I had managed to mix into the walking street crowd, trying to figure out how the hell I was gonna get back to my car.

Why do I keep getting myself in these situations, I thought. I picked up the phone and called Day-Day's ass, ready to tell another lie.

2

Tori

I stepped up to the dirty full length mirror inside my bedroom, smiling like a pastor during Sunday tithes and offerings. Always tootin' my own horn, I knew my body looked good as shit in the new $300.00 deep purple corset 'dat I'd just copped from my weekly visit to Agent Provocateur. They knew me by name up in 'dat mufucka. Every time I rolled up in there, I always dropped at least a 'g' on new lingerie, so a bitch was definitely considered VIP.

By the time my eyes made their way down to the matchin' purple thong, I'd started to do a little dance, which instantly caused my big voluptuous-ass to bounce. Beyonce didn't have shit on me. I'm queen of the fuckin' booty clap, and could make any nigga come up off they paper whenever I performed. Shit…and 'dat was only one of my many talents.

Born and raised in the grimy streets of Watts, I'm what you would call a hood chick, and more importantly a certified hustler. A fuckin' thoroughbred in the money makin' business. Ever since I was thirteen, I'd done it all, from sellin' dope to stealin' cars, and didn't have plans to retire anytime soon. Hustlin' is and always would be in my blood, and I was out to get mine by any means necessary. 'Dats why I knew when I moved to Vegas three years ago, makin' money would be a piece of cake. And so far my predictions were on the money. Sin City had definitely been good to my pockets.

Comin' from a cramped, roach infested house in the projects to a nice two bedroom apartment twenty minutes from the Vegas strip was a serious upgrade, but I didn't have plans to settle. In my mind, I still had a few more dicks to suck in order to be livin' in an 8,000 square foot mansion like 'dat spoiled bitch Jewell. From my count, I was only a testicle away from the good life, especially once I was done wit' my latest hustle.

With the thought of Jewell's crazy-ass, I wondered what happened between her and Kenny at the pool hall. Knowin' 'dat I had some important shit to do 'dis evenin', I ain't have time to fool around wit' 'dat crazy girl, or be her rowdy sidekick like I normally did when she went postal. I'd dropped her ass off at the front door of the pool hall and burned the road up, headed home to my latest gig. I couldn't help but think…one of these days Kenny was gonna kick her ass for flippin' out like 'dat all the time. 'Dat bitch needed to take some anger management classes! For real.

Hearing my annoyin'-ass Mexican neighbors argue for the third time today immediately caused me to snap outta my trance. I often wondered when them funny talkin' mufuckas ever got any sleep, 'cause all they do is argue, play 'dat loud-ass La Bamba music, and fuck. Today wasn't a good day to disturb me.

"Will y'all damn Amigos shut the fuck up over there!" I yelled, and banged on the wall at the same time. "Don't let me have to call immigration on y'all mufuckas." I knew they heard me through the thin-ass walls, but didn't give a fuck. I'd had enough of they asses for one day.

While I waited to see if the arguin' would continue, Lil' Kim's old school song, *Big Momma Thang* suddenly started to play. It was my ringtone…and had certainly become my theme song.

I used to be scared of the dick
Now I throw lips to the shit
Handle it like a real bitch
Heather Hunter Janet Jack me

Take it in the butt yah yazz wha

All I could do was smile because she needed to pay me my royalties for describin' me wit'out permission. Well, except for the part 'bout bein' scared of the dick. I ain't never had 'dat problem.

I walked over to the bed, then picked up my new I-phone. "Who 'dis?"

"Yo, Tori. This Q. Me and the crew are at your door."

I looked confused. "Then why the fuck didn't you knock on it. I ain't no damn psychic, nigga."

"I did. You didn't answer."

My eyes instantly shot toward the wall. 'Dat loud- ass yellin' from next door is probably the reason why I ain't hear nothin', I thought. *I'ma fuck them damn taco eatin' mufuckas up one of these days.*

"You live in apartment 226, right?" Q asked.

"Hell no dumb-ass. I'm in 224. No wonder I ain't hear shit. Look, I'm not payin' you to be fuckin' up. I need perfection."

"My bad. I guess I wrote down the wrong..."

Before he could even finish, I hung up. I didn't have time for excuses. 'Dis was business, and time was money. My money.

Checkin' my appearance in the mirror one last time, I made sure my expensive wig was in place, then checked to see if my Double D's were still sittin' nice and high, before walkin' out of my bedroom. After finally hearin' the knock, I strutted toward the front door, checked the peephole, then opened it nice and slow.

Q's eyes said it all, along wit' the other two dudes he was with. "Damn," they all seemed to say at the same time.

I turned around and gave a little model spin, rubbin' my hands across my thick thighs. "Yeah, I look good don't I?"

"I can't wait to shoot you again," Q said, lickin' his full lips. "You look even better this time." He sat his professional-looking camera down on the table.

Q was a director who I'd met three weeks ago at Vegas' highly acclaimed porn convention where we clicked instantly. It had always been one of my passions to make my very own sex tape, and Q was gonna help make 'dat dream a reality. We'd already completed the first half of the short film, and already had tons of niggas lined up to buy my shit the moment Q edited, and put the final touches on the movie. If 'dem bitches, Paris Hilton and Kim Kardashian could become famous off they tapes, then so could I. My sex game would run circles around they shit.

I looked at Q and placed my index finger into my mouth. "You wanna be the one inside my pussy 'dis time, instead of behind the camera, don't you?"

I wasn't known for being shy, especially when being around a fine-ass dude like Q, whose dark skin and beautiful smile reminded me of Morris Chestnut. I could see him swallowin'…hard.

"Tori, you're crazy. Hey, speaking of the film. Let me introduce you to Vince. He's gonna be your partner,"Q said.

When my eyes shifted to the wide nose, pale lookin' dude, I didn't waste anytime showin' my disappointment.

"You mean to tell me 'dis the person I'm supposed to fuck?" I asked. "Oh hell no. What happened to the Jamaican dude from the other day?" I didn't wait for his lame response. "Dis not what the hell we agreed on, Q!" I shouted. "I told you I wasn't into no red niggas. How the fuck am I supposed to cum like 'dat?" Shit I was already a red bone so I liked most of my niggas nice and charcoal.

Vince seemed offended, but I wasn't in the biz of carin' 'bout his or anyone else's fuckin' feelings. I'd given Q a thousand dollars as a down payment to shoot 'dis shit, so I wanted my moneys worth. I was too close to the end for him to fuck somethin' up. Wit' a three thousand dollar balance remainin', he needed to come correct, or get ghost.

Q scratched his forehead. "Yeah, I know. I'm sorry Tori, but the actor from the other day pulled out on me at the last minute."

"What the fuck does 'dat have to do wit' me? 'Dat shit ain't my problem!" I yelled. "Well, if I'm supposed to fuck the red dude, then who is 'dat?" I asked, pointin' to the third guy, holdin' a large black duffel bag.

"Oh, that's my assistant, Trevor. He's here to help do things like oil you all up, and whatever else I need," Q said.

"Nice to meet you, Tori," Trevor spoke, preparin' to extend the tripod.

"What? So, you don't care 'bout oilin' niggas wit' dicks?" I asked.

Trevor smirked. "Hey, welcome to world of pornography. And no...I'm not gay if that's what you're thinking."

Shit, oiling another nigga up...you could've fooled me. "I think I want a refund," I stated, givin' Q an evil eye. I still wasn't satisfied; maybe because I really had no intentions on payin' him the balance anyway.

As I continued to dig into Q's shit, I noticed Vince slowly takin' off his pants. Stoppin' in mid sentence to see what the hell he was doing, it wasn't long before he dropped his boxers, and exposed the biggest dick 'dat I'd ever seen. My mouth immediately fell open, and my eyes opened wider than the size of a cue ball. I'd fucked plenty of niggas in my time, but had never seen anything like 'dis in my life. My clit began to throb instantly.

Is 'dis mufucka part horse or some shit, I thought as I continued to stare at his long, thick shaft. *If his shit is like 'dis now, I can only imagine what it looks like once it's hard*. It had to at least be twelve inches.

"Are you still not into red niggas?" Vince asked, makin' his dick jump up and down.

It almost had me hypnotized. "Wit' a dick like 'dat, I don't give a shit what color you are now." I finally turned to Q with a smile. "Where do you want 'dis to go down? I'm ready to fuck."

He returned the smile. "Let's start in the bedroom."

Like clockwork, Trevor carefully picked up the tripod and movie camera before headin' to my room. They all seemed to be on point, so I smiled my approval. But inside, I laughed wickedly, 'cause I still wasn't payin'.

$$$

Twenty minutes passed, and everythin' was finally in place. Wit' both of our bodies butt naked and oiled up, Vince and I were laid on top of my king-sized bed and ready to get things poppin'. Q had made a stupid-ass suggestion 'bout us gettin' inside my bed, but I looked at 'dat nigga like he was retarded. Even though I knew my apartment could use some serious spring cleanin', it was one thing up in 'dis bitch 'dat was never dirty- my sheets. I loved sex and would damn near fuck anywhere, but I had one strict rule when it came to my bed. Never allow a man inside. The thought of my ass rollin' around on mufuckin' pubic hair was nasty as shit.

At 'dat moment, I looked over at Vince to see what type of pubic hair he was workin' wit', 'cause I hated the nappy-ass kind 'dat looked like fuckin' taco meat. However, my hair inspection was instantly cut short when I saw 'dat his dick was finally fully erect. *Damn*, I thought. A part of me wanted to fuckin' salute, 'cause 'dat shit looked just like a tall-ass flag pole. I couldn't wait to feel it inside of me. 'Dis was sure to be my best hustle yet.

"Okay, guys, here we go. Just have fun with it," Q instructed, before closing one eye and gazin' into the camera.

Shit, he didn't have to tell me 'dat. I was gonna enjoy

'dis. It was show time.

"Look Vince," I instructed, while playin' wit' my clit. "Remember, I need a lot of noise. People who buy 'dis shit are freaky. They want sound effects. Understand?"

"Got it." He stroked his dick and pushed me onto all fours.

"Oh, we startin' like 'dis, huh?" I barked like a dog to let'em know 'dis was 'bout to be some animalistic type shit.

"We doing multiple positions in this scene," Q shouted from behind the camera. "Action!"

All I heard was Q's finger snappin', and the sound of Vince's condom slappin' his meat as he popped it on. No lube was needed. His dick already had me soaked, so I pressed back forcefully on what I'd been dying to get. Without hesitation, Vince drove his manhood into me as deep as possible. In return, I shouted like crazy!

"Oh yes! Damn it!" I started poundin' and absorbin' every inch of Vince. "Work i-i-i-i-t-t-t-t-t," I repeated at least three times in the first three minutes of our grindin'.

It didn't take long for a light sweat to produce in light of our increased speed. Hump after hump our bodies meshed well under the instruction of Q's hand signals.

Although Vince had me doggy-style, I kept throwin' my ass back at him like I was runnin' shit, all the while still givin' up facial expressions into the camera 'dat would help skyrocket my sales once the word got out.

"Fuck me, baby!" I said, pickin' up more and more speed. I reminded myself of a dog in heat with one leg raised midway in the air, gettin' fucked under a tree.

Wit' my ass jigglin' like jelly, Vince grabbed hold wit' a tight grip, then moved his hands down to my best asset, my thighs. He was feelin' good from the sounds of his moans. I just hoped he wasn't 'bout to let loose, 'cause his strokes had become suddenly violent and uncontrollable.

I held on for dear life while Vince banged my back out. It felt gooooooooooder than a mufucka, but I couldn't allow myself to cum. My movie, my money, and my scam was all on the line. I needed 'bout ten more minutes of fuckin' to make my shit complete. Q had already told me wit' a little bit of creative editin', he could use the quick fuckin' scenes a few times throughout the movie, so I kept bangin'.

Luckily, within the next few seconds, Trevor moved near us and motioned for me and Vince to change positions. Vince had to be nudged, but 'dat was a part of the original plan. We had four more positions to complete for 'dis final session. The Cowgirl position was up next, my favorite. I straddled him forcefully, and rode Vince like an unstoppable bull-ridin' bitch at a top notch rodeo. My hands swung in the air as Q zoomed in for a facial close-up. I ate it up, givin' mad exotic expressions, even slobberin' at the mouth.

"Yes...... Daddy," I hollered sensually.

"Ahhh!" Vince moaned back. "Ahhhhhhhhhh!" he repeated, as his eyes rolled up into his head. "I-I-I-I can't..."

I kept on mashin' him wit' my pussy dance. After a while, Vince's hands gripped my calves as he thrust harder and harder. I knew 'dat nigga was 'bout to mess my shit up and cum...so I abruptly slid back off the dick. He looked at me like I was crazy until Q started yellin' 'bout gettin' 'dis shot. We both listened to Q yell for about two minutes. Vince lay there lookin' pissed, blue balls and all, while I secretly had one eye on his still erect dick.

Before I knew it, we were on the cold, fake hardwood floor doing our oral sex scene. The dick was good, but I'd had enough. While I laid flat on my back, Vince squatted above my forehead allowin' my tongue to sweep his balls. Amazingly, Q had gotten on the floor and had the camera right up in the mix.

I started thinkin' 'bout the remainin' steps for the tape.

Editin', then mass producin' was next. I'd already been promotin' on several sites on the internet, so knew I needed 'bout 1,000 copies to start. The thought of makin' $15,000 'dat easily had me pumped. Wit' just the thought, I sucked Vince off like a hungry lion. I grabbed a hold of his nuts and licked him like a crème-filled lollipop.

"Ohhhhhhhhhhhhhhhhhhhh!" he hollered. "What the fuck! Damn girl!" I kept suckin'.

"Damnnnnnnnnnnnn, girl. Oh-Oh-Oh."

Punk ass, I thought. I went ballistic, and made Vince cum like crazy. I was done. I needed to make my next move. I hopped up like I was in charge, and pushed the stop button on the camera. "Q, change in plans. I want you."

"What?" he asked in disbelief. He stepped away from the camera.

"I don't care if you don't want yo' face in it. But I need you to make me cum, so I can get the facial expressions I know I'm capable of givin' up." I looked over at Vince like he was a sorry son-of-a-bitch.

I threw him his pants straddled across my chair. "You and Trevor may leave," I instructed.

They both looked at Q, who was in shock. Luckily, he wanted me, so I knew I had'em.

"Bet. I'll take it from here," he stuttered. He peeled off a few hundred for Vince, then looked at me. "I'm paying Vince now so I need that final payment before I leave."

I nodded real sexy-like with my arms crossed.

Within minutes, Vince and Trevor had exited wit' an attitude, and left me and Q ass-naked in the middle of my bedroom. I had them leave everythin', oil and all, lettin' them know everythin' else would be taken care of. We'd set the camera on automatic and laid missionary style across a large chaise in the middle of the room. My plan was to fuck Q, quick and fast, and send him to the showers pussy whipped.

No sooner than he entered, I felt his meat throbbin'. So I grinded like a chick on a mission, clutchin' him by the ass. Q was obviously a wanna-be porn star, 'cause he started chantin' all these obscenities into the face of the camera.

"Oh, you made a big mistake!" he shouted. "You gon' get fucked, baby! You gon' get what you asked for!"

"Oh yeah." I pounded back like he hadn't said shit to intimidate me. "Fuck me, Q. Show me what'cha got, boo."

All of a sudden my insides exploded. Q started gyratin' slower and his dick pulsated. "Ahhhhhhhhhh," he moaned.

I started throwin' the pussy at him real hard, but he seemed to be in a comatose state. I let loose 'cause I knew I had the nigga. I went out with a bang, and ended with a loud opera-like holler. "Ahhhhhhhhhhhhhhhhhhhh. Shit!"

I felt good 'bout releasin' 'dat much cum in one settin'. My only disappointment was 'dat I couldn't capture 'dat on camera. 'Dat woulda been a helluva sellin' point, I laughed, pushin' Q off of me.

"Okay, Q. Go get in the shower. I got somethin' for you when you get out."

'Dat stupid nigga just smiled; didn't even ask what, why or nothin'. He just got up and walked real funny into my bathroom, with cum drippin' down his left leg. The moment I heard the shower water start, I hopped into action. I quickly removed the tape from the camera, and ran into the kitchen. The Swanson's TV dinner was perfect. I snatched open the freezer, ripped open the TV dinner, and replaced it wit' the tape.

Next, I called Brisco, the neighborhood gangster. He'd been waitin' for my call. "Yo, c'mon. You outside?" I asked him anxiously.

Briscoe confirmed, so I ran to open the door. As soon as he entered, I heard the shower water stop. I rushed into my room wit' Briscoe on my heels and packed up all Q's shit. By the time he walked out wit' a towel wrapped around his waist, I was fully dressed in an over-sized sun dress.

"I thought you had something for me?" he asked with a puzzled expression.

"I do," Briscoe answered on my behalf, while exposin' his .357 from his waist.

"You know, Q, I'm just not satisfied wit' the tape." I had my hand clutched beneath my chin. "I thought about it. It's just not gonna work."

His eyebrows crinkled. "What do you…"

Briscoe cocked the gun.

"Here's all yo' shit, Q. I'll be in touch if I ever need yo' services again."

"You bitch," he mumbled, while grabbin' his duffle bag and camera equipment.

As Q headed out the door, I beamed inside. Little did he know the tape he recorded was missin' from the bag. I had a copy from the first session, and had another editor on standby who agreed to charge me $300 just for puttin' it together. In addition, my guy who was gonna produce the first 1,000 copies was on standby too.

I counted out two crisp hundreds and handed it to Briscoe. He'd served his purpose so I was ready for 'dat nigga to go, too. I had moves to make, I snickered walkin' him to the door. Mentally, I calculated. I'd spent $1,200 out of pocket total, but stood to make a mint.

"Dats what the fuck I'm talkin' 'bout!" I shouted, slammin' the door behind my accomplice.

3

Jewell

I was ready for war as I walked inside the Cue Club on Sahara Avenue like the fucking Terminator. Kenny knew better than to fuck with me, and I couldn't even believe he'd allowed this shit to get to this level. On my way to the pool hall, I just knew he was going to have enough sense to call me and plead his case, but to my surprise the only phone call I got was from Nadia. She was always trying to get me to calm down whenever I got like this, but she should've known by now. Once I got to the edge, there was no pulling me back. Besides, I wasn't going to let Kenny's sorry-ass get away with me hearing some bitch in the background. Didn't he know? I was the only one allowed to cheat in this relationship…not him.

Even though Kenny's favorite table was all the way in the back, I didn't even have to take but a few steps before I spotted him…and he wasn't alone. I was ready to take off my eight hundred dollar pair of Christian Louboutins and throw them right in his face when I saw him talking to some ugly-ass Wesley Snipes looking girl over in the corner.

Is this nigga smoking crack now? He had a lot of nerve being all bunned up with someone else, especially considering how she looked. I could've easily posted up in another area and watched them from a distance, but fuck that. I needed to know the focus of their little conversation. I stormed over to the two lovebirds and invaded their personal space.

"Muthafucka, you got about three seconds to tell me

what the hell is going on or it's about to get crazy up in here!" I yelled over the loud Ne-Yo music playing in the background.

I couldn't believe he looked surprised to see me. Didn't his dumb-ass know that I knew exactly where to find him? Hell, I knew his routine like the back of my hand.

"Jewell, what are you doing here?" he asked, stepping away from the girl. Even though I was mad, I loved the way his tall 6'3 frame still managed to tower over mine. At 5'9 myself, I needed a big man.

He tried to grab my arm, but I snatched it away. "Don't fucking touch me. So, is this the bitch I heard in the background? Huh? You trying to play me for her ugly-ass?"

Kenny's mouth began to twitch a little bit, which was a sure sign that he was pissed, but I could have cared less. He was the muthafucka cheating with this Too Wong Foo looking broad, not me.

"Who in the hell are you calling ugly?" She-Man asked.

I glanced around the hall like I was looking for someone. "Umm…you bitch." I pointed dead in her face. "I don't see anybody else up in here looking like a transvestite."

Kenny immediately stepped in between us as the girl tried her best to get near me. "Get the fuck out the way, Kenny. I ain't about to let this bitch keep talking shit about me!"she yelled out.

"Yeah, Kenny get out the way," I repeated. I wanted She-Man to try her hand.

If it was one thing I wasn't worried about, that was getting my ass kicked by another woman. I'd taken several private Tae Kwon Do and Jiu-Jitsu classes, and even though I didn't stay around long enough to get a black belt, I knew how to defend myself. Luckily, my long jet black hair was in a high ponytail, just in case this bitch managed to find her way in my face. I took off my shoes, ready for battle.

Kenny held both of us back with each of his hands. "I'm not going anywhere." He looked at me like a disappointed parent. "Jewell, what the hell is wrong with you? Are you drunk…again?" His eyes were piercing.

I couldn't believe that he was taking up for this girl and not me. "What the fuck did you just say to me?" I stared at the small gap between his two front teeth.

"He asked if you were drunk, bitch!" She-Man added.

"Shut up Alyssa. I'll handle this," Kenny replied. Taking a chance, he let her go, but made sure to have a firm grip on my arm, as he quickly led me to the other side of the pool hall.

"I told you before to take your hands off me!" I screamed.

He wasn't listening. He continued to hold my arm until we were a good distance away. "What the hell is your damn problem, Jewell? Coming up in here starting shit." He finally let me go. "I thought you were supposed to have some class. You up in here acting like a straight hood rat."

"Well, if you weren't in here cheating on me with that gorilla looking bitch, then I wouldn't have to act like that, would I? What the fuck do you expect me to do? Greet you with open arms." Before he could even answer the question, I went off. "So, your broke-ass can take money from me, ride around in that brand new Range Rover that I just bought, lay up in a rent-free apartment, but still have the audacity to cheat on me?"

I waited for him to answer, but he didn't. "Are you crazy? I take care of your ass! Any man would love to be in your fucking shoes. On top of that, I look damn good." I paused, giving him time to look at me.

Coming from a mixed Hawaiian and black descent, my honey coated complexion and long legs had plenty of modeling agencies beating down my door at one point. Not to mention, my natural 36C cups, tiny waistline, and slender build would've looked great on any runway.

"That fucking alcohol got you trippin' as usual. I'm not cheating on you. That's my damn Godsister. She just flew in from Chicago," Kenny finally said.

"You expect me to believe that shit?" I glanced back over at Alyssa, who surprisingly was talking to another guy. *Does that dude need glasses or some shit*? But even though she looked like the bottom of my shoe, I did have to admit her body was a work of art. Eyeing the cheap looking mini skirt she wore, her big ass and thick thighs, did have me a little jealous.

"Yeah, I do expect you to believe me, 'cause I don't have a reason to lie. She's never been to Vegas, so I told her to come visit me for a few days. Oh, and yes, that's who you heard when we were on the phone earlier."

"So, why the fuck didn't you just tell me that?"

"I tried, but you just kept yelling. Why in the hell would me and her be at this pool hall if I had something to hide?"

"Muthafucka, it's not like you knew I was coming. I didn't exactly get an invitation to this little celebration."

Kenny sighed…hard. "Listen, I'm tired of you and these fucking tantrums that you constantly throw when shit don't go your way, or when you assume I'm up to something. Why do you always have to act like that? Maybe you need to slow down with that bottle."

Nigga are you crazy? I could use a few shots of Grey Goose right now.

"Besides, I thought all you cared about was money. That's all I ever hear. You damn sure don't care about me," he added.

As mad as I was, he did have a point. *Maybe I am*

overreacting a little bit. Besides, this nigga would have to be a fool to cheat on somebody like me, I thought, as my warrior mode turned me into a shy, little girl. I walked up to my man and threw my arms around his waist. I had once again made an ass out of myself, and needed him to forgive me. Just like with my father, normally all I had to do was poke my lips out a few inches and things would go my way.

"I'm sorry, baby. I guess I just love you too much…that's why." I looked at him and batted my long eyelashes, then gave him a sad puppy dog expression. But for some reason it wasn't working this time.

He snatched my arms away abruptly. "I'm also tired of you throwing what you do for me up in my face. If the shit ain't genuine, then don't do it, Jewell. I mean let's keep it real. You don't even have a fucking job, so it ain't your money…it's Daddddyyyy's."

I was heated, especially by the way he dragged out that last word. "For a broke muthafucka, you sure are talking a lot of shit, Kenny. My father's money is my money. Don't get mad at me because your family ain't paid," I shot back. "You know what, if you don't want any of the perks you're getting, then hand the shit over. As a matter of fact, give me the keys to that shiny new truck outside. You know…the one I just put $4,500, 26" rims on."

His mouth began to twist again, but he didn't respond.

"That's what I thought. You ain't got shit to say now, huh? Don't ever come out your mouth about my money. Shit, I didn't hear you talking like that when you just asked me for that thousand dollars."

His tone changed almost immediately. "When are you gonna give me that money anyway?"

"When I feel like it." I turned around and made my way back over toward Alyssa, with Kenny following a few steps behind. He probably thought I was trying to start some drama again, but the only thing I was about to start was a bar tab.

Surprisingly, Alyssa felt it was necessary to walk toward us and invite herself into our conversation.

"Can I help you with something?" I asked. For some reason, I still felt uneasy about this whole Godsister shit.

She ignored me and looked right at Kenny. "I'm hungry. I need money for some buffalo wings or something."

"So, pull your own damn money out, or go get some," I added. "I saw an ATM machine on my way in."

"Jewell, please we just squashed this beef," Kenny replied. He then looked at Alyssa. "Why don't you ask the nigga you were just talking to if he can get you some wings? Who was that anyway?"

She frowned. "Umm…the last time I checked I was grown, and why do you even care anyway?"

"Yeah, why the fuck do you care?" I badgered.

Kenny shook his head. "Man, both of y'all are tripping. I'm just tying to make sure I protect my Godsister, that's all."

He seemed a bit uneasy about the whole situation, but quickly tried to get himself together. Trying not to stress about it anymore myself, I put my shoes back on, and headed toward the front door. I'd wasted enough of my time.

Damn, I wish Tori had waited for me. Now I gotta catch a cab.

"Where you going?" Kenny asked.

I turned back around. "You're at your favorite spot, so now I'm going to mine."

"Well, I can go drop Alyssa off at the crib if you wanna stay here and chill with me. You haven't let me beat you in a game of pool yet anyway."

I laughed right in his face. "You can't be serious. Why in the hell would I hang out at a place like this? You know better than to suggest some stupid shit like that."

"Well, can you at least apologize to my Godsister for the way you acted?" he pleaded.

I looked at She-Man one last time before letting out a huge laugh. "No, I can't. Call me when you take her ugly, broke-ass back to the airport." And with that said…I was out.

$$$

Forty minutes later, I was in my element. But I also wanted to come across the damn table when the scrawny Asian dealer turned over her card to reveal an ace of hearts. An ace of hearts that went perfectly with the king of clubs laying in front of her. Fucking blackjack! This was her third time in a row getting twenty-one, and I was beyond pissed. Why I'd gone against my better judgment and sat down at this table in the first place was beyond me. Well, actually it was probably the alcohol, because I never played at tables with Asian dealers. They were known to be ruthless with their long- ass nails and jade bracelets, and never offered a smile while they scooped up your life savings. I also didn't play at tables with dealers who had on lots of jewelry or blank expressions. I only liked fat or older white people, because they were always happy for you when you won, and very sympathetic when you lost. Yeah, I had a lot of rules when it came to gambling.

I need to start counting cards or something, I thought, as I took my fourth Belvedere and Cranberry to the head. Normally, the Casino gave out the cheap liquor for the free drinks, but not for me. I'd been coming to the Bellagio forever, so they knew I always got the top shelf shit.

"Are you betting on this hand, Miss?" the dealer asked me, with no expression of course.

Looking down at my last fifty dollar chip, I knew it wasn't enough for the minimum two-hundred dollar bet. Besides, this fried rice bitch had managed to take me for $3,000 in a little over an hour, and I didn't have anymore cash. The shit was embarrassing.

"No, I need to get some more money. You completely drained me," I replied trying to force a fake smile. In reality smiling wasn't something I wanted to do at the moment. All I wanted was one or two things…more chips or more drinks, and didn't care what order they came in.

Sliding off the chair, I took a few steps over toward some slot machines, when one of my favorite Pit Bosses called out my name.

"Hey, Jewell, why are you leaving so soon? You just got here?"

"Oh no, Frankie. I'm not leaving. Just gotta get more money."

Knowing there was only a certain amount that I could get out of the ATM machine, and I didn't particularly want to get a marker, there was only one person who could make things happen for me. My father.

I went into my new Yves Saint Laurent bag, and pulled out my faithful Blackberry. Knowing it was late in the evening, I hoped like hell my father was still at his office. Crossing my fingers, I hit the speed dial number and waited patiently for the phone to ring. Actually, money was the only thing I had patience for anyway.

Seconds later, I was crushed when the call went directly to his voicemail. Crushed because when calls were routed there, it usually meant he was gone for the day. Crushed because more than likely that meant he would be at home.

"Fuck," I said to myself.

I was dreading the phone call already, but knew it had to be done in order to get the gambling monkey off my back. Normally, when I called my parent's house my mother always answered the phone, and I wasn't in the mood for her shit today. My mother and I never had a good relationship because she said I was a spoiled, ungrateful bitch, and made sure I was reminded of that almost everyday. However, I knew the name calling was just a way to cover up all the jealously that consumed her body everyday. She was and always would be jealous of the relationship my father and I share, which had caused a great deal of resentment on my end.

Every since I could remember we'd always been in competition for his love, attention and affection. Sadly, that same competition existed up to this very day and would probably continue until somebody decided to give in. Call me stubborn, but this was one battle that I didn't have plans on losing.

I let out a huge sigh as I dialed my parent's number. A number that would never be in my speed dial as long as her ass was living there. The phone hadn't even gotten into a second ring, before she answered...as usual.

"Hello. Givens residence."

I hated her chipper voice. "Is Dad around?"

"You can't tell me I didn't raise you better than that," she belted in an uppity tone. "What happened to speaking to the person who answers?"

"Hello…is my father around?" I was already annoyed.

"You know what Jewell. I should hang up on you right now since you want to be so damn disrespectful. Besides, what do you want with him anyway? Oh, let me take a wild guess, money right?"

Here we go, I thought. "The reason why I called is actually none of your business. But yes. I'm calling because I need some money, so if he's home, can you put him on the phone?" I was becoming even more annoyed.

"Well, the answer to that question is no. It's no way in hell you're gonna keep calling here everyday asking for money, when we already give you $20,000 dollars a month. Jewell, I don't know why the hell you even graduated from UNLV if you don't ever intend on putting the degree to use. I mean, it looks like that was a complete waste of our money to me."

She'd finally struck my last nerve. "I didn't know you'd started speaking French, because everything you've been saying is *we*. The last time I checked, *you* don't give me anything. It's my father's money that takes care of me. The same way it takes care of you. Speaking of jobs, when are you going to get one?"

She immediately started yelling. Now, I'd struck her last nerve. "You're such a disrespectful bitch. I can't believe you're talking to me like…"

I could hear my father in the background asking her why was she screaming at me. It wasn't long before he grabbed the phone. Thank God, he'd stopped the boxing match before it got too ugly.

"Jewell, sweetheart," he said.

My angelic voice was ready to go. "Yes, Daddy."

"Joyce tells me that you're being nasty. What's going on?"

"Oh, Dad, please. You know how your wife likes to exaggerate. It's nothing." I tried to change the subject. "Hey, why aren't you at the office? You always work late."

"Yeah, I know, baby. I was just so tired this morning that I decided to take the entire day off. Besides, I had some meetings at home with your Uncle Louis today."

I was in shock. Ever since I could remember, I'd never known for my father to miss a day at work. "Is everything okay?"

"Everything is fine. I just needed some rest, that's all."

"If Uncle Louis is still there, tell him I said hello." I loved my father's attorney, who'd been around the family for years. He was just like a real uncle. He'd literally watched me grow up.

My father chuckled. "When is Louis not here? He practically lives in this house. I should charge him for rent."

I could still hear my mother yelling something about being disrespectful as my father tried to calm her down. I needed to go in for the kill before she fucked up my chances of getting what I called for.

"Hey, Daddy, I'm in a little bit of a bind. Do you think you could loan me some money? I'm really in need of a few suits for some job interviews that I have lined up." I couldn't dare tell him that I had a slight gambling problem.

He laughed. "Jewell, please stop talking about me loaning you money, because you always say that and never pay me back. If you need money just ask. How much do you need anyway?"

"Umm…about $10,000."

"Wow, those are some pretty expensive suits, don't you think."

"Well, it's only the best for me, right?"

He paused for a brief moment. "Yes, only the best for you. It's late princess. Come by the office tomorrow morning. I'll have the money ready."

It was like taking candy from a baby.

4

Nadia

"Ten more minutes, and I'm outta here," I smirked toward Lisa, the only white female supervisor who I even considered liking in the cage.

She was a certified Diva, showing up in all designer gear, each and every shift. I could never rock the few fly outfits I owned, cuz of the strict uniform policy for cashiers working in the cage. On the real though, working in the MGM cash booth made me feel like a correctional officer in a maitre 'd uniform. *My boring job-priceless*. I laughed to myself. *It's the same thing everyday. Guard the money, until some sinful individual walks up to the booth to cash in. How exciting.*

"How much," a thin, Vietnamese guy rudely asked, sticking his hand through the slight opening in the window. He slammed his chips on the counter arrogantly, like I worked for his ass.

I wanted to shout back. "I don't know muthufucka... lemme count it first." Instead, I looked over my shoulder to see Lisa eyeing me…so I started stacking the chips into piles of hundreds. The fact that I cringe each time a rich Asian muthufucka walks up to the booth, cashing in thousands of dollars, pisses me off. I couldn't understand. Why not me? Why is it that I was so broke? I wallowed in my own pity party.

"Nadia," Lisa called, walking up from behind. I knew she was just doing her job, but I didn't need anybody to count behind me; math had always been my specialty. "Don't forget to ask if he has any markers," she whispered. "You forgot to ask the last person. You've been working here long enough to remember by now."

I gave up a fake smile. "Do you have any markers, sir?"

"No," he snapped, like I was taking too long.

I frowned and counted out his eight thousand like I'd made a new enemy.

As soon as Chung Lee walked away, Lisa felt the need to remind me again about the markers, but she didn't have to. I knew that people take out markers from the casino on credit, which is just another way of borrowing cash. That is, those who are lucky enough to have good credit. They get credit on the spot, and in return we give them cash, with the hopes that they lose their asses off. People are supposed to pay back the money when they cash in their chips from winnings, but instead, most fools just cash everything in, and wait for the MGM to take money out of their checking account. *Losers*, I thought.

This was the perfect time to ask Lisa about an opening. "Hey Lisa, you know if they have any dealer positions open? Lord knows I need more money."

"Not sure. But I'll ask around."

Instantly, my eyes zoomed in on the clock. "Two more minutes," I mumbled.

Just then, a glimpse of Day-Day walking near the five dollar slot machines reminded me that my raggedy-ass car had broken down on the way to work. Just my luck, I needed a ride home on a Saturday night. A party night. A night where all the potential money makers would be out, ready to spend cash.

It was bad enough that I'd missed last night's festivities cuz I had to work. When I listened to Tori babble about the playas she'd hooked up with from the East Coast with all the cash, I became sick.

At the thought of the word cash, I remembered the bag

of clothes I left in my car this morning that was supposed to be going back to the store today on one of my many return sprees. If only Jewell knew how many times I bought outfits just to showboat with her, then pranced the items right back to the register the following day for a return, she would probably be disgusted.

Standing a few feet away, Day-Day smiled at me relieving me from my miserable thoughts of not being able to return my shit for some weekend cash. But I flicked him a nonchalant wave to let him know I was coming.

I gave Lisa a nod, twisted my hands back and forth toward the cameras, and headed out the exit door of the cashier booth.

By the time I clocked out and stepped onto the casino floor, Day-Day had already ruined my night. I watched him stand like a tall, lanky, robot with his hands clutching both arms. On the real though, he was too formal for me. I needed excitement and a little spontaneity. I gazed at him thinking, everything about him always remained the same, even the toothpick wedged in his mouth, which seemed to be a permanent fixture for him. Day in and day out, he chose to have that little stick fixed between his teeth.

I walked up on him with my lips twisted into a nasty scowl. I wanted a rough neck, or at least a man with charisma. A "G", somebody who stopped traffic when he hit the room. Somebody who I wanted to fuck as soon as I smelled the stench from his cologne. Day-Day did none of the above.

"What's up, Nadie?" He puckered and moved close, invading my space.

"Nadie?" I questioned then jumped back. "Didn't I tell you I don't do pet names?" I rolled my eyes and turned away from him.

As usual, Day-Day followed like a lost puppy. "This the thanks I get?" he uttered. "The minute you called to say you needed a ride, I dropped everything. Didn't I?"

I smacked my lips loudly.

"Why you gotta act like that, Nadia?"

"Cuz."

"Cuz what? Speak…you know, talk like normal people. Not like your hood rat-ass cousin, Tori."

"Whatever. I'm just tired." I started walking fast through the growing crowd, my body brushing swiftly past the partygoers and gamblers. "Look, I've been working all day, that's it. No harm intended."

"Yeah, sure. You tired until Jewell or Tori say they wanna go shopping or out to some club."

I stopped in my tracks, put my hands on my hips, and spat. "My biz is my biz! Until you start taking care of me…let me do me!" I pointed to myself like I'd really done something, then turned around and started walking again.

Day-Day stuck his toothpick back in his mouth and followed me to the parking garage.

By the time we made it to Day-Day's Ford Explorer, and jumped inside, I'd already decided that I needed to butter him up. I needed money bad. Although he couldn't contribute what I needed, the goal was to get all he had.

For the average woman, Day-Day's pay would probably come across as decent. After all, he was a senior account manager at Alize Liquor Company and made close to $60,000 a year. He just had no intentions on splurging his hard earned money away. Fancy cars, rims, jewelry, or anything of flaunting status didn't excite his ass. It just wasn't him.

"Day-Day, I need some money," I blurted out, as he turned the corner out of the lot.

He looked over at me and stared. The fact that he gave me no response bothered me.

"Nadia, I'll help you out whenever you need it. But I don't have any money to give you if you think you're gonna go spend it at some store with your girls. You know, I wish you would just be yourself and not try to keep up with them all the damn time."

"Why would you think that? I got bills to pay, damn it."

"Well in that case, I got you, then."

"That's the problem. I wish you had me a little more."

He looked at me like I was ungrateful. "Look, I suggested that you move in with me so you could save some money. Hell, I even gave you a key, but you were the one who said no. So, don't try and make me feel guilty."

He was right. Because of Tori's crazy advice, I did decide not to move in with him. "So, since you didn't move in, can I have my key back now?" he asked with a slight smile.

Now I looked at him with a crazy expression. "Yeah, whatever."

"I just thought I'd ask." He tapped my leg and laughed. "Oh, I almost forgot to tell you, I'm taking you out tonight."

I slouched deep down in my seat, and prayed I'd heard incorrectly. Out? With Day-Day? On a night like this? Instantly, I reached for my phone which was on its last leg, and text Jewell as quickly as I could. For some reason, my old-ass Razor phone took me forever to type. I looked over at Day-Day, angry as hell wondering why I didn't have a Blackberry or something a little more fancy.

Jewell- Sumthin came up. Can't go 2night...Don't bother callin.

I raised my palm to my forehead, closed my eyes, and pressed the side of my face against the window. Of all fucking nights.

$$$

Luckily, I'd fallen asleep and didn't have to listen Day-Day preach to me all the way to my house. The last words I heard him say was that we had to get to my house fast, so I could shower and get dressed…and that we were going out as a couple. On most days I would've told him to kiss my ass, and that I was going out with my girls. But shit…I needed money! I sat up in my seat and thought, *Damn...a bitch will do anything for a few dollars*.

When Day-Day whipped his truck in the parking lot to my complex, my eyes did a double take. I saw my mom's car and frowned, but the fact that my dad was standing near the fire hydrant shaking his head meant trouble. I grabbed my purse, and popped open the door before Day-Day could even stop the truck.

"What's the problem, Dad? I see it all over your face," I said, moving closer in his direction.

"I tried to get your car towed here, and I gave them your phone number to call me once they got here, so I could pay."

"Sooooooo." I crossed my arms just as he did. There always seemed to be a power struggle going on between the two of us.

"They never called. You know why!"

"Noooooo," I belted with all the sarcasm I could muster.

"Because your house phone is turned off, again! See, if you hadn't been fooling around with that niece of mine, and graduated, you would've landed a decent job! And you'd be able to pay your bills on time like normal people! Here, take your key. You figure out how you're going to get the car towed here."

I never reached for the key being handed my way. Luckily, both my mom and Day-Day walked over toward us about the same time.

"Nadia, didn't I meet this young man before?" my mother asked. "Dashawn, right?"

"Yes, Ma'am," Day-Day interjected politely.

My mother smiled. I remember her telling me how much she liked Day-Day the first time she met him. She commented on how respectful he was, and all the wonderful things she liked about him.

"I'll get her car towed here," Day-Day finally said to us all. "I can handle it. And I'll make sure her phone gets turned back on, Sir."

My father nodded Day-Day's way and hurried to the car. My mother waved like a school girl and smiled like a laughing hyena. I hated that about her. She always seemed too happy. Thankfully, she rushed off, shouting my father's name.

I walked toward my apartment, which sat nestled near the back of the first floor garden-style apartment complex. The neighborhood seemed to be unusually quiet for a Saturday night. I guess that's why when Tori came flying around the corner in her red, customized convertible Corvette with her music blasting, it shocked us all. Especially my father, who was slowly pulling out of the lot in a nasty funk.

"Hey, Uncle Earl," Tori stopped abruptly and shouted from her car. She knew he hated her. "Call me the next time you throw somethin' on the grill." She laughed crazily, and zoomed forward, zipping into the only available handicapped space. Her V8 engine made it sound like the militia had arrived.

My father never responded.Instead, he kept going.

I knew drama was headed my way cuz Tori couldn't stand Day-Day and he triple hated her. Just as I opened the door to my place, Tori grinned, hopped out of her car and made her way inside behind us.

"Day-Day, what's up, love? Long time no see. I missed

you," she joked with a sheepish look.

"Same here," he dryly responded.

When I scanned the form-fitting dress she wore, and the way she'd worked her make-up to perfection, I knew she was trying to score big for the night.

"So what's up, Tori?" I wanted to see what she needed, so she could go.

"Same shit different night. The question is…what's up wit' you, bitch." She removed her Fendi sunglasses and shot Day-Day a scrutinizing look. "We hangin' tonight, right?"

"Uhhhhh…"

Tori looked at Day-Day, who was already staring her down in disgust.

"Day-Day is taking me out. I promised him…"

"What the fuck!" she yelled to my backside, cuz I'd already taken off down the hallway headed to my room. I was too embarrassed to look her in the eye.

"Why you not goin' wit' me and Jewell?"

"Cuz."

"Cuz what! I hate when you say 'dat one word shit! Cuz," she mocked. "If I didn't know better, you couldn't tell me you was enrolled in 'dat stupid-ass college." She slipped her shades back on, even though the sun had gone down and not a drop of light filtered through my room. "Cuz," she repeated again. "'Dats some stupid soundin' shit. And you wanna say I'm hood. Ha!"

"Look, Tori, I'm going with Day-Day. That's final."

"Ughhh! Nadia, you disgust me," Tori added. "I thought I taught you better. But yo' ass is just weak. Plain ole' weak!" Tori spoke extra loud, hoping Day-Day would hear her.

I hit the button on my CD player nailed to my bedroom wall to drown out our voices. "I'm not weak! I gotta plan. He's giving up some serious paper so I can buy that house in

Pinehurst that I've been looking at."

Tori's eyes lit up. She knew Pinehurst was a new, exclusive gated community out in Henderson. I sighed, hoping she'd let it go. Maybe she'd think I was getting something out the deal. I needed her to simmer down. Besides, if I chose to go with Tori, I knew I'd need at least four hundred to get me through the night.

"Tori, is everything about money to you? Do you give a shit about anything else?" I asked.

She pointed to the tattoo of Chinese lettering on her arm that was the symbol for money. "No, bitch, I don't," she quickly answered. "Look, what you need to do is go out there and give 'dat nigga some magic pussy."

"Magic pussy?" I hated not knowing what she meant. I seemed to always be the last to find out everything. "What's that, Tori?" I stood with my hands on my hips.

"Go out there, fuck 'dat nigga on the couch, hard! He gives you cash…and then he disappears!"

Tori grabbed her purse and laughed her way through my living room. She stopped just to laugh at Day-Day directly in his face, who was still in the same spot where we left him, then headed out the door.

"Have fun fuckers." She continued laughing hysterically, then closed the door.

"Day-Day, I'm hopping in the shower," I shouted, and shut my door too. I was pissed...extremely.

$$$

Two hours later, I'd forgotten all about Tori's nasty remarks. I knew she and Jewell were talking about me like a dog, but the feel of Day-Day's dick print against my leg, dismissed any thoughts I had of them. The music blared, while we grinded to the slow beats on the dance floor.

The Sky Lounge wasn't my original choice, but I was

glad Day-Day chose it. It sat off the strip, away from all the major happenings, and gave me a chance to just be me.

I had my hair gelled down to my head. It wasn't the cutest, but short, wet, and smelling good was how Day-Day liked it. Maybe cuz it gave him enough room to kiss all over me. As he licked, and allowed his tongue to dance all over my neck, the four shots of Ciroc had me feeling wild.

While we danced, I thought about the fact that Day-Day was a good, hard working man. He wanted to be with me solely, and wanted the same from me. I just needed to get my mind off finding a money man, just so I could keep up with Jewell and Tori.

My other issue was a big one! Day-Day had the right tools down below…he just needed to know how to work it better. I needed excitement and variety. I smiled up at him thinking…*he could be taught.*

All of a sudden, I felt a hand swipe my butt. I stopped completely, turning to locate the culprit. Strangely, no guys were nearby. I did see a thin, fair-skinned young woman standing behind Day-Day circling him slowly.

"So, to catch up wit' a nigga, I gotta spot you at a club?"

I started thinking, *damn, I gotta fight a hoe on a night when I got my freak'um dress on.*

"Oh, what's up, Monae?" Day-Day spoke hesitantly.

He reached over and gave up a tight embrace. My face reddened and tightened the moment he kissed her cheek. The chick was pretty, but had nothing on me by the way she was dressed. I wouldn't be caught dead looking like that. No sexiness at all; baggy jeans and a white-tee. Shidddd…

Then I checked out her hair. Yeah, she had the good stuff. It was short like mine, but curled naturally, no chemicals needed. Still in all, I had her beat.

"What's up, baby girl. You need a kiss too." The

Monae chick grinned, showing her sparkly set of braces. I saw nothing funny, so I didn't crack a smile. "She a feisty lil' thing, Day-Day. I like that though,"she continued.

I thought, *damn...she talks more like a dude than a girl.*

Day-Day pushed me aside like he was protecting me. "Monae, this my girl, Nadia. Nadia this my cousin, Monae."

I held out my hand, sorta calling a truce. Monae grabbed my palm softly and ended with a light kiss. "Pleasure is all mine."

I snatched my hand, and shook it several times, like I needed to shake off some deadly disease. Monae reminded me of Day-Day in a sick sorta way. Their light complexions resembled fair-toned Indians. Day-Day was tall, but not athletic at all. While Monae's tall, lanky body appeared to be slightly muscular, as if she worked out a lot, or even played a little ball. A certified dyke if you ask me. I laughed at myself when I thought, she sure was pretty though.

Beyonce's, *Get Me Bodied*, blared through the speakers, and the dance floor swarmed with partygoers.

"That's my shit!" Monae announced, and started dancing in a circle around me and Day-Day. All of a sudden, she pulled out a red bandana and waved it in the air like one of the dudes off a Lil' Wayne video. The crowd was feeling her. Hell, she made the party!

I was feeling good, so I swayed back and forth into Day-Day's body. By the time he got into the grove, Monae had grabbed a bottle of VeVue Clicquot champagne off the waitresses tray, and handed her three crisp hundreds.

I thought, *Monae got it like that , huh.*

Before long we were all fried with alcohol and having a blast. We'd danced nearly five songs straight. I'd kicked off my Nine West shoes, and had my dress hitched up a little too far, when Monae whispered in my ear, "You doing some real sexy shit!"

I tried to brush it off, cuz Day-Day had me wet between the legs from grinding up on my coochie. Although Monae made me feel a lil' weird, my nipples hardened a bit. Next thing I knew she grabbed me by my waist. The feel of her rings on every finger had me looking down to verify that her hands were indeed gripped to my sides, and that she was riding my ass.

Day-Day stopped in mid-motion and walked off the dance floor. I followed, feeling a lil' crazy about what had just happened. "What's wrong, Day-Day? I thought we were having fun?"

"We are. You just don't know about my cousin that's all. Why you let her ride up on you like that? Don't tell me you didn't realize that she was gay."

"I'm half drunk, Day-Day, but yes, I did realize it." I could tell he was serious, so I was careful not to make light of the situation even though I was curious. "If she's so bad why would you leave me on the dance floor with her?"

He nodded a forbidding look my way. "Just watch her."

"I find it odd that you're saying that about your own family."

"So what if she's family. You don't know about her."

"Know what about me?" Monae interrupted. She invaded our space knowing she'd caused a problem between us. "What? That I'm fine as hell, and fun to hang around," she replied, with a small grin. "Look, I'm about to roll…but Day-Day you better keep in touch, nigga."

She grinned again then reached out to give him a pound. He grinned back with a half-ass smile.

"And you, miss lady…this is for you." She passed me a piece of paper. "Dats my number. Keep in touch. We all family. If you Day-Day's girl, we should be friends too.

Peace."

Yeah, I'm thinking we should, I thought to myself.

When Monae walked away, I had mixed emotions flying through my head. One, she had my attention. Two, she knew how to party. But three, I knew from the disturbing look on Day-Day's face, I needed to stay away.

I crumbled her number in my hand as if it were trash. But the moment Day-Day turned his head, it was shoved deep into my pocket with the thought, *I'd definitely call her*.

5

Tori

"Damnnnn, you got a fat ass, girl!" a dude yelled from a car window.

"I know it, nigga," I shot back, doin' my normal sexy strut down Las Vegas Boulevard.

Shit, he didn't have to remind me. I knew I looked good in my leopard print Dolce & Gabbana cocktail dress 'dat hugged my body like a glove. A dress 'dat I'd worn on purpose, 'cause I certainly had plans to jump on somebody's dick before sunrise. Not to mention my four-inch stilettos and lack of underwear had my ass sittin' extra high and jiggly.

It was the night of the big Floyd Mayweather vs. Oscar De La Hoya fight, and I couldn't believe how many damn ballers were in town. I almost got whiplash every time a Bentley or a Mercedes Maybach would pass by. It was obvious 'dat money was floatin' around like a fuckin' airborne virus, and I definitely wanted to get sick.

My cheesy smile showed my excitement. "Me and my pussy gon' work 'dis town tonight, baby!" I yelled makin' sure I switched even harder.

As crowded as the strip was, a few people looked at me like a mental patient, but I paid it no mind. I was a professional gold digger and damn proud of it.

When I made my way past the Excalibur Hotel, my cell phone started to vibrate. Knowin' exactly who it was, I rolled my eyes before grabbin' the phone out of my Chanel clutch. "What up?"

"Tori, girl, where you at? I'm missing out on all these

John's out here. You were supposed to be here fifteen minutes ago. I need those pills."

"Look, I'm walkin' toward yo' spot now. Calm the fuck down." **CLICK**

Even though I knew I was never on time for anythin', mufuckas rushin' me was a big pet peeve of mine. *The only fuckin' time schedule I ever plan to be on is my own,* I thought, placin' the phone back in my purse. *I don't know how people do 'dat 9-5 bullshit.*

However, before I could even put the phone back in my purse, it vibrated again. Now 'dis bitch was really testin' me.

"Didn't I just fuckin' tell you 'dat I was almost at yo' spot? Keep on callin' me, and you ain't gettin' none of 'dis shit!" I shouted into the phone.

"So, I'm sitting here waiting on you to go into this party, and you're about to fuck some dude," Jewell responded.

I gave a slight smile. "I would love to have a big fat dick up in me right 'bout now, but no, girl. I thought you was Dixie."

"Dixie. Who the hell is that?"

"Dis prostitute I fuck wit'. Yeah, word on the street is 'dat she supposed to suck the best dick in town, but I doubt 'dat very seriously, 'cause mufuckas ain't seen me in action."

"So, you into women now?" she asked. "Does Dixie suck clits too?"

I wanted to hang up on her ass. "Bitch, don't get mad when I smack the shit outta you, okay. You know I don't get down like 'dat. Are you drunk?"

The crazy thing is even though I wasn't into chicks now, back in Watts I did it all. One could definitely call me a tri-sexual back then.

"Well, I'm just asking. I never know what your crazy-ass is into. Hey, where the hell you at anyway? I'm standing outside this club looking like a damn groupie, and you should know I don't get down like that." The phone suddenly became muffled. "Hit me."

"You lyin', bitch. I thought you said you were standin' in front of the club. Yo' ass is somewhere gamblin'."

Jewell laughed slightly. "What are you talking about?"

"Don't play dumb wit' me. I just heard you say hit me when you tried to cover the phone. You playin' blackjack, ain't you?"

Jewell's second giggle confirmed my suspicion. "I just had to come put a couple thousand on the table before we go into the party."

Between booze and gamblin', 'dis girl had it bad. "Then why fuckin' rush me! How the hell are you on the phone at the tables anyway? Casinos don't allow 'dat shit."

"Don't worry about that. Just worry about getting here."

"I'll be there in a minute. The strip was so packed, I had to park my car on Tropicana Avenue and walk."

"Is Nadia with you?"

I smacked my teeth like a poutin' ten year old. "No, 'dat silly bitch ain't wit' me. She was actin' all dick whipped when I went by her house earlier. Talkin' 'bout she goin' out wit' Day-Day. I can't wait 'til she get rid of 'dat dead weight nigga."

"Well hurry up, Tori. I've already been waiting for twenty minutes, and you know these heels have timers. I don't want my time to be up before I even get in the damn club. Ain't shit cute about walking around a party barefoot."

"Stop buyin' cheap shoes then, bitch," I joked. I knew she wouldn't find 'dat joke funny, 'cause her ass didn't even associate wit' the word cheap.

"Oh, so you got jokes?"

It didn't take much for Jewell to get upset. She was like a tickin' time bomb.

"Damn, it was just a joke. Calm down. Yo' ass could use some dick. Look, I'll be there in a few minutes, but I gotta handle some business first." **CLICK**

Hangin' up on her was the only way I was ever gonna get off the phone before day break. Whenever Jewell didn't get her way she always fuckin' whined, and I wasn't in the mood for 'dat toddler shit. Besides, I wondered when she was gonna realize 'dat temper tantrum stuff didn't work on me anyway.

Finally makin' my way to the corner of Flamingo Avenue a few minutes later, I spotted Dixie, who was pacin' the concrete like a straight crackhead. She even looked like a fiend the way she scratched her neck and bit her nails. Her behavior immediately took me back to the hood.

"Damn, girl, you need a hit?" I asked walkin' up to her wit' a huge grin. When she turned around it was the first time I'd ever paid attention to her figure, which was quite shapely, especially for a white girl.

She swung her long, platinum blond hair over her shoulder. "I can't believe you had me waiting this long, Tori. Is this how you're going to do business from now on?"

My smile faded instantly. "Who the fuck you talkin' to? You better shut the fuck up before you get stomped out here! Don't let 'dis pretty face fool you."

I balled up my right fist, just in case the bitch was feelin' confident. However, when she saw how serious I was, she changed her tone, quick.

"Oh…no, I didn't mean it like that."

We stared at each other for a few minutes, while I tried to calm myself down.

"I didn't think you did," I finally responded. I reached inside my purse and pulled out an empty Newport cigarettes pack, then handed it to Dixie. "You owe me $200.00."

Her thick eyebrows were wrinkled as if she was confused. "Two hundred dollars? For what?"

"What the hell do you mean for what? 'Cause it's ten Ecstasy pills in there, 'dats why."

"Oh, I only wanted one pill. That should hold me over until tomorrow."

'Dat was all I needed to hear before I went the fuck off. "You mean to tell me yo' ass been blowin' up my phone all day for one damn pill. Do you think I would waste my time for twenty dollars?" I snatched the pack back out of her hand.

"But…but I only need one, Tori," she whined.

"Well, you better increase yo' quantity, bitch, 'cause the minimum amount of E pills I'm sellin' tonight is ten. Shit…I ain't got time to be runnin' around all night. Didn't you get the memo? There's a fight in town tonight. I gotta get some paper off these niggas too." I held out my hand. "So, you comin' up off the two hundred or what?"

It looked as if she wanted to cry. "But I only got forty dollars to spare until my next John. The rest of my money has to go to my man."

"Yo' man? Do you mean yo' pimp?"

Dixie shook her head up and down.

Damn, they got pimps in Vegas? I thought all these hoes out here were self employed. Oh, shit... maybe I could be a pimp 'cause I know them crayon suit wearin' mufuckas make money. I made a mental note to try and recruit some girls later on.

"Look, Dixie, time is money. All my other clients just pay and go. If you such a good dick sucker, then go slob on some more knobs then get back at me." When I turned around to leave she called my name which pissed me off.

Jewell is gonna kill me, I thought. "Dixie, I gotta go.

Just go get yo' one pill from somebody else. I'm only dealin' wit people who like to spend..."

Before I could even finish, she was already in her purse. "I already missed three John's waiting on you. By the time I find somebody else, I'll miss even more."

"Not 'dat I care, but you 'bout to get yo' ass beat over some Ecstasy, huh?" I asked.

"You don't understand, I can't perform without it," Dixie replied, handin' me the money. She then looked around like she was already nervous, which instantly made me look too. If her pimp was 'bout to come up and punish her, I needed to get out the way.

See if she was a real professional like me and not a phony, she wouldn't even need 'dis shit, I thought, after quickly countin' the money and handin' her the cigarette pack. "It was nice doing business wit' you again, Dixie. Make sure you tell all yo' friends, 'cause I give nice referral fees."

Givin' me a crazy look as she walked away, I could tell Dixie didn't find my joke too funny, but I did. Wit' a wide smile spread across my face, I placed the money inside my purse, and finally headed toward the club. Ready, willin' and able to shake my ass.

$$$

By the time I arrived in front of the 40/40 Club, located inside the Palazzo Hotel, I wasn't surprised when Jewell wasn't anywhere to be found. I knew she'd pulled one of her spoiled-ass 'everythin' gotta go my way' moves, and went inside the club without me, but it didn't matter. I was the kind of chick who could make moves, and would find a way to make it inside...regardless.

However, it wasn't long before Jewell made her way back to the front door and peeked her head out. By the look on her face, I could tell she was beyond pissed 'dat I was late, but she could go ahead and kill 'dat attitude. I wasn't gonna let her ass fuck up my chances of havin' a good night.

Once Jewell spotted me, she got the attention of one of the front door attendants, then handed him my VIP pass. I was excited when the metallic green badge was placed around my neck, and the red velvet ropes were unhooked so 'dat I could pass through. A bitch was born to be a very important person.

"You finally decided to show up, huh?" Jewell stood at the entrance wit' a bitter expression and a drink in her hand, of course. Her eyes were a little glassy, which was a sure sign 'dat she was drunk or almost there.

"Hey beautiful. I see your girl is here," one of the massive security guards called out from behind me. "You need anything else?"

I turned around wit' a sexy stance. "No, I'm straight, Moe, but don't forget to call me a'ight."

"You know him?" Jewell asked, takin' another sip of her drink.

I turned back around. "No, I just met him outside, but you know how I roll. When I wasn't sure if you were gonna come back to the door, I offered him a sweet deal on some pussy if he let me up in VIP. So, we good friends now."

Even though she tried to act mad, the comment immediately forced her to smile. "Tori, you're such a hoe," she stated in her sophisticated voice.

I shook my ass back and forth, just in case Moe or another cutie was watchin'. "I know. Don't you just love it?"

"Why do you have to be hood all the damn time? I can't go with you anywhere."

"Look, ain't nobody got time for 'dat Fresh Prince of Belair shit tonight, a'ight. Stop actin' all stuck up."

She gave me a friendly push. "Shut up."

Makin' our way to the VIP area, I couldn't help but notice how good my friend looked. Always remindin' me of the R&B singer, Amerie, Jewell's skin glowed in her strapless aqua blue Chloe dress and some hot Valentino heels. Not to mention the iced out diamond necklace and matchin' bracelet she wore made her look even more like a rock star. Yeah, next to me she was definitely one of the baddest chicks 'dat Vegas had to offer.

As soon as we walked inside the plush VIP area, I was completely star struck and could barely keep the drool from oozin' out my mouth. Every A-list celebrity 'dat I admired, from rappers and athletes to actors and even the fine-ass Tyson Beckford, were all sittin' around like we were at a family cookout or some shit. I pinched myself two times, just to make sure I wasn't trippin. Jay-Z had definitely brought out the heavy hitters.

"Girl, I'm so glad yo' father be hookin' us up like 'dis. I'm in fuckin' heaven!" I shouted to Jewell over the loud music.

Jewell took another sip of her drink. "Yeah, I know. I'm not sure what I would do without him."

"I knew I shoulda gave yo' pops some coochie. I could be yo' step momma by now." Jewell cracked up laughin'. "No, I'm serious, 'cause I know yo' momma ain't throwin' it on him like she used to."

"The only thing that bitch throws is his wallet on top of a cash register."

"Shit, at his age I know his ass don't nut no more. But I'm willin' to let him piss on me or whatever the fuck he be squirtin' out instead of cum these days."

'Dis time we both laughed.

"Hey, I gotta go to the bathroom. You wanna go wit' me?" I asked. I hated to leave the VIP area for even a second, but in order for me to make my rounds, I had to make sure my make up was flawless. I also had to check on the new wig I was rockin'. All the long cinnamon colored tresses had to be in place.

Jewell raised her glass 'dat was now empty. "I'll walk with you until we reach the bar, and from there you're on your own."

"I shoulda known," I replied. "Make sure you got some damn mints in yo' purse before you be all up in a nigga's face. Ain't nobody checkin' a bitch wit' dragon breath."

Turnin' around, I only managed to make it a few feet before I spotted two potential candidates. Lookin' at the big titty women up and down, they were perfect for the new scheme I had in mind. I had to make my move, and hoped Jewell wouldn't fuck it up for me.

"Hello beautiful ladies," I said, extendin' my hand. Hopefully my white girl voice was still in tack, 'cause it had been a while since I used it. I could already sense 'dat Jewell wanted to know what was goin' on, so I had to make it quick.

"Hello," they both replied.

It was at 'dat point when I noticed how ugly these two broads actually were.

"My name is Tameka, and this is my assistant, Brandy. Have you ladies ever heard of Fabulous or Ludacris?" I could see Jewell shakin' her head out the corner of my eye. She hated associatin' wit' anyone who wasn't gettin' money.

The two girls looked at each other like they were thinkin' 'bout the answer before one of them spoke up. "Yeah."

"Well, I'm the manager for both platinum selling artists, and I'm always in need of beautiful ladies for their videos. Has anybody else approached you about being in a music video yet?"

"No," both of them replied in unison.

Damn, do these bitches ever say more than one word? "Well that's great because I would love for the two of you to be in the new Fabulous video that's coming out next month.

Do either of you have a manager?"

"Oh my God, are you serious! We would love to be in a video. Shoot, that's why we even came to this party in the first place, to meet some people. Hey," one of them said.

"Ooohh…can you be our manager?" the other asked.

Wow, I thought I was ghetto. What in the hell happened to the shy role? I thought.

"I sure can. I ran out of business cards tonight, but here's my number." I reached inside my purse, and pulled out a piece of paper that already had my number written down. "Call me so we can set up something for you all. I would love to add you to our roster. However, I gotta be honest. There's a $1,000 start-up fee for new clients, which would have to be paid before we send you to any shoots."

"Oh, that ain't a problem. I get $1,500 a month for my child support," the taller girl stated.

"Umm…Tameka, we have to go. We were supposed to met with Fat Joe about his new deal over by the bar a few minutes ago," Jewell butted in.

My eyes told her to shut up. "She's right. I do have to go, ladies, but make sure you call me, so I can get your start up fees right away."

"We will. Tell Fat Joe we said lean back," I could hear one of them saying as Jewell pulled me away. I knew she was going to mess up my scheme.

"Tori, you got fucking problems. You should be ashamed of yourself lying to those girls like that. You know they're too ugly to be in a damn video. You always got a scam going on."

"Don't be hatin' on my hustles," I replied. "Just look at it 'dis way, you like the bottle, and I like to make deals."

"You call that shit a deal?" Jewell asked, finally walking up to her second home.

Before I could even reply, my eyes became glued to a

Boris Kojoe lookin' dude on the other side of the room. From a distance he seemed to be my type…paid. I had to get a closer look. Not even tellin' Jewell where I was goin', I strutted over to Mr. Soul Food himself and got up close and personal. I could care less if he had a woman, and hoped like hell 'dat he didn't have a man.

"You fine as hell, and I hope to get to know you better."

"Are you always this blunt?" he asked, wit' a sexy smile.

Good set of teeth, another plus, I thought. His huge diamond earring almost blinded me. "What's yo' name, sexy?"

"Adrian."

"Well, Adrian, I hope you don't have a girl or a wife, 'cause if you do, you might as well tell her now 'dat you ain't comin' home tonight."

He smiled again. "Don't worry. The only thing I'm married to right now is football."

The juices in my pussy instantly started to flow. "So, I take it you play pro ball, right?" I checked out his physique. He had to be at least 6'5' and weighed quite a bit. At least three hundred pounds.

"Yeah, I've been with the Raiders now for about four years. You trying to tell me that you didn't recognize me?" he questioned me suspiciously then smiled.

A football player in less than an hour…Jackpot, ladies and gentlemen.

6

Jewell

I finally reached in my purse and grabbed my annoying Blackberry, which for some reason hadn't stopped vibrating in the last five minutes. My initial thought was to ignore the damn thing, because more than likely, it was Kenny trying to see where I was. Trying to keep tabs on me, especially since he thought I was helping Tori move. I chuckled at the thought of his dumb-ass actually believing that stupid shit. Since when had he known me to do any type of manual labor? I hated the fact that he'd interrupted me while I was surrounded by my favorite friends...three shots of Armadale.

I had to make this phone call quick. "Yeah," I answered, even though I could barely hear.

Suddenly, it felt like I was going to pass out. "What?" I screamed. "Are you serious? What happened!" I only listened for about three seconds. "I'm on my way!"

Frantically, I took all three shots of vodka to the head and threw a hundred dollar bill up on the bar before looking for my shoes. I'd taken them off about twenty minutes ago, because my time with the painful pumps was up. But for some reason, the designer shoes were nowhere to be found.

"Did somebody take my shit?" I yelled while looking all around the bar. I knew all the alcohol I'd consumed was starting to take effect, but I wasn't crazy. "Fuck it!"

Racing out of the club like an Olympic track star, I ran barefoot toward the front of the Palazzo at top speed, headed for the main lobby. As my feet glided across the cold titled floor, I was prepared to bust my ass at any minute, but surprisingly I never fell. I did however gain the attention of several hotel employees, so by the time I reached the cab stand, everyone, including the hotel manager, a male desk clerk and five security guards were all on my heels. Even though I hadn't done anything wrong, I'm sure they were more than suspicious about my erratic behavior, and weren't going to go away until they had some answers. I didn't blame them though. Everybody in Vegas was always up to some bullshit, so I wasn't an exception.

Finally slowing down, I walked quickly to one of the cabs, and had almost made it to the door when one of the hotel's fat security guards grabbed my shoulder.

"Miss, we're gonna need you to step back in the casino," he stated.

I turned around with a devastating expression. "Why? What did I do?" Everyone seemed to be looking at my bare feet at the same time.

The guard seemed tired and annoyed, and applied even more pressure to my shoulder, which actually started to piss me off. "Miss, I'm only gonna ask you one more time." He looked back at the other guards. "I smell alcohol. She's probably drunk."

"Get your fucking hands off of me!" I yelled. "Don't you have a chicken dinner or a twinkie to get to?" The whole situation was becoming embarrassing, and immediately gained a small audience. "Do you see what they're doing to me? All I'm trying to do is catch a cab. This is harassment!" I looked at the few people who were standing around watching the scene unfold.

The look on the manager's face caused the guard to finally remove his hand. The manager then tried to get better results. "Miss, we just need to ask you a few questions, that's all. It's nothing to get upset about. Have you had anything to drink tonight?"

"Why yes, I have...several of them to be exact. But what the fuck does that have to do with Shamu putting his hands on me?" I pointed my index finger at the fat guard. "I wasn't upset until then." Not even wanting any type of explanation or apology, I continued. "Look, if you're wondering why I was running through your hotel, it's because I just got the news that my sister died, so I need to get out of here!"

Everyone seemed to take one step back at the same time, as tears began to trickle down my cheeks. Little did they know, I wasn't crying because of the lie I'd just told. It took a few uncomfortable seconds before the manager cleared his throat.

"Umm…Miss, I'm so sorry to hear that." Without saying another word, he quickly placed his hand in the air, and signaled for a cab.

When the cab pulled up, no one else said a word as I climbed inside and shut the door. I guess any sort of sympathy or support was out of the question for them, and although it didn't surprise me, it would've been nice to hear.

"Sir, I got a fifty dollar tip for you if you can get me to Country Club Hills as fast as you can," I said to the driver. "1717 Enclave Court is the actual address."

"Is everything okay?" he asked, looking back in his rearview mirror.

Tears strolled down even faster, and I began to quietly sob. Stranger or not, I needed somebody to talk to, especially since I didn't even get a chance to look for Tori before I left the club. Not that she would've cared anyway. Whenever she was on dick or money duty nothing was more important than that. "No, I just found out that my father is sick, so I need to get to him fast." On a normal day, the drive to my parent's house from the strip would've only taken about twenty minutes, but with all the traffic tonight, it would probably take us much longer.

"No problem. I know a short cut."

Finally in route, panic began to set in as I began to think about life without my father. A man who has always shown me unconditional love and support, and who has enriched my life in so many ways. It was going to kill me to see him any other way than what I've known during my twenty-three years, so I knew I had to prepare myself. Besides, I didn't know what to expect.

Reaching inside my purse, I pulled out my cell phone to call Kenny. After hitting the speed dial button, I wiped a few of my tears then waited for him to answer.

"Hello."

I could barely hear him with all the noise in the background. "Where the hell you at, Kenny?"

I could tell he hesitated to answer the question. "Umm…I'm out right now."

"You out. Where and with who? I thought you were staying in tonight?"

"I was. But Alyssa wanted to go out, so I changed my mind. Besides, why are you calling me anyway? I thought you were helping Tori move."

"First of all, I can call you whenever the fuck I feel like it. I told you about coming out of your mouth wrong, but you refuse to listen. Do you get a kick out of pissing me off?"

The cab driver looked back in his rearview mirror again with concern, but kept driving.

"Did you call to argue? 'Cause if you did, I'm not in the mood," Kenny replied.

"I don't give a damn what mood you're in. You and your so-called Godsister are getting on my fucking nerves. Who told you that it was okay to take her ass out tonight?"

"I don't need your permission," Kenny boldly stated.

My eyes bulged. Ever since Alyssa had strolled into

town, Kenny had been getting awfully cocky. "Muthafucka, I own you. Do you hear me?" I yelled damn near at the top of my lungs. "I can destroy you!" Again, the driver looked in his rearview. I know he must've thought I was insane.

"Oh, let me guess. Instead of helping ya girl move, you've been out with Gin and Juice," Kenny replied. "Don't you ever get tired of being drunk?"

He still wasn't taking me seriously. "That's all you think about."

"That's all you do."

"You know what, I'm on my way to my parent's house because I just found out that my father is sick. You need to come be with me…your girlfriend. I could use the support." The line went silent for a minute, before he finally spoke up.

"Can't you just get one of your father's cars and drive yourself? Since this is Alyssa's last night in Vegas, I already promised that I would show her a good time."

I'd had enough. As hard as it was for me, I had to stay calm until I figured out how to get Kenny back for treating me like this. *Maybe I'll hold off from buying those custom suede seats he wants for that truck.*

"No problem, asshole. Have fun," I said.

"Hey, what about that $1,000 dollars. When are you gonna give it to me?"

"You inconsiderate muthafucka. Didn't I just tell your ass that my father was sick! Why would you ask me some shit like that?"

Seeing that the cab was about to pull up to my parent's gate, I hung up the phone, not really caring what Kenny's response was. "I'll deal with him later," I said to myself. Seconds later I instructed the driver to pull up to the call box, and press the button.

"Yes, may I help you?" It was our housekeeper Rosa.

"Rosa, it's me Jewell. Can you open the gate?" I could

hear one the many cameras posted up outside the gate zooming in on the vehicle.

"Jewell, why are you in a cab, sweetie?"

Even though Rosa was from Peru, she'd been with our family for over eighteen years, so my father had taught her how to protect herself and our family well. Taking his protection lectures to heart, Rosa was always very suspicious of everyone.

"It's a long story."

"What is the password?" she asked.

Now I really knew she didn't think it was me. I stuck my head out the window, so the camera could get a better view. "Rosa, the password is pineapple."

It didn't matter that the driver had heard the code because my father normally changed it every week anyway. This week it happened to be the one item that he was allergic to. Now it would have to be changed immediately.

"Okay, Jewell, I'm so sorry. I will buzz you in now," Rosa replied.

Seconds later, the eighteen foot black iron gate finally opened. As the driver slowly crept up the circular driveway to my parent's 14,000 square foot home, I could see Rosa standing at the front door already.

"Well, at least you don't need another code," the driver joked. "This is a nice house. You guys are rich, huh?"

Normally I liked to brag about my dad's money, but for some reason I wasn't in the mood. "I guess you could say that. How much do I owe you?"

He placed the car in park and stopped the meter. "$26.50."

Going into my purse, I pulled out eighty dollars, and handed it to him. "I didn't forget about the tip I promised. Thanks for getting me here so fast." I opened the back door then hopped out, placing my bare feet on the pavement.

"My pleasure. Oh, and don't worry. Your father is going be fine. Just have faith."

After counting the money, he drove away with a smile. It was sad how I had to count on a fucking cab driver to cheer me up, and not my friends or even my so-called boyfriend.I shook my head before walking up the front steps.

"Hola Jewell. How are you, sweetie pie?" Rosa asked with a huge smile. She'd gotten so much better with her English. "What are you doing in a cab? Did something happen to one of your cars?"

"Oh no, I just decided to take a cab over so I could get here faster. The traffic is crazy out there."

"I see. Well, I haven't seen you in a while. Give me a hug."

Being that my own damn mother was never around when I was growing up, Rosa was like my surrogate and I loved her just like family. "Thanks for calling me, Rosa. How's Daddy doing?" I asked after we embraced.

She looked concerned, but still kept her smile. "He's coming along."

"Why am I just learning about this? When did he get sick?"

Rosa looked around before answering. "I don't want to get into that. Let him talk to you."

From that response, I knew I had to find out what the hell was going on.

"Mr. Givens has been asking for you, Jewell. Go on up to the bedroom he's..." She looked down at my feet. "Where are your shoes? Are you sure everything is okay?"

"I'm sure, Rosa. I'm gonna go up and see him. Thanks again for calling me."

"No problem, sweetie."

Walking through the grand foyer with its custom made Italian marble floors, instantly brought back special memories of my dad and I taking pictures on the day of my prom and graduation. Trying not to get too emotional, I placed my purse on the table before making my way up the mahogany colored staircase, and straight into my parent's bedroom. Luckily the door was wide open, because I didn't feel like knocking anyway. I couldn't wait to see my father.

When I walked into the beautiful and spacious champagne colored room, I noticed that my father was in the bed watching T.V., which is something he rarely had time for. I ran straight toward him and into his arms.

"Be careful, baby, I got old bones now," he said, with his usual charming smile. My father looked damn good for his age. At sixty-one he still had smooth butter pecan skin and a nice body. Not to mention, his thick goatee.

"Oh my God, Daddy, are you okay? I was worried sick about you."

"Yeah, I'm okay." He rubbed the back of my head like he always did to comfort me. Then out of nowhere, I got a light tap on my back. "I smell alcohol, young lady. You were supposed to be done with that stuff. Haven't you wrecked enough cars or gotten into enough trouble?"

I couldn't even look him in his eyes. "I know, Daddy, but I was out celebrating. I think I got the job that I was telling you about the other day. It's not something I do all the time anymore." It killed me to lie to him, but I hated to be a disappointment.

"Really, that's wonderful. What company is this with?"

"Dad, I'm not here to talk about me. I'm here because of you." I had to hurry up and change the subject. "What's wrong? Is it something I should be concerned about?"

"Oh no, sweetheart. I'm gonna be fine. I'm just a little overworked at the office, that's all. I guess all those artists at the label are taking its toll on the old man. My doctor said its just stress. Nothing major."

I finally raised my head. "Are you sure, because you're never sick. I'm not used to you being like this."

"I'm fine, baby. I promise."

"Well, I'm gonna make sure you get plenty of rest from now on. We can't have you all stressed out."

He shook his head. "Yeah, my doctor has definitely put me on bed rest for a while, so I guess I'll be doing work from home."

"Oh…no, you're not doing any work from home. All you're gonna do is rest," I demanded.

"Jewell, the label can't run properly if I don't do any work. Not unless…"

"Not unless what."

He flashed the same charming smile. "Not unless you finally take over and run the business for me."

My father knew I hated talking about the label, or any kind of work for that matter. He'd asked me a thousand times to take over as CEO at the record label, but for some reason I just wasn't interested. I guess I would rather sit back and enjoy the perks from all the hard work. Not be the one who had to work hard to get the perks.

I got up off the bed and walked over to one of the huge bedroom windows and stared out onto thc golf course. "Hey, Dad, how come you don't play golf anymore? That should be relaxing. If you want, I'll even go out with you. They have cute golf outfits, right?"

My father laughed. "Well, I don't bother going anymore because your mother started complaining about me spending too much time out there. Shoot, speaking of Joyce, where is she? I was supposed to get something sweet to eat after her workout."

You could almost see smoke coming from the top of my head. "After her workout. It's two o'clock in the morning." A curse word was begging to come out. "So, let me get this straight. You're sitting here hungry, and she's in the gym working out!"

He could tell I was getting upset. "Jewell, don't get yourself all worked up. I'm not starving. I just wanted a snack. You know I have a bad sweet tooth."

Thinking about how my father probably wanted a slice of red velvet cake made me even more upset. Why was he waiting for something he wanted? Hell, I never had to wait and neither did my mother. "Why can't Rosa get it?"

"She asked, but I told her not to worry about it. It's okay, sweetheart, really."

"No, it's not okay. Stop making excuses for her!" I shot out of the bedroom like a loose canon, and headed for the stairs, drunk and all.

I could hear my father calling my name, but I wasn't gonna let him talk me out of this one. Taking two steps at a time, I reached the bottom of the stairs in less than five seconds and ran straight to the gym. Hopefully, Rosa was in her wing of the house and wouldn't be able to butt into our conversation like she normally did, because I didn't want any interruptions this time.

Storming into the gym like the Tasmanian Devil, I walked directly over to the treadmill and pulled her ass right off.

"So, you're down here trying to get that wack-ass shape together, and my father is upstairs starving? Trust me, the only thing you got going for you are those big boobs my father bought." Even at fifty-six, those silicone things still sat up high.

Sweat rolled down her bronze coated forehead. "Have you lost your damn mind, Jewell? Who the hell do you think you're talking to?"

"You obviously. I'm tired of the way you treat him. He's sick, and you act like you don't even give a shit. What kind of fucking wife are you? Your ass didn't even call to tell me that he was sick. Rosa had to do it!"

She pushed her sweaty natural black bangs out of her face. "Don't you dare stand here and disrespect me in my own house!" Now the shouting match had begun.

I let out a slight chuckle. "Your house? This is not your house! You don't pay any damn bills around here!"

My mother looked at me with her deep Hawaiian features. "You know what? I'm sick and tired of you, disrespecting me all the time. Get the hell out of my way. Your little spoiled-ass is just jealous of me anyway!" She tried to brush past me and head toward the door, but I blocked her path.

"Jealous? Jealous of what? Some gold digging broad. Don't flatter yourself, bitch, my father will always love me more than you!"

All I remember seeing was the deranged expression on my mother's face before she lifted her French manicured nails in the air and slapped the shit out of me. With the force of the blow, along with the countless number of drinks, my head started pounding immediately and my face throbbed like a pulse. However, that didn't stop me from taking action.

Instantly, I charged at my mother's mid-section like a linebacker, causing both of us to fall to the floor. As she started yelling for Rosa, I didn't waste anytime climbing on top of her and placing my hands around her neck. I could feel my fingernails digging into her skin once I began to apply pressure. I wanted her to feel all the pain she'd caused me over the years. I wanted this bitch to die.

"Get…off," was all she managed to say, as I forced my fingers deeper into her skin.

"Who's jealous of you now, huh? Who?" I asked.

"Oh my God, Jewell. What are you doing?" I could hear Rosa asking, as she rushed into the room. She dropped to the floor, and quickly grabbed my arms. "Let her go! She's choking!" I wanted to tell Rosa that was the point.

Seconds later, she was finally able to pry my hands away, but it wasn't easy. Not exactly knowing where the strength came from, I felt like a wild animal as I jumped up, and began to walk around the gym in circles. My mother started coughing uncontrollably.

"Oh my goodness. Mrs. Givens, are you okay?" Rosa asked.

"Leave her alone. The same way she left my father upstairs." My body was still filled with tons of anger.

"What is wrong with you, Jewell? That's your mother," Rosa cried out.

"I don't wanna hear that shit!" I yelled.

For the first time in my life, Rosa looked at me with extreme disappointment, then said something in her native tongue. I'm sure she was probably cursing me out or calling me all sorts of names, but none of that really mattered at the moment. What did matter was that both my mother and I finally got the message of just how much we really hated each other.

"Rosa…call…the police," my mother struggled to say in between breaths.

I wanted to choke her ass all over again. "So, you're gonna call the cops on me?" I walked back over in her direction, but Rosa quickly jumped back up in order to intervene.

"Jewell, please leave. This is going too far."

"No, maybe I should finish what I started."

"Leave now!" Rosa screamed. She looked like she'd turned two shades of red.

"I can't. You know I came in a cab."

"The keys to your father's Jaguar are on the table in the foyer." When I didn't respond, Rosa screamed again. "Go!"

Whether she was trying to protect me or my mother, I

could tell Rosa was serious as she stared at me with a blank expression. For once, she was the one in charge.

Out of the love and respect that I'd always had for her, I decided to turn around and walk out of the gym like I was told. When I got to the staircase, a part of me wanted to go up to my father's room so I could give him my side of the story, because I knew my name would be dragged through the mud. But something told me to leave.

Let me get the fuck outta here before I catch a charge.

7

Nadia

Monday rolled around faster than expected. It seemed stupid how I had allowed one of the wildest weekends in Vegas pass me by, only to face another day still broke and still hooked up with a regular working class Joe Blow. Although I vowed to try to keep things popping with Day-Day, something in me just wouldn't behave. I felt like I needed to lift my shirt, and let my little tits hang loose until some paid nigga came by and licked the shit out my nipples.

It seemed like I was missing out on life. Just the thought of all the fun Jewell and Tori said they had at the club made me sick to my stomach. It caused me to walk uneasily. I rubbed myself just a bit in a circular motion, just as I glanced over at my date.

Instantly, shame filled my spirit. *How could I? What would my mother think? All for a buck*! I thought to myself. I walked in a daze hand in hand with my Sugar Daddy while the onlookers gave us both evil eyes. I laughed at the thought. *Should I say Daddy*? My goal had always been to find a nigga who would treat me like royalty, but damn...this was pushing it. I couldn't find a nigga, but anybody with a wallet would do for now.

"You like this, baby girl?" Monae asked me, holding a black Christian Dior, halter dress in the air.

I switched both my bags to my left arm and sighed. I wanted to say hell yeah, but didn't wanna appear too greedy. Yes, I knew I was pressed for a dollar, and would date anybody who would keep me in the runnings with the Jones',

Jewell, Tori, and anybody else I came in contact with. But Monae? Day-Day would kill me if he ever found out.

"I like it," I finally said.

"Good. 'Cause I think you'll look damn sexy in this shit. It's yours," she said, walking toward the counter.

I froze right in the middle of a footstep. Of all people to catch me out with a dyke, it had to be Karen, a salesperson in the Christian Dior store.

Damn…damn…damn… My fist banged against my moist forehead. Although, our acquaintance wasn't personal, she knew me well enough to know I was always up to something, and had seen me come into the mall with Day-Day on several occasions. We'd fallen out several times about me bringing back worn merchandise for a full refund.

"So, what'cha bringing back today?" the woman shot, with a sarcastic grin. "Jeans too long? Shirt didn't work out?" She laughed like she had one up on me.

Out of the blue, Monae grabbed me by my waist and pulled me close. As usual, her presence demanded respect, so Karen shut her mouth with the quickness.

"This pretty lady can bring back whatever the fuck she wants, when she wants. I got plenty of money to spend. 'Dats what it's like to roll with me." Monae shot me a smile.

Now I had one up on Miss. Karen. I just wanted Monae to loosen her grip. I loved the way she stepped up to bat for me, but on the real, the attraction just wasn't there.

"Oh yeah, well since you're spoiling her, just know she brings all your gifts back for a cash refund. Now what?" Karen asked.

Ms. Employee of the Month shot me the one up on you smile, then turned to scrutinize Monae. For the average person, the first impression of Monae would be to say- yeah she's a girl. Her smooth skin, and pretty face deters you from the fact that her pants were two sizes too big, and the thick link chain that hung from her neck read: Money.

"While you finish up, I'ma head outside," I told Monae, trying to distance myself from her hold.

Karen seemed to become more and more suspicious about our relationship, so I didn't want her tripping on me if she ever saw me with Day-Day again.

"Don't go nowhere," Monae barked in her light boyish tone. She blew me a kiss. "Stay right here so Miss Karen here can see what it's like to be spoiled."

Monae looked at me with the deepest lustful look I'd seen in a while. My skin cringed, yet I stood in my place. In totality, I'd done pretty well for a first date. Three outfits, several matching pieces from Victoria Secret, and a pair of Giuseppe sandals; not to mention the five hundred dollars she'd given me for taking the day off from work.

I crossed my arms and waited like a kept woman. Even the small screen on the register that read $842.89 didn't even ease the tension I felt. A dress priced that high would definitely put me in the league with my girls.

Just as Monae grabbed the bag from our hating-ass sales lady, my cell rang. I was mad at myself for not putting it on vibrate. Monae's phones had been going off like crazy, so I knew mine needed to be silenced. I fumbled with the phone for a few seconds from being crazy nervous. There was nobody I could think of who would understand why I was with Monae for the day. Then, after glancing at the caller ID, my simple mistake had me shaking like a junkie suffering from withdrawal. It was Day-Day of all people!

"Who 'dat?" Monae laughed, as if she knew it was her jealous cousin calling. "Want me to get it?" she asked. Her hands spread open wide. "Tell 'dat broke nigga I said, to keep a chick, you gotta do some whining and dining."

I smiled and clicked ignore. Then rushed to type Day-Day a text message

OMG- u keep callin. In a study sess @ school. Call u later.

Monae ignored the worried look on my face as I slipped my phone back into one of the large front pockets on my oversized shirt. She reached for my waist again, but I swiftly moved away. She was clearly a lovey-dovey type-a-chick; the hand holding, touchy feely shit. Outwardly affection wasn't for me, even with a dude. I damn sho wasn't 'bout to be booed up with a chick. What Monae didn't know was that, this was business. Strictly business. I needed money and whoever on two legs that came through with some dough, I'd hang out with.

"Let's go," Monae turned to say. "Let's go talk. You know…get to know each other a little better."

Her words seemed to come out in slow motion. For some reason, I'd allowed her to intimidate me just as I'd seen her do to so many others, especially Day-Day. I kept walking in front of her, afraid to look back or respond. I prayed that wasn't her way of making a move on me. I imagined pulling up to a hotel, and having to tell Monae I didn't get down like that. I was strictly dickly and in this relationship just for the money!

"So, where you work at baby girl?" Monae asked. "Fucking with me, you might be able to quit that muthafucka one day,"she called out from behind.

Shiddd...that's a nice thought. "At the MGM. I work inside the cashier's booth."

She seemed pleasantly surprised. "Ummm…sounds interesting."

Somehow Monae passed me. She shot me a smile showing off her shiny braces. When I didn't respond favorably, she flipped open one of her cell phones and gave up some short conversation. She seemed to be on a mission as I followed her out the Forum Shops at Caesars like a trained puppy. I watched her square shaped thin backside closely, not sure about her next move. Although tall and thin, Monae had a bit of muscular mass that could be defined easily through her clothing. Obviously she liked wearing her jeans low, hanging slightly from her ass. From the looks of things, she loved high dollar, blinged out jeans and white tees. She followed the same format the first night we met. Just a different pair of pimped out three hundred dollar jeans I'd seen in the front window of Neiman Marcus not even a week ago.

Within minutes, my breaths had shortened. The walk to the car didn't seem that far, but my body needed water.

Monae flicked the alarm on her key ring, popped the locks, and hopped in. Luckily my hair appointment was tomorrow cuz I knew Monae was gonna drop the top on the Benz again. That's how she rolled; dropped top, spinning rims, loud music, and me of course. It was clear-she loved showboating.

Prior to her actually calling me early Sunday morning, I'd already had one up on her when I started asking questions about Monae to a few of my old classmates from high school, who'd swayed into the street life. They quickly confirmed my suspicions. Monae had made a name for herself. If any drugs got sold in the Southern part of town, it was on her block. If large shipments of guns came into the city, she either sent for them, or was the negotiator for the sale. Her hands touched everything illegal in Vegas and on the outskirts.

It was evident by the way both her cell phones rang consistently she was the woman. I laughed at my thoughts and glanced over at Monae, whose mannerisms confirmed why I was so confused about her sex. She gripped the steering wheel hard, and leaned like a pimp on a mission.

"So, where we going now?" I blurted out.

"Why...you got a curfew?" she snapped.

"No, but can't I ask."

She gave me a mean grimace to stare at for a few seconds. "This how you treat people when they take you out? Huh? What about Day-Day?" She opened up a piece of gum and threw the wrapper on the ground. "You treat Day-Day like this?"

"Uh-Uh…"

She reached for her cell. "Let's call 'em." She shot me a devilish grin just as I caressed the palm of her hand.

"Look, Monae. Day-Day don't know I'm out with you today. He doesn't even want me to talk to you without him being around."

"Fuck 'dat shit! How old are you?"

"It doesn't matter. We sorta go together. So can you keep this on the hush for me?"

"We just chilling. Why we gotta tip-toe around Day-Day's lame- ass?"

I hunched my shoulders.

"You act like we fucking." She laughed hysterically, and whipped the corner like a race car driver. "Or are we?" Her outburst of laughter filled the car once again.

I didn't think shit was funny. "Look, just keep our little outing between us. Day-Day wasn't too happy about the fact that you tried to give me your number from the start. You sorta cool to hang out with, so keep this hush…okay."

Monae didn't respond. Instead, she answered her thin cell phone that lay clipped to her side.

"Yo, talk to me. Umh-huh…umh-huh. I'll be there shortly," she ended, just as the 500 SL zoomed into my parking lot.

By the time she slid the gear into park, I'd already grabbed my bags from the back seat hoping she wouldn't want to come in. It was almost eight o'clock, and all Day-Day's calls had been shuffled straight to my voicemail. He was no fool, and on numerous occasions in the past, popped up at my spot unannounced.

"Monae, it's been real," I said, throwing a heavy hint that she wasn't invited in.

She turned the ignition off and yanked the key out. "Let's get you inside. I got a few more dollars for you, but you know a lot of thirsty-ass niggas is probably watching."

She hopped out and led the way, like we were going to her apartment instead of mine. My feet trailed uneasily as I watched behind, hoping Day-Day wouldn't pull up. I pulled my phone out to see if he had texted me back. Nada!

Once I finally reached my front door, it seemed as if Monae had taken complete charge. She gripped my hand and assisted me with turning the key, then the knob, and pushed the door wide open. My heart raced when the door flung open. Monae walked inside and immediately made herself at home.

"Nadia, Nadia, Nadia," she repeated, sitting back on my sofa with her legs wide open. "You cool peoples."

For some reason she made me feel so inferior. Why, I wasn't sure. She weighed probably about a buck forty, only twenty pounds more than me, so my fears couldn't be explained. I closed the door then walked over in her direction. As crazy as it sounds, for some reason she was like a magnet.

I thought about Monae's comment, calling my neighbors thirsty. She was the one with the thirsty look in her eyes. I wanted to offer her a glass of water, and send her on her way, but knew it wasn't H20 she wanted. It was me.

The way she grabbed my inner thigh, and pulled me close had me wanting to shit in my thong. Even the coldness from the numerous rings on her fingers gave me chills. I'd never been in a situation with a chick before, especially one who intimidated me the way she did.

In a flash, Monae stood to her feet. While her height towered over me slightly, she covered my mouth with one hand, the intent of silencing me. She knew I'd say no, but wasn't taking no for an answer. Strangely, her hands felt soft…soft like mine, yet her nubby clear nails were far from girly. I shook nervously, cuz I wanted to tell Monae to get the fuck off of me. Yet, a part of me, wanted to see her again to see if money would still flow as freely as it had so far.

While my thoughts brewed around in my head, Monae took full control. Like a snake devouring it's prey, I felt her swallowing my tongue. With so much action twirling around in my mouth, it felt as if I'd swallowed a bag of pop rocks.

"Whoa…whoa…whoa," I stammered. "Be easy."

I stepped back and smiled, praying her reaction would be easy. I'd done my research and heard how bad of a temper Monae had. The story that stood out the most came to mind. It was crazy how they said she pistol whipped her last girlfriend in front of a crowded club for flirting with a guy right in front of her face. I snapped from my daze instantly as my phone vibrated inside my shirt pocket. For a moment, I figured Monae was packing a pistol, ready to whip me for not complying.

I looked down and almost pissed on myself.

Ur foul. I been tryna get wit u all day. Where the fuck u@
Ur not studying!

"Monae, I-I-I gotta studddddy for a test tomorrow," I stuttered. "I hate to be rude."

"So study," she said with confidence, while cracking her knuckles. "I like to watch beautiful women work."

Damn. This chick had an answer for everything. I sighed. "No seriously…"

"No…I am serious. I got everything you need, so relax. Here's a few extra ends as promised," she accentuated, letting me know her word was good. "And there's more where that came from."

She handed me three crisp hundred dollar bills and squeezed my hand tightly around the money. Almost simultaneously, her lips met my neck. She pecked, sucked and did some exotic shit that made my soul melt. All kinds of thoughts invaded my head. *Why? Why me? Why would I let this happen to me? Besides, what would I actually do with Monae?* After all she didn't have a dick. And my dildo was on the blink. The cord caught a short a while back when Day-Day cut me off for a couple of months.

While I tried to stay focused, Monae's deliberate attempt to seduce me was working. My insides tingled like crazy. No matter how hard I tried to fight it, I couldn't. I started moaning and breathing heavily. Before I knew it, her hand dove deep into my pants, and caressed the hell outta my clit. Not sure how to respond, I threw my head back and let my mouth open in ecstasy. I wanted to say no- really!

Luckily, I opened my eyes momentarily, only to see Monae with a mischievous smirk. Her face rubbed gently against mine, yet I still could see the devilish look from the corner of my eye. Something told me to turn around, and look toward the door. But when I did, nothing.

"Be easy," Monae instructed, and tried to turn my body back around. "That's what you told me, right?"

I knew something was up. I looked toward the door again, and when I did, Day-Day's face flashed before my vision outside the living room window. He'd obviously been peeking outside my window and had seen enough.

My first instinct was to run after him, but my feet remained stuck to the floor. I was so embarrassed, I had no idea what I'd even say. Even if I wanted to, it didn't seem possible. Monae had a tight grasp on my arm, and her other hand was caressing my ass.

"Oh, he ain't coming in. He know better. Don't worry."

She grinned.

Her words shocked me. Did she have something over Day-Day's head, or was he just not willing to fight for his woman? Or was there a fear in going up against his own cousin? My mind began to race. I wondered how much had he seen. I was confused.

"Monae, let me go. I think I need a minute."

"Nadia, all you need is me."

Monae forced her tongue back in my mouth before I could respond. This time she gripped my tits and pushed me onto the couch. The roughness had me spooked for a sec until she dropped down to her knees. My heart skipped a beat just as I looked back at the window again. Monae had a way of making you feel like nobody else existed, and if they did, they wouldn't matter anyway.

I almost forgot she was a girl by the way she ripped my jeans down below my knees. The fact that I wiggled to help her, was the craziest part. So much chaos circled around in my head, but Monae's tongue moves kept me from thinking clearly. She'd cropped my thong to the side, and was feasting on my shit like a sweet country watermelon within seconds. My head tilted back in delight while Monae spent the next five minutes pleasing me like no other. Before I knew it, two things happened…a knock sounded at the door, and I think I had an orgasm.

8

Jewell

"I'm not waiting for her ass all day," I mentioned to Tori, who swung her hips back and forth to Mary J. Blige's hit song, *Just Fine*, and paid me absolutely no attention. I still couldn't believe she'd gotten to my house before Nadia anyway. However, regardless of how much I bitched and moaned, somebody was always late for our weekly 'get money meetings.' I guess they didn't give a shit how much it pissed me off or the fact that I was a stickler for time. Besides, we needed to catch up, especially since our last lunch meeting at Manchelli's was ruined by Kenny's ass.

Looking down at my Cartier watch, I shook my head after realizing that it was almost four o'clock. "She was supposed to be here an hour ago!"

Again, there was no response from Tori. Obviously having a one woman party, she began imitating a few old Michael Jackson moves. *Maybe I shouldn't have installed that surround sound out here*, I thought, watching her switch to the hideous Roger Rabbit dance.

"Sit your ass down!" I yelled. "Soul Train was cancelled, hoe."

I'm sure she thought the dark blue booty shorts, blond wig, and tight Bebe tank top that she wore was cute, but it wasn't. It screamed hoochie.

Tori finally stopped and looked at me. "Would you shut up. For the last three years, yo' spoiled-ass been try'na rule us. My cousin ain't on yo' time schedule."

"She doesn't have to be," I snapped back. "The meetings need to start on time if they're going to be at my house. Besides, it's hot out here." Sitting under my Moroccan style cabana allowed some relief, but the unseasonably hot ninety-five degree weather was working overtime.

"What the hell is wrong wit' you? You been bitchin' since I got here." Tori smacked her lips. "Don't let me have to push yo' ass in the pool."

I made myself laugh, even though I wanted to keep going back and forth. But in reality, I guess she was right. For the past four days, I'd tried my best to get my mind off the dispute between my mother and I, but couldn't. Not that I was worried about how she felt because I could care less. However, it was my father who I was most concerned about, and once I talked to him right after the unpleasant incident, I knew that I'd fucked up.

Seeing my mother and I come to that point hurt him beyond measure, and the last thing I wanted to do was cause him any more pain. I loved my father more than life itself, so in order to make him happy, I knew I had to find a way to get along with that bitch. It would be hard, but I'd made a promise to him and vowed to keep it. I just hoped that she'd made the same commitment, because the minute she couldn't keep her hands to herself, it was going to be a situation. Suddenly, my thoughts were interrupted.

"Here you go, ladies," my chef, Devin said, walking over with six Mimosa's, a drink that I'd requested specially for this occasion. "It's freshly squeezed orange juice in there, so I hope you enjoy it." He handed each of us a champagne glass and placed the other ones down on the table.

"I want to enjoy you," Tori boldly stated. "Why you so stingy wit' 'dat dick of yours, Devin?"

I wasn't surprised to hear my friend go there, because every time she came over my house, she spent more time trying to get with Devin than visiting me.

"You know what, I better not ever go in my kitchen and find y'all fucking on my granite," I said. "See, Devin, this is why I always tell you to wipe the countertops down with Lysol after she leaves."

Devin smiled, showing the cutest dimples ever. I had to admit, he was cute, but I couldn't sleep with the hired help.

"Don't worry, Ms. Givens, everything is sterile in the kitchen."

"Don't listen to her. She's just mad 'cause ain't nobody got her ass bent ova the stove, 'dats all," Tori replied.

I rolled my eyes, even though I knew she was telling the truth. Thinking back, it had been a while since Kenny and I had sex in that part of the house. "Actually, I prefer the dishwasher," I shot back, causing Tori to snicker. "Devin, you can bring the hors d'oeuvres out to the pool once Nadia arrives. Oh, and call out for a few more bottles of champagne. We might need it."

"Yeah, and don't forget the Grey Poupon," Tori joked, in a snooty tone.

Again Devin flashed his melting smile. "Okay. Well ladies again, I hope you enjoy the drinks," he said, before turning around to leave.

"Oh, don't worry. 'Dis drunk bitch will drink anythin' wet, so it won't matter," Tori felt the need to add.

"You mean like this?" I asked, downing the entire contents of the champagne glass. I didn't have anymore time to entertain her sarcasm. Instead, I had more serious things to discuss and needed to be slightly tipsy before I said anything.

Placing the empty glass on the table, I reached for another one, then swallowed the second Mimosa within four seconds. Tori could call me what she wanted, but that shit was good. Now, I was ready to let her in on a few things. Before now, I'd kept the whole incident away from my friends, and now it was time to let it all out.

"I choked the hell out of my mother the other night. Tried to damn near kill her," I blurted out.

Tori stared at me with her mouth open for what seemed like forever before finally responding. "Whatever. You lyin'. I don't believe 'dat," she said. "And then you woke up, right?"

"Look, I'm dead serious."

Again, she stared for a moment. "Well, what the fuck happened? Why didn't you call me? You know I ain't got into no brawls since I left the old neighborhood."

"Basically she slapped me first, and after that it was on. I just lost it."

"Oh snap, 'dat sound like some shit I would do." Tori was so hood. She started swinging and jabbing her fist into the air. "See, I told you I shoulda been fuckin' yo' daddy a long time ago. 'Dat bitch woulda been livin' up in the Holiday Inn by now."

We both started laughing until my housekeeper, Julia walked up. "Umm…excuse me, Ms. Jewell. Your other guests have arrived."

"It's about damn time," I said, looking back at my watch, the time had moved to four-fifteen.

Tori looked at me. "Hold up, she just said guests. Man, don't tell me Nadia don' brought Day-Day's ass over here." She turned her attention back to Julia. "Do she got a nigga wit' her?"

Julia seemed confused by the question. Although she was from Peru like Rosa, she didn't understand English as much. She began to shake her head until Tori spoke up again.

"A man…a man. Do she got a man wit' her?"

Finally she understood. "No man. Two women," Julia informed.

Both Tori and I looked at each other in a complete daze, and were probably thinking the same thing. Who was this other woman, and why was Nadia bringing her to my house?

Still confused, I said, “Send them out here, I guess.”

As we watched Julia walk away, Tori started back up. “I know my damn cousin ain’t got no friends other than you, so I wonder what ‘dis is all about.”

“Yeah, I know.”

Things did seem a little strange that Nadia would be willing to bring someone to our weekly get together, especially since they were personal. I’d known Nadia since our days back at UNLV, and met her crazy-ass cousin soon after. So we’d all been close friends for a while. Our meetings were our way of discussing how we were going to continue to stay on top, chat about our love life, figure out what dudes were out, and most importantly, who was in for the week.

“What’s up y’all?” I heard Nadia say when she walked into the cabana.

However, it was the only thing I heard, because what I saw next didn’t even make sense. I almost fell out of my chair. Following a few steps behind Nadia, She-Man looked like she had an attitude as soon as she made her grand entrance. She even had the nerve to have her hands on top of her hips like she was running shit.

I sat straight up in my chair. “What are you doing here? How did you find out where I lived?” I asked. Both Nadia and Tori looked at me, then at Alyssa.

“I found the address in Kenny’s phone,” she replied.

“Hold up! What the hell you doin’ in her man’s phone? Who ‘dis bitch?” Tori asked in her usual ghetto tone. When Alyssa shot her a ‘oh no you didn’t’ look, it only added fuel to the fire. “What bitch, what? You gotta problem!” Tori continued.

“Tori, I’ll handle this,” I informed. “What’s up, Alyssa?” For a brief second I became nervous, thinking that something terrible might’ve happened to Kenny.

She folded her arms. "Can we go somewhere else to talk?" She looked over at Tori, who began cracking her neck, then her knuckles. "That girl looks unstable."

I shook my head. "No, these are my girls. Whatever you have to say, you can say it in front of them."

"Yeah, 'dats right. And I got yo' damn unstable," Tori interjected.

Nadia sucked her teeth then placed a box of chocolate covered strawberries on the table. "Tori, shut up. You always trying to start something." She wasn't one for drama.

Alyssa's confidence seemed to come back as she placed her hands back on her hips "Well look, there's no other way to say this...but I'm not Kenny's Godsister."

I quickly stood up. "See, I knew that shit. I knew y'all were lying. Who the hell are you then?"

"Who else…the other woman," Alyssa responded in a cocky tone.

Tori went ballistic. "You raggedy bitch! How is yo' ugly-ass supposed to be his girl?" She turned to me. "You ready for me to fuck her up, 'cause I don' heard enough."

Looking down at Alyssa's cheesy tunic dress with the words 'Apple Bottoms' spread across it, and her fake Gucci bag, I did have to wonder what Kenny saw in her if she was really telling the truth.

"It's true. Kenny lied to you about everything. I don't live in Chicago, and I wasn't just in town for a few days. I live right in Spring Valley, but most of the time I stay at his crib. Well, when you're not there anyway," Alyssa stated.

Seconds later, all I heard was glass breaking. Looking over at Tori, I noticed that she had a jagged edge champagne glass in her hand, and appeared damn near deranged. "Fuck 'dis!" She took two steps toward Alyssa, before Nadia sprung into action.

"What are you trying to do, kill her? Put that glass

down!" Nadia yelled. Her petite frame was only able to hold one of Tori's arms back.

Despite having a weapon pointed at her, Alyssa's smile was still conniving. "You wouldn't do that to a pregnant woman, would you?" Nadia, Tori and I looked at each other for answers. "Yeah, that's the reason why I'm here. Do, you remember Kenny asking you for $1,000 dollars? Well, that was for my abortion. And…"

Tori instantly cut her off and looked directly at her stomach. "Yo' ass don't look like you in no second trimester. Who the fuck you tryna fool wit' 'dat price? Trust me I don' had plenty of abortions, and first trimester gigs ain't nothin' but 'bout $300."

Alyssa patted her stomach. "Well, if you must know, I'm about sixteen weeks."

"Bitch, you lying!" Tori shouted.

"I'm not lying," Alyssa replied, then looked at me with a little smirk. "And since Kenny can't get the job done, I just thought I'd come and ask for the money myself."

As soon as the words left her mouth, I hauled off and punched Alyssa right in the mouth, catching her completely off guard. It happened so fast, even Nadia and Tori didn't have time to react. Two more punches followed. This time, directing my fist toward her eye.

"Yeah…'dats right. Fuck her ass up!" Tori yelled with excitement. "Hit her in the stomach!" she taunted, jumping up and down.

Nadia almost had a heart attack. "Are you crazy? No…no…no. Jewell, stop it!"

I stepped back, waiting for Alyssa to retaliate, but she was so busy holding her face that she didn't even bother. Besides, the girl had to be on drugs if she thought she could beat me, especially with crazy-ass Tori in my corner.

"This shit ain't over!" Alyssa belted out. It looked and

sounded like she wanted to cry. Turning around, she tried to leave, but Tori obviously had other plans.

Walking up behind Alyssa with the broken glass, Tori quickly stepped in front. "Oh no, bitch, where you think you goin'? Since yo' dumb ass wanna come up in my girl's spot and talk some shit, give me 'dis," Tori said, snatching her purse.

Nadia immediately started shaking her head in disbelief.

"What are you doing? Give it back!" Alyssa demanded. She tried to grab the purse, but Tori held up the glass.

Nadia and I just stood back and watched as the two went at it.

"Fall back before you get sliced." Tori held the bag upside down and began to dump out all the contents. "Hmm... let's see what I want." She grabbed Alyssa's wallet first but quickly threw it back down after realizing there was no money it in. Next, she grabbed what looked like two cards. "Hmm…what are these? Oh, two tickets to see Alicia Keys at Mandalay Bay. I guess that was for you and Kenny, so I'll take those." After going through a few more things, she grabbed a key. "I know yo' broke-ass ain't got no Range Rover. Is 'dis Kenny's shit?"

Both Alyssa and Tori immediately directed their attention toward me. "So, you had the nerve to drive over here in the truck I fucking bought?" I wanted to pound on her again. "Toss me that key, and get her ass out of here," I instructed.

"Wit' pleasure," Tori replied. She grabbed Alyssa by the arm.

"Noooo. Kenny doesn't know that I took the truck. He's at the gym. How am I supposed to get home?" Alyssa asked like a scared little girl. The overconfident attitude she once had was gone.

"How you think? Walk, bitch!" Tori ranted.

Nadia seemed to be in shock. "Just get her outta here. I don't want anybody to call the police, or if that girl has a miscarriage, we might get locked up."

"Nadia, why the fuck you so damn scared all the time? Damn. Be a soldier for once! Her ass probably ain't even pregnant!" Tori yelled, before ushering Alyssa to the front.

"I can't believe this," Nadia said, shaking her head again.

"Me either," I replied, looking down at the key. "I wonder how long Kenny's been playing me."

There was a short awkward silence between us until Tori returned. "Now 'dats what the fuck I call a 'get money meetin'. 'Dis been the most excitin' one yet!" Tori raved.

"But we didn't even talk about anything," Nadia announced.

"So what. We were entertained by ole' Mike Tyson here," Tori joked. She walked over to me and smiled. "Damn girl, you on a roll. First yo' mom, now 'dis shit. Maybe we shoulda had yo' ass in the ring instead of Mayweather."

Nadia looked confused. "What are you talking about?"

I hadn't even gotten a chance to tell her about the drama with my mother, and didn't feel like talking about it now. "It's a long story. I'll tell you later. All I want to think about now is how I'm gonna fuck Kenny up."

Tori shook her head. "Hell yeah. I can't believe 'dat mufucka been cheatin' on you wit' that pit bull lookin' bitch. See, I told y'all not to fall in love wit' these nigga's. Just fuck 'em and role out like I do."

"But everybody ain't built like you, Tori," Nadia spoke.

"Well, you should be 'cause..." She stopped dead in her tracks and stared at Nadia like it was her first time seeing her. "What the fuck did you do, hit the lottery? Where you get 'dat outfit from? It looks expensive."

I eyed the olive colored off the shoulder shirt. "Oh, yeah, that is cute. When did you go shopping, and why didn't you call us? We normally tear the malls up together." The thought of Kenny cheating on me still played around in my head.

Nadia giggled. "I went a few days ago, but didn't bother calling cuz it was spare of the moment."

"Let me guess, you spent yo' own money, right? See, if you had a real nigga instead of Day-Day, you wouldn't..."

Nadia cut her off. "I didn't spend my own money. Somebody else bought it, and it wasn't Day-Day. I'm on vacation from him for a minute," she said, in a softer tone.

Tori and I gave each other strange looks. "If it wasn't Day-Day, then who was it? You mean to tell me you been fuckin' some other nigga, and we don't know 'bout it?" Tori asked.

Nadia giggled again like she was having a teenage love affair. "It's something like that."

Obviously seeing that Nadia wasn't going to spill the beans just yet, Tori finally let her off the hook. "Fuck it then. I'll leave it alone for now, but don't think you gettin' off the hook." She gave Nadia the once over again. "Well, whoever it is, must got some paper, 'cause I was just in the Dior store the other day and saw them sandals. They like seven hundred bucks," she said, pointing down to Nadia's shoes. "I'm proud of you, baby girl. You might be movin' up to the big leagues." Walking over to the table, Tori picked up a champagne glass and handed it to me. "I know you could use 'dis."

"Hell yeah," I replied.

She then picked up two more glasses, and gave one to Nadia. "Let's do our toast, ladies, on the count of three. One…two…three."

"Rich girls for life!" we all screamed at the same time.

Just then Devin walked in and dropped off six bottles of Perrier-Jouet champagne that had obviously been delivered from the liquor store. For sure, we'd get smashed tonight, and Kenny would definitely be dealt with.

9

Tori

I felt like a queen dressed in my sultry Kimono style satin robe. The material made me feel at ease, like everythin' was okay. But the sound of my lengthy fingernails tappin' on the kitchen countertop shoulda warned me. Clearly, I was 'bout to blow my top. I held my cell phone in anger and listened to dis' dumb mufucka Dante on the other end come up wit' his own plan.

"Whoa…Whoa… Hold it!" I shouted. "I'm runnin' 'dis operation and I'm not into freezin' sperm. Either you gon' follow through usin' my method and get paid, or keep yo' nasty-ass sperm. You probably got a low sperm count anyway, nigga!"

I felt like a low jab was necessary to bring his ass back down to reality. Dante was one of my homeboys who I met when I first moved to Vegas. He normally got down wit' all my schemes, just lookin' for a couple hundred to stock up on his weed. But today, he seemed to have attention deficit disorder.

I'd put together a quick way to make a lil' cash when my older sister back at home turned me on to these ladies in their mid-forties who'd been searchin' for good sperm. They wanted to get pregnant by a good-lookin' man. I guess the sperm bank in the hood wasn't much to look forward to. So, of course, I volunteered to collect some good ole Vegas sperm, for a small fee of course. I laughed at how I shoulda been on the BET show- *The Ultimate Hustler*. I woulda won- hands down.

Yet instead, I sat listenin' to Dante babble and spit out

more excuses as to why he couldn't deliver 'til tomorrow. But the reality was…I had two other niggas lined up ready to get paid for their baby makers. Eight ounces is what I had committed to. And $3,500 was the fee. It was a quick flip, but Dante appeared to be the weakest link.

I'd had enough. "Look," I shouted. "These bitches I got are really tryna get pregnant. Tonight! I spelled out the letters one by one "P-R-E-G-N-A-N-T. Understand?" My voice had gotten so much louder in the last five minutes it was startin' to get hoarse. "I mean, what you tryna do, Dante?"

"I mean…"

"Dats it. Yo' ass is weeded out. I only wanted yo' shit 'cause you're a sure shot. You fathered seven babies 'dat I know 'bout, and who knows how many more are out there. Damn stallion gone bad!" I shook my head and looked for the number to my next victim.

"Fuck you, Dante! I gotta get 'dis money!" **CLICK**

I figured I would take a moment for myself before I called my connect 'dat had his shit ready for me to pick up. I hopped from my chair and opened the top cabinet above the microwave. Four Domino Sugar bags sat just where they were supposed to be. One by one, I pulled them down and dumped the contents onto the table. There was nothin' like the smell of green. Of course since I didn't have a bank account, and couldn't get approved for one if I tried, 'dis was my savings account. Unfortunately, my name was in the Chex system, which kept any decent company from givin' me any type of legit account or credit card.

So, I sat with my Jack Daniels and Coke and counted my loot, just as I did every Thursday. It had been a week since I pulled off my sex tape deal. My shit had been edited, finalized, packaged, and was being sold like crack in the eighties. If my calculations were right, the tape had added 'bout five thousand to my stash in just a few weeks time. 'Dat made me say fuck goin' to Paradise Strip Club tonight. I'd promised the owner I would come by and grace his joint wit' a set like I'd been doing once a week for $500. It was easy money, but I didn't need it, especially if I could get good money like 'dis off my tape.

Besides, a personal night was in order. A night to sit here in my robe, no panties, and even shave my pussy if time permitted.

I started countin'…twenty, forty, sixty… Just as I got into a rhythm my damn phone rung.

"Who 'dis?"

"Yeah…we do need to talk. And you need to come up with my money. Don't think I'ma lie down easy."

"Q, is 'dat you, boo?" I chuckled a little.

"Let's see if you laughing when you six feet under, bitch!"

I thought it was cute how Q tried to be tough. He was the same nigga 'dat I'd found out was a momma's boy and spent most of his time at the library studyin' books on film producin'.

"Look, Q. Just chalk it up as a loss. You didn't provide good service," I said, in a nonchalant manner. "Move on. Okay."

"I did give you good service! And I want my money. I don't care whether I gotta take you to court."

I fell out laughin'. 'Dis nigga was half-crazy. He was keepin' me from my me time, so I was ready to end the conversation. "Q, hear me out. It's over. You not gettin' no money outta me. Sue me."

"Bitch, you doubting me. You really don't know me. I'll have you killed and your momma out in Cali too!"

I got to thinkin', what did he know 'bout my mother? I did tell him where she lived. What else did he know?

"Who the fuck you talkin' too!" I shouted. My veins got to jumpin', 'cause 'dis nigga was so outta pocket. I didn't even fuck wit' my family, but I wasn't gonna let nobody talk 'bout'em or threaten'em, even though they had written me off.

Just then, there was a knock on my door. I jumped, thinkin' 'dat nigga, Q might have a hit on me.

"Who is it!" my voice sounded off like a guard dog. I held my nervousness inside as much as I could.

"It's me," the voice sounded from the other side of the door. "Tori, open up."

"Me who?" I asked, walkin' closer to the door. I pressed my ear back to the phone to make sure Q was still there. I heard'em breathin' hard, which led me to believe he had nothin' to do wit' the knock at the door. I still stayed on point, 'cause niggas I know are tricky like 'dat. He was probably waitin' for me to open the door, hear the bullet pierce through my head, then hang up.

"Tori, I just wanna talk for a minute. It's important."

At 'dat moment I recognized the voice. I quickly swung the door open, and stared, givin' up an uninvitin' gaze.

"Yo, what you doin' at my crib?" I said, with a puzzled look on my face. "Q, I gotta go," I announced into the phone. "Go jerk yo'self, nigga." **CLICK**

Day-Day stood on my welcome rug wit' a strange expression. His hands were tugged in his pockets, and his stance told me he had something important to say. Oddly, he was dressed real jazzy, nothin' I'd seen before. His fresh jeans looked to be costly, and the glistenin' diamond in his ear told me he'd ran into some money.

I still didn't like the nigga for my cousin, but he looked like he'd stepped his game up a notch. I looked him over from top to bottom, thinkin' he looked pretty good. I just didn't know what he wanted. I walked a semi-circle closely around his body.

"What can I do for you, Mr. Day-Day?" I asked.

"I need to ask you something."

"Shoot. Time is money. And since you don't have none, start now."

"You'll never change, Tori," he laughed slightly, and shook his head. "For starters, I got money. I just choose how I spend…"

I interrupted quickly. "You call 'dat 'lil measly nine to five havin' money?" I wanted to take him in my kitchen to show him some real money, but I didn't want him going past the front door.

"Umph…" He shook his head again, then hit me with a confident smirk. "I got a raise, Tori. A big raise." He watched for my response. "I make over $200,000 now. See, hard work pays off. Everybody don't have to rob, steal, and strip to make good money."

I wanted to spaz out on Day-Day's new ass. If he thought a lil' new money was gonna allow him to dis me, he was wrong. Negative. Nada! But I did like his brand new style.

"So why are you here?" I spat.

He stepped forward, invadin' my space. His presence and closeness to my body made my nipples rise. When he spoke, I thought my mind was playin' tricks on me. I couldn't believe my ears. Now 'dis nigga was speakin' my language.

10

Nadia

I stood at the cash booth window with my arms folded like a tight mummy. For a Thursday night, the casino seemed dead and awfully cold. There were only three of us working the booth, and neither of the two people scheduled had anything in common with me; so talking was out.

The only person I'd said anything to within the last hour was a worrisome-ass parking attendant named Reggie. He drove me crazy most of the time, but we were real cool. He came up to the booth and asked me out damn near every time I worked, but I don't know why, cuz I always said no. Maybe one day he'd stop. Shiddd, maybe one day I'd finally get a job as a dealer, and come from behind this strict-ass cage. If the rules for working with cash in the MGM weren't so tight, I woulda whipped out my Sister to Sister magazine and started reading the latest gossip.

Instead, I stood shivering, bored out of my mind, waiting for the next customer to walk up and cash in chips. The fact that I had nothing to do wasn't a good thing for me. It seemed as if lately, too much idle time had my mind wondering off thinking about Monae. After three weeks of following her around like a fish swimming after bait, I felt like I was falling for her. Hard! The worst part of it all, was that I couldn't lean on my girls for support. They knew I hadn't seen much of Day-Day, but how could I tell them about Monae? Everything we'd done, and everything we planned on doing. Maybe if I told them she owned two houses in Vegas, and a penthouse in LA, Tori would accept it. But Jewell, hell no.

Monae would have to be a member at the most elite country club, and rub elbows with Diddy, Tiger Woods, and fucking Oprah to even sit at the dinner table with her.

My emotions were twisted when it came to Monae. I fought hard to keep my feelings under wrap. I didn't consider myself a dyke, and wouldn't dare allow anyone to label me as one. Besides, I'd never been into women, nor did I even think about experimenting. I was in this for the money. But somehow Monae had turned the tables. I found myself calling her five and six times a day only to have her say- "I gotta get back wit' you."

What the fuck? I asked myself. At first, she put the chase on me…and now that she'd gotten what she wanted, her ass was treating me like yesterday's garbage. I mean, even returning my calls seemed to be trouble.

I thought about our conversation this morning when she dropped by to give me the money I needed to pay my high-ass credit card bills. She told me she'd seen Day-Day out last night and that they'd called a truce. She also said that Day-Day told her she could have me. But then she shot me some smart-ass comment. "Now I gotta decide if I want you."

I called her back countless times after she left just so I could ask, "What the fuck is that supposed to mean?" But just as she'd done a lot recently, my calls were ignored.

My heart sank thinking about my situation. I'd sold my soul to a manly chick over some money; trying to keep up with my girls. The crazy part is; Monae didn't even dish out the loot anymore like she did when we first met. Every time I asked for two hundred, I got a hundred. If I asked for a hundred, I got fifty. Just like this morning, I asked for six hundred, but she only gave me four hundred. The crazy thing is it wasn't like that at first. All I had to do was open my mouth and I could get whatever I asked for. It was fucking humiliating having to ask for money all the time.

I just gotta stop depending on other people, I thought. I could by all means make it on my own. I just needed to lower my standards, live like a college student, and stop hanging out with Jewell and Tori, spending crazy money.

Because of my sulking, I didn't realize I'd gotten a line all of a sudden, until my co-worker nudged me. A freckled-face giant was at my window, looking as if he'd waited far too long.

"And how are you today, Sir?" I asked, trying to get myself pumped back up.

I grabbed his chips and started counting. His red-ass never responded, so I took my time, and moved extra slow. He had about eight thousand and some change from my estimation, so I stacked the money in five hundred dollar stacks slowly. My plan- once I'd finished counting- I'd do a double count on his ass just to piss him off. I could only estimate from his huge six foot seven height that there were about three more people behind him, who would probably get pissed and move to another line, but I didn't care. His arrogant persona had rubbed me the wrong way.

"How about I take you out tonight?" he finally said.

My insides tingled instantly. My first thought, he cashed in $8,800, and the Breitling watch on his arm was worth at least $14,000. So he probably had a little money.

"Oh, so you didn't really want to speak at first." I smiled. "But now you wanna take me out." I turned to see if a supervisor was standing behind me on watch, or if the other two workers were even looking my way. Luckily, one had gone on break, and the other person was busy doing a marker.

"You seem like a confident woman. That's what I'm looking for. Besides, I'm only in town for a few days. I got basketball practice on Monday," he ended with what was supposed to be a sexy smile. I thought, *damn, he's ugly*, but *maybe NBA perhaps?*

"Can we make it happen, beautiful?"

I nodded slightly, letting him know I was unsure. But my money alarm bell went off instantly. I counted out his cash in all hundreds, trying to buy myself some time before answering verbally. All kinds of thoughts rolled around in my head. I imagined myself as an NBA wife sitting lovely on the front row on game night.

Then I saw myself standing ass-naked at a stainless steel Viking stove cooking my red nigga a luscious meal. He wasn't much of a looker, but if he was any kinda professional baller, his money was probably right. I just needed a few dates to show him I could be wifey material. After all, Day-Day was out.

"So, what's it gonna be? Yes...maybe?" He hunched his shoulders.

I took my time answering, putting him on ice. I didn't wanna seem too excited. I noticed from the corner of my eye people jumping from my line to the other lines. It was crazy how people behaved when it came to cashing in chips for real dollars. However, there was still one person behind my potential victim, but I couldn't see his face to even know if he was agitated by my slow demeanor.

"What's your name?" I asked, pulling out some paperwork that I pretended I wanted him to fill out. I knew if a supervisor came out and saw me just standing here talking, I'd get fired. Lord knows I needed my job.

He scribbled his number down on a piece of paper along with the name Quentin Styles and said, "Call me when you get off. I'm staying at the Venetian."

Quentin Styles! I'd definitely heard his name in the league before. He wasn't a Kobe Bryant rich type of dude, but he was getting enough paper for me. I grinned so hard all my back teeth showed, including my wisdom teeth. As expected, I watched his backside as he turned and left the line. When my next customer stepped forward, he must've been pissed for waiting so long 'cuz he slammed the chips on the counter, snapping me from my daze.

"Uhhh…ummm," I stuttered. I was at a loss for words. At first my body became numb. Then I felt my blood pressure rising. Monae stood before me with an angry, enraged expression on her face. Had she heard all that went down? I wondered in fear. Surely she did cuz she stared at me wide-eyed, like I'd been terribly insubordinate. It was real weird, almost as if she didn't know me. It really had me puzzled by the way she laid her drivers' license on the counter.

"I need a marker," she spat between her grinding teeth.

I was so confused. I knew she was pissed and that we needed to discuss what had just gone down, but I was caught in a bad position. One of the supervisor's had just walked through the cage, checking to see if all was well, so I said nothing. He stood back behind us as usual, just watching and monitoring. His name was Jaron, and although I'd only worked with him twice, he seemed to be cool. I whipped out the small informational form, and handed Monae a pen.

"Fill out the information here," I said professionally, yet nervously. "You do have an account set up with us already, correct?"

I asked that question because I knew Monae wouldn't be able to collect her money here at the cage without setting up an account first. Besides, she never mentioned to me that she had a credit line at MGM. I thought maybe she was asking for a marker to fuck with me because of what she'd just seen. But from the looks of things, she was filling out the form in its entirety, and within seconds, had pushed it back my way. My eyes showed my confusion, but I remained silent. Monae had written $5,000 on the line which asked how much money you wanted to borrow off your credit line. The bigger problem was that she wrote the name Kelsey Brown on the paper, and the name matched the identification she'd given me.

I did a double take. My eyes gazed from the license to Monae. Then from Monae to the written information. My eyes asked the question, are you serious? But I never said a word. Neither did Monae. Her expression never changed. She maintained her intense look and gazed at me as if she wanted to kick my ass all across the casino floor. I was no longer cold anymore. I'd become hot, uneasy, and wanted to go on break.

All of a sudden my supervisor, Jaron, walked up behind me, moved Monae's license toward him slightly, and quickly glanced at her request. "Is there a problem, Nadia? Your face looks a little flushed."

"No, I'm fine. I just had a quick hot flash, that's all."

I grinned in his direction and started processing Monae's marker request while he watched from behind. I kept my head tilted downward as I typed her information into the system. Monae's scowl could be felt strongly, even though I'd chosen not to look her in the eye. After a few moments of typing, sure enough she had an account opened three days ago under the name Kelsey Brown. One of two things were possible, either she had a fake ID, or I really didn't know as much as I thought about her, or whoever the fuck she claimed to be.

I was heated, but had to maintain my composure, cuz my supervisor was obviously in the cage to stay for a while. So, I tore the marker check off the printer and passed it to Monae for a signature. I was supposed to double check the signature with identification before giving up the cash, but it didn't matter, I knew something was up with my ex-lover. She'd dissed me for over a week, then showed up at my job, either pretending to be someone else, or exposing her real name to me in an awkward fashion. If I were really her girl, as she'd claimed in the past, I'd know her real name.

I counted out the five thousand in all hundreds quick, and with attitude. As soon as the last hundred hit the counter, Monae was out.

Instantly, I turned to Jaron. "Can I get a break, please? I'm not feeling too good."

"Sure," he responded.

Without hesitation, he motioned for someone from the back to come out and relieve me. I'm sure he could tell from the moistness of my face, something was indeed wrong. I raised my hands and twisted them back and forth in front of the cameras, before walking toward the small employee area in the back. I held my stomach tightly, so Jaron would think I had serious female problems going on.

After grabbing my belongings, I quickly made my way out of the cage. The moment the coast was clear, I snatched my name tag off, and yanked my sweater from my new oversized Prada bag. I threw the sweater on over my hideous uniform in a hurry in search of Monae. My first guess- the crap tables. She was a high roller, and loved to roll dice. My bet-with five thousand she would be front and center at a hundred dollar table for sure.

With quick strides, I made my way over to the high dollar pits. I stood on my tip-toes, hoping to get a good ariel view. I saw young dudes, older Texan looking white men, and even a few Asians, trying their hand on the dice. But Monae was nowhere to be found. My heart pounded, thinking she could be watching me. I turned from left to right, but there was still no sign of Monae. My breaths quickened, as I made my way over by the black jack tables, and then roulette. Monae said she'd never be caught dead on roulette, but I tried anyway.

After fifteen more minutes of searching, I realized Monae was nowhere to be found; not the bathrooms, the food establishments, nowhere. Finally, I whipped out my cell and called her phone, hoping she would pick up. I needed to get back to the cage. The phone rung and rung, but Monae never answered. I strutted back to work like a lost puppy, wondering why she'd stop accepting my calls regularly. Then, just as I opened the door to the cage, my phone sounded. It was a text.

Meet me @ Fat Burger when u get off. 11 is good...Monae
The Good Dick!

That bitch! I thought. I closed the phone and smiled at Jaron.

$$$

Three hours later, I sat at the bar in the one of the lounge's at the New York New York Hotel, thinking about what I would say to Monae when we met up. I'd gotten off over an hour ago, but decided not to call her earlier than the time she quoted. She was a stickler like that, always so controlling. So I downed my last glass of Ciroc, and headed out to the street.

As usual, excitement filled the air. As soon as I stepped onto the glitzy Vegas strip, full of blinking lights and shimmery décor, I felt like I didn't belong anymore. I'd lived here most of my life, but needed a change. I wanted something different out of life. I just didn't know what. The more I looked around, it all seemed so fake. Vegas was the place to make you feel like all was well. No reality at all.

I made my way across the street, noticing how the area around Fat Burger was jammed packed. But it was always like that on Thursdays, cuz of Hip Hop night at the Spy Club. A club that was only five yards away from the famous burger spot, and where I'd first met Day-Day. He was known to hang out at the rowdy hot spot.

Shit, I forgot Day-Day be coming to this spot on

Thursdays. I hope Monae ain't trying to start nothing, I thought, looking at her white Escalade that was parked up on the curb directly in front of the club.

She's always over does shit, I said to myself. I searched for her, but kept walking toward Fat Burger as she instructed. My arms were folded, which made me look outta place. Suddenly, I heard my name. I turned, but didn't see anyone. Then, out of the blue, I felt a rough tug on my elbow.

"What up, trick?"

When I turned around, I saw Monae standing behind me with a toothpick in her mouth. It immediately reminded me of Day-Day, cuz he always had the little wood stick between his teeth too.

"Monae, I'm not gonna be too many tricks," I snapped. "What's gotten into you?" I had a serious look on my face.

"No, what's gotten into you, besides Quentin Styles? I knew you was a tramp. That's my boy though," she laughed, and rested her butt on the hood of a 5 Series BMW. "I sent his ass in there to see how you would get down. You showed your true colors, boo."

My heart raced, and I jumped on the defensive instantly. "I did nothing but remained polite. It's my job, Monae! I didn't give him my number, did I?"

"You didn't get the chance." She laughed as if I meant nothing to her. "We could do a threesome though."

She turned and looked away from me, gazing down into the screen of her phone. She seemed preoccupied with leaving me hanging.

"So what now?"

"What do you mean? We still girls," she told me. "We'll kick it from time to time," she added, with hunched shoulders.

"Oh, so that's it?" I thought, *damn, my money is gone. And over somebody without a real dick, or without a real name*. "So, let me ask you something. Is Kelsey your real name, or Monae? I'd like to know who I was really fooling around with."

Suddenly, we were interrupted by a short guy wearing a baseball cap. He walked up to Monae, handed her a brown paper bag and kept walking. It definitely looked like some type of drug deal.

She turned to me like nothing happened. "Look, Nadia, you wanna make some real money?"

The sound of the word money distracted me from getting to the truth. "Sure." I twisted my lips a bit.

"You see how I came in there and signed for that marker all easy."

I nodded, wanting to know more.

"Well, 'dat Kelsey Brown ID is fake. Top notch fake. Kelsey doesn't exist and neither does 'dat debt I just created with the casino. I walked in a few days ago and set up an account in the MGM credit office. It was gravy." She switched the toothpick from one side of her mouth to the other. "All I needed was ID and the bank account I opened last week. They checked to see how much money I had in there, and then gave me a credit line of $5,000. You know the rest. I come to the cashier booth, show my ID, and request as much of the credit line as I want. Obviously, they'll never get paid back." She laughed hysterically. "And when they go to withdraw the money out my bank account, nothing will be there! But fuck'em, they making billions."

My eyes lit up. She was into everything. "Why me, Monae? I don't wanna lose my job. I need my damn job!"

"Lose your job! It has nothing to do with you, stupid. I coulda gone to anybody's window. It's all laid out. The fake ID and opening the real bank account is the key. Tomorrow morning I'll withdraw my $8,000 out of the Kelsey Brown bank account and never use it again. Next week it's a new ID, and more money. You down?"

I stood stiff. I was stunned.

"You need money, don't you? Or you gon' call Quentin?" She burst into laughter like I was some kinda joke.

"I don't know, Monae."

Her face frowned. "Bitch, do you realize that your ass is broke?"

I shook my head up and down. "Yeah, but…I'm not sure what you want me to do."

"All I want you to do is what you did tonight. I'll open up the bank accounts and the credit lines at MGM with the fake ID, then come to you to collect on my marker. I'll give you twenty percent for looking out. Now, if you wanna make more money, you can start getting the fake ID's too. I got the guy on lock who does it."

"I'll let you know," I blurted out.

"Yeah, you do that." Again, she looked away. Then typed into her phone.

Just then a few shabbily dressed females walked by. "Hey Monae," they slurred in unison. One waved, while another one winked.

"You're into everything." I shook my head in disgust.

"Yup. I do it all. Just remember this, never settle." Oddly, she looked like she was referring to me.

"Look, we really need to talk," I said.

"So talk," she shot back sarcastically.

"Why don't you come over tonight so we can discuss some things?"

"Nah…I gotta make a run."

I was disappointed. "Oh, well be careful," I said in a lighter, more caring tone. "The streets talk, so I know you doing some foul stuff."

"Umh…I'm straight,"she snickered. "I'm invisible."

I moved forward and reached in her direction, but instantly, she dodged my potential hug. She was about to make a statement until her phone rang. "What up?" she answered.

I watched her closely as she said a few lines into the phone then hung up. I knew in my heart it wasn't business. It sounded more like a bootie call.

"Look, I'll holla at you later, Nadia," she uttered, strutting toward her truck.

"Monae," I called out.

She turned back slightly. "What up."

"Can I hold a lil' something. I gotta register for summer school."

"Huh, that's funny. You missed two of your damn finals last week chasing me. Your ass probably failed."

"So what? If I did, I'll just take the classes over," I shot back. "I need about three hundred."

"Don't have it," she said, without the least bit of remorse.

Before I knew it, I was standing on the corner alone, as Monae quickly hopped into her truck and drove off, zipping past me, and taking in the last minute waves and shout outs she received from her groupies.

I felt like a complete idiot. I opened up my phone to call Day-Day, hoping he would take my call. Deep down inside I missed him a lot. His life was simple, uncomplicated and peaceful. It's crazy how life works. When I had him, I wanted more. Now that I'd lost him, I was willing to do whatever to get him back.

I dialed his house number while standing on the curb, only to get the shock of my life. My jaw dropped when the recording came on. "The caller you're trying to reach, does not wish to receive calls from this number."

I couldn't believe it. He'd done the ultimate and blocked my number. I thought about trying his cell, but decided against it. I'd gotten embarrassed enough for one night.

Instead, I hit the end button on my phone and called Tori. Her crazy-ass was just the right person to give me some 'fuck it' advice.

"Yo' what up?" Tori answered.

"Tori, I need some advice," I pleaded.

"You got 'dat shit right. The streets been talkin' 'bout you boo. And I don't like it. But check it; I gotta business deal goin' down on the other line, so I can't kick it right now. I'll call you back."

And just like that Tori hung up, leaving me wondering what the hell she'd heard about me.

11

Jewell

You couldn't wipe the smile off my face as I walked into the Alexander McQueen boutique located inside the Wynn. It had been over three weeks since I'd been in the up-scale couture store, so I was definitely going through with-drawal. In light of all the drama that had been going on in my life recently, I'd taken a small hiatus from shopping just to get a few things in order. Now everything seemed to be falling into place, especially with Kenny.

After Alyssa showed up at my house, I drove straight to his apartment complex the next day and paid $6,000 to break the lease. Luckily, I was the only person on the con-tract, so even if he wanted to challenge my decision, he couldn't. An extra five hundred was added in order to get the management company to change the locks right away, and three hundred went to some local Mexicans to move every-thing out. Shit, I was like Morgan Freeman in the movie *Lean On Me*, I needed things done expeditiously.

From what I hear, once he caught a cab back home from the gym a few hours later, all of his belongings, which only amounted to his clothes, a pool stick, and a few pairs of shoes, had been escorted to the sidewalk. I know all of this because Kenny had been calling my phone non-stop since then. But leaving mushy-ass messages didn't matter. He even had the nerve to say the reason why he cheated was because all I cared about was money. However, I didn't give a shit what his reason was. Since he'd decided to fuck up, I wanted to make sure his ass left out the relationship the same way he came in… **WITH NOTHING.**

Everything else, from furniture and electronics to plants and food were given to Nadia. The last thing I had to tackle was figuring out what to do with the Range Rover. I thought about letting Nadia drive around and floss in it for awhile. But until I discussed it with her, it would just have to sit at the airport parking garage. I'd moved it from in front of my house, just in case he or Alyssa wanted to get cute.

"Ms. Givens, I'm so surprised to see you here," my regular salesperson, Lena said.

I'd been immersed in thought so long, that I almost forgot where I was. However, before I could reply, my phone started to vibrate inside my purse. Something it had been doing all morning, but I'd elected to ignore every call just like this one. I wasn't in the mood for any of Kenny's bullshit lies.

"Oh, hi Lena. I know it's been a while, but you shouldn't be surprised. I'm always gonna shop here. It's my favorite store on the strip." I walked straight over to a nice wine colored chiffon top. "Oh, this must be new because I didn't see it the last time. I'll take that in a medium. As a matter of fact, if it comes in another color, I'll take that one as well."

But, for some strange reason Lena didn't move. She continued to stare at me with a blank expression. Normally, when I wanted something she was at the register before I could finish my sentence. Something was wrong.

Again, my phone started to vibrate, but I disregarded it and kept talking. "Is everything okay? You look sick or something."

"Yes, I'm fine but how are you holding up?" she asked sounding concerned.

What the hell is Lena talking about? I know she's not referring to that Kenny shit, I thought. *Nah...how would she know anyway*. "I'm not sure if I know what you're talking about."

Again, she looked at me crazy. "Oh, well pardon me for assuming. I guess I just didn't expect you to be in the store so soon after the news about your father. But it seems like you're okay, so I'll mind my own affairs." She turned around to pick up the top. "Now, yes, this is a new piece that just came in, and I must say, it's even more stunning once you put it on."

Everything she'd said after the word father was a complete blur, because I wasn't paying attention. "What do you mean the news about my father? What news?"

Lena once again transformed from a highly trained salesperson, to a concerned friend. "Ms. Givens, I don't think I should…" she seemed loss for words.

"What news?" I repeated. This time with a little bit more volume.

"The news about your father's death. It's…it's been on the television all morning."

I stood aimlessly in silence for what seemed like an eternity before collapsing onto the floor.

$$$

When I opened my eyes, the first thing I saw was an all white ceiling, and several people, including Lena, kneeled over my body. Looking at all the people, most of whom I didn't recognize, for a split second I wondered what the hell was going on. But then in almost an instant, I remembered why I was on the floor in the first place.

My father. My father was gone.

I felt numb.

Could barely breathe.

My mind literally went blank.

"Miss…Miss, are you okay?" one of the strangers asked.

I opened my mouth in an attempt to respond, but nothing would come out. After exchanging stares with a few of the other people, I decided to nod my head.

"You must've bumped your head during your fall, because you were out cold," Lena informed. "The EMT's are gonna take you to the hospital. You need to be examined."

This time I managed to force a whisper. "No."

"Miss, you could have a serious head injury. You need to go to the hospital," the same stranger replied. I assumed at this point that he was an EMT.

I knew I had to force myself to act as if I was okay even if I wasn't, because there was no way I was going to anybody's hospital. Taking what little bit of strength I had left, I slowly began to lift myself up.

"Oh no, Ms. Givens. Please lie back down," Lena instructed.

I never stopped moving. "No, really I'm fine," I spoke in a soft tone. "I just have a headache, that's all." By now, I was sitting all the way up.

"I'm so sorry you had to find out this way," Lena continued.

In an instant, tears began to stream down my face like a river. I couldn't believe this was happening. Why? Why would this happen? I buried my face in my hands, as a million thoughts started to run through my head. Lena rushed to console me.

"I…need to…get…out of…here," I said, a few seconds later.

You could tell that everyone was still concerned about my well being, but obviously didn't want to compete with my overwhelming pain.

"Are you sure? Would you like someone to drive you somewhere?" Lena asked.

I shook my head. "No, I…need…to be…alone right…now…PLEASE."

Twenty minutes later, and after more convincing, I was finally back in my car and on my way to my parent's house. Just as before, my phone continued to vibrate, but now I really didn't answer. I wasn't prepared to talk to anyone with the state I was in. The more I drove, the more I couldn't wrap my mind around the thought of my father passing. *Maybe this was all a mistake*, I thought. *Maybe Lena had me mixed up with somebody else*. It was as if I still wasn't convinced that she was telling the truth. It was like nothing had sunk in.

Quickly, I turned on the radio to 97.5, and sure enough, as soon as I heard my father's latest artist saying what a wonderful person he was, I knew it was true.

"Just in case you guys are just tuning in, we want to inform you that the CEO of GMG, which is Givens Music Group, Joseph Givens has passed away. Reports say that Mr. Givens, 61, died late last night, of what appears to be a heart attack, but that has yet to be confirmed," DJ Franzen announced. "We'll give you all more details as they…"

I hit the button for the radio, turning it off instantly. Suddenly, my head started spinning, and my hands began to shake. I couldn't believe what I was hearing. My father…gone? This couldn't be. Besides, I'd just talked to him the night before, and he told me he was feeling much better.

"But I didn't even get a chance to say goodbye," I said out loud, like someone was listening.

Tears began to flood my eyes once again. I could barely see, and was surprised that I hadn't run off the road yet. Who was going to be there to walk me down the aisle now? Who was going to be there to watch my first child being born? Who was going to be my constant cheerleader no matter what I did wrong? Who was going to love me now that he was gone? Why would he leave me? What was I going to do without him? The further I drove, more and more questions began to consume my mind, causing me to weep uncontrollably. I was hurt. Bad.

Minutes later, I pulled up to my parent's gate and was surprisingly able to drive straight through, which was odd, something that my father would've never approved of. He wasn't even in the ground yet, and my mother was already going against his rules. However, despite our differences in the past, I'd already told myself those issues were no longer worth it anymore. At this point, we would both just have to establish civilized relationships with one another, and learn how to get along. My father would've wanted that.

There were at least seven other cars lined up in the driveway, as I pulled up behind the last one and placed my car in park. Scanning the high priced vehicles, I immediately recognized my Uncle Louis' car, but not the other ones. I'm sure there were tons of people here to extend their condolences. Any other day, I would've probably checked my appearance in the rearview mirror, but not today. No matter how good I wanted to look, it wasn't going to bring my father back, so beauty would just have to wait.

I turned off the ignition and stepped out, doing damn near a power walk type of strut to the front door. It was at that moment when I realized that I'd left my purse in the car along with my parent's house keys, so I was forced to ring the doorbell. Something which I didn't want to do, because it made me feel like a complete stranger; like I didn't belong.

Rosa appeared at the door several moments later, but couldn't speak. She cried, sobbed and hugged me at least five minutes before she was even able to utter the words, "Your father." But actually she didn't have to say a word. I knew exactly how she felt.

"I can't believe he's gone," I said, wiping my overflowing tears away. "He was supposed to be okay."

Rosa was visibly upset. "Mr. Givens was such a good

man. He will be missed." She could say that again. Words couldn't even begin to express how much I was going to miss my dad.

"Rosa, why didn't anybody call me? I'm just finding out today."

She looked confused. "What? Mrs. Givens told me she called you."

As crazy as my mother was, even I knew she couldn't have possibly had enough nerve to do something so foul. I had to give her the benefit of the doubt. *Maybe she was too upset to call*, I thought trying to entertain positive thoughts.

"I'm sure she was going to," I said, trying to convince myself.

Rosa desperately tried to get herself together. "Well, we can't stand by the door all day. Go on in the solarium, sweetheart. You have a few relatives that just got in town inside the house, and some of your dad's business associates."

I had no idea who any of those people could've been, even the relatives. "Okay," I said.

However, before I could even lift my foot, my mother came strutting around the corner with a huge smile on her face. That smile disappeared once she saw me. "What are you doing here?" she coldly asked.

I wasn't prepared for the blow. I even turned around to see if she might've been talking to someone else. Even Rosa was surprised. "I don't understand."

"What the hell is there to understand? The last time you were in this house, you tried to kill me, so you're no longer welcomed here anymore. As a matter of fact, I have a restraining order against you."

I was beyond speechless. "A restraining order. Why? Why are you acting like this?"

My mother's face frowned like she ate something sour. "Jewell, your father's no longer here, so that innocent shit is not going to work with me. Yes, I have a restraining order. You better be glad I didn't press charges for attempted murder." She turned to Rosa. "Don't let her back in this house." When Rosa didn't respond, my mother's voice escalated. "Did you hear me?"

It looked as if it killed Rosa to say anything. "Yes, Mrs. Givens."

When my mother chuckled, I looked at her and noticed that she had on a long flowing robe with furry open toed heels; something that I'd never seen her wear before. Not to mention, she looked like a hooker. *If she has company, then why the hell is she walking around looking like a fucking Fredericks of Hollywood model?*

"Rosa, you don't have to call me Mrs. Givens anymore. Call me Joyce," she instructed. "Now, go check on our guests."

Rosa nodded, then hurried off.

I didn't understand. Where were her tears? Wasn't she supposed to be grieving like everybody else? Hell, they'd been married for thirty-two years. Thinking about how my father was always too good for her, my tears once again began to make their presence. But something told me I had to be the bigger person this time.

"Mom, do you think we could work out our differences? For daddy at least?"

"What's there to work out?" she asked. "Look, let's be honest, Jewell. You've never liked me, and I certainly never liked you."

Normally, I had no problems taking her cheap shots, but the tears proved that my heart was broken. "I just wanted you to be my mother. To spend time with me. Take me to ballet recitals and cheerleading. Instead, you always pushed me off on Rosa or Daddy."

She looked me dead in my face. "And you know why?

Because I didn't want you to begin with. When I got pregnant, I wanted to get an abortion so bad, but Joe wouldn't hear of it. He made me give birth to you. I never wanted to be a mother."

Her comment pierced my heart. I knew my mother, and I had an overdose of animosity and jealousy toward each other, but I never knew her feelings ran that deep. I wanted so badly to run up and hug her, to ask her if we could start over, but I knew she would never allow it. Affection wasn't in her vocabulary. In twenty-three years, I'd never even gotten a pat on the back. Now, I was finally convinced that she'd purposely decided not to inform me about my own father's death.

At that moment, Uncle Louis walked into the room and stood beside my mother. "Hello Jewell." I hoped like hell he would talk some sense into her.

Still upset, I raised my hand and waved.

My mother snapped. "Don't you know how to talk?"

"Joyce, please. It's not the time for that," Uncle Louis said, placing his hand on her lower back. An area that was too low in my opinion.

She looked at him and smiled. "Yeah, Lou, I guess you're right." She then looked at me and scowled. "I know I can't keep you from coming to the funeral, but you need to stay as far away from me as possible. There's no need to be phony." She walked over to the front door. "Now, get out."

I looked at Uncle Louis, who stared back at me like he agreed with her decision. Growing up, he always took up for me. What was the difference now? Again, I didn't know how to respond. The only thing I could do was respect her wishes. The humiliation was simply unbearable, and there were no words for the severe pain that I was in. As I walked toward the front door, I wasn't surprised when she didn't try and stop me. I don't think she even stood around long enough to watch me leave.

12

Tori

I slapped a crisp fifty dollar bill into Eduardo's hand while rushin' him out the door. He'd cleaned extra good and had the apartment smellin' like fresh pine. I didn't get my spot cleaned very often, but for my special guest it was necessary.

"Eduardo, get all 'dis shit!" I hollered, knowin' he didn't understand a word I said. "I got power moves to make. Time is money."

Instead of movin' faster, he grabbed his bucket full of rags and cleanin' supplies, and moved just two feet before sittin' the bucket on the floor again. His short Mexican-ass was a nice piece of eye candy, which is why I wanted a guy to clean my shit. But he was startin' to get on my nerves.

"Tori," he called.

"What the fuck! Eduardo, let's fuckin' go. I got company comin'."

It was funny as hell watchin' the dumb-fuck look on his face, while I cursed and smiled all in the same breath. "Come the fuck on!"

I snatched the front door open, never wantin' to hear him out. Then pushed his broom and mop to the outside area of my door, hopin' he would grab his supplies and get the fuck out. But he stood still lookin' crazy in my doorway wit' his eyes widened and his hand extended like he wasn't gonna leave. I jerked my neck backward showin' my offense. I had told the mufucka I would lace him good for comin' on such short notice, but now his ass was being downright ungrateful.

I got up close up in his face like a Canon camera zoomin' in.

"Senor, let me tell you one mufuckin' thing." I pointed so close to his eye, he had no idea he was 'bout to lose an eyeball. "You being real ungrateful." I nodded and scrunched up my face, lettin' him know he was fuckin' wit' the right one. "I gave you a fifty thinkin' I was helpin' you out. You could be on yo' way back to Tijuana or some shit, instead of ova here makin' a lil' change."

I guess he could tell I was fired up, 'cause he started speakin' 'dat fast, ebonics-type Spanish, then managed to get out a few English words. "No enough."

He was holdin' me up. My new business partner, who I'd planned to fuck if everythin' went my way, was due to arrive within minutes.

I twisted my arm to check the time on my J12 Chanel watch. "Okay, 'dats it. Get the fuck out."

I dug into my pocket and grabbed two tens before holdin' my hand out. "Eduardo, give me 'dat damn money back then!" I ordered.

He turned and handed me the fifty wit' a smile. I in turn, handed him two tens, and pushed his short ass on the other side of my threshold.

When I slammed the door in his face, it sounded like the hinges were about to rip off. Then the loud babblin' sound of Eduardo speakin' Spanish resonated through the halls. I turned, walked toward the kitchen, and pulled my Domino Sugar bags from the cabinet and onto the table. I didn't give a fuck if he stayed out there all night. He wasn't gettin' back up in my spot.

"Stop bangin' on my door!" I shouted as loud as I could. "Yo' ass shoulda took the fifty!" *I really am gonna call immigration on them fuckas one day.* Thinkin' 'bout my annoyin' neighbors.

I whisked my way around the kitchen, grabbin' rubber bands and anythin' else I needed to count up my loot. I had been makin' money like crazy, but spendin' out of control. I settled down at the kitchen table to count up before Adrian arrived. 'Dis way, if I had to give him a lil' money for information up front, I'd have it ready.

I laughed at myself sittin' at the table like a banker. Jewell always talked shit 'bout me not havin' a bank account. But for what? Why did I need a white man to hold on to my paper? Then when the IRS or the FEDS wanted to take my shit, they could wit' no problem.

"Dats why I keep my own loot right here in my damn Domino Sugar bags." I smiled and blew kisses at the bulk load of money.

Just the fact 'dat I now needed four bags to hold my cash made me grin inside. Nothin' else mattered to me, but havin' paper. I guess 'dats why my family really had nothin' to do wit' me.

At 'dat moment I thought 'bout callin' my mother who'd pretty much written me off. She said I was no good, trifilin', stood for nothin', and needed Jesus. I agreed wit' some of what she said, but not all. One day I knew I would change my life, and hoped I could redeem myself. From time to time I yearned for a mother's love, but since I'd been on my own since the age of sixteen, now wasn't the time to get soft.

I dumped the money onto the table, and refocused on the goal. From the looks of things, I was makin' moves. Ecstasy, pussy, movies, strippin'; whatever it took, I vowed to stay up.But again my bankin' session was quickly interrupted when thoughts of my girl, Jewell entered my mind. I could only imagine the pain she was in by her losin' her pops. I'd been callin' her non-stop, but she still hadn't answered, so I told myself it was only right if I gave her a lil' bit of space.

Suddenly, I realized 'dat the bangin' had stopped. Walkin' back over to the peephole, I looked out and realized 'dat Eduardo was finally gone. "I guess he finally got the picture," I said, walkin' back into the kitchen.

Fifteen minutes passed, and before long, I'd bundled up $45,000. There was about six or seven thousand left on the table when my cell rung.

"Who 'dis?" I spoke into the phone.

"It's me," a deep, seductive voice sounded on the other end.

My first instinct was to say, who the fuck is me? But the voice made me feel all tingly inside. "And you are?"

"Stop playing. It's Adrian. I'm outside."

"Oh shit. C'mon up."

I pressed end, jumped up from the table, and started stuffin' the loose cash into the bags, followed by the thousands wrapped in bundles. My fingers quickly folded the bags at the top and pushed them to the center of the table. I figured they'd be okay until I freshened up, and rushed back to open the door for Adrian.

I was impressed already, 'cause the nigga had me excited. I didn't rush like 'dat for too many people, but since the nigga was in the football league, he had potential. I ran to the bathroom toward the back of the apartment, thinkin' 'bout his tall, solid ass. He was the sexy bun I'd hooked up wit' ova a month ago at the Jay-Z party, but his voice had more of an appeal than it did before. We rapped on the phone a few times, but he never said anythin' about money to get my coochie wet.

'Dat is, until yesterday when he said he had a few connects to get my sex tape distributed internationally. Of course dollar signs invaded my mind. Up until now, I'd only sold 'bout 12,000 copies; mostly via the internet and a few thousand from my own hustle to a few independently owned DVD stores. But ‘dat wasn’t shit. My tape was ‘bout it ‘bout it, and deserved to be sold all ova the world. I smiled at the thought.

The fact ‘dat dude was ‘bout to get me paid made me consider givin’ him some ass. But then again, ‘dat shit depended on how many contacts I got out of ‘em. He had told me ‘dat he pitched my sex tape to the head guy over at Trojan Distribution, one of the largest straight to DVD distributors in the country. I just needed a name and a phone number.

Of course, Adrian thought he was gonna be involved. Over the phone we had discussed him gettin’ twenty percent of whatever he set up for me, but ‘dat wasn’t gonna go down like ‘dat. I wasn’t born in the hood for nothin’. I just needed his info, and my shit would go platinum on its own.

By the time he found out I was a scam artist, I’d be on to the next dude and have his ass dealt wit’. Although I thought about it, he was a big, thick nigga, so I’d probably need extra man power to handle his ass. His body reminded me of Deeboe from the movie *Friday*, but his face was workable, even a little sexy from what I remember.

I pranced outta the bathroom swiftly, when I heard the knock on my door. The settin’ needed to be right for big business to take place. I wanted him comfortable and at ease with me, so I hit the button to my CD player as soon as I walked into the livin’ room. Number two was perfect. Angie Stone, ‘dat soulful shit. *No More Rain* blared through the speakers, makin’ me feel good and bringin’ back memories when my momma used to blast Earth Wind and Fire every Friday night. *Enough reminiscin’ ‘bout ‘dat bitch for one night*, I thought.

I sang along to the music and adjusted the newest addition to my wig family on my head. I didn’t want ‘dis one to fall off. It wasn’t a lace front like I normally wore. ‘Dis was just a lil’ somethin’ I threw on to entertain ole’ boy. It was perfect for tonight; a black short, sexy type wig. Almost like the page-boy cut Rihanna rocked now.

I shook my body, feelin' real good while struttin' up to the door. I'd already applied my bronze lip gloss, and had touched up my lashes a bit. So, I was ready to give my new victim a taste of Tori.

I checked the peephole before grabbin' the knob. When the door swung open, he didn't have to say nothin'. The saliva leakin' from his mouth said it all.

"Close yo' mouth and c'mon in, nigga."

Adrian stepped inside, but couldn't take his eyes off my red Versace shirt-dress.

"You look good. Damn, I don't remember all that from the club," he commented, referring to my breast.

"I'on remember all of 'dat," I pointed, referrin' to his bi-ceps. He was a big dude, just like I liked'em, straight outta jail type niggas.

We walked over to the couch and sat down to talk a bit. Immediately we hit it off. We sat like old friends and discussed his crazy past in detail. Then it dawned on me. I was being rude.

"Let me get you somethin' to drink," I offered, standin' slightly.

"Oh no, sit down. You all I need. I'm enjoying your company."

I sat back down, but 'dis time made sure my dress was raised a little higher. I wanted to get his appetite wet so we could move onto business. In less than thirty minutes he had told me his whole life story. I had to sit and pretend to be interested...torture!

Then all of a sudden he turned the tables. The conversation suddenly focused on me. He started askin' way too many questions.

"So, you a hustler, huh?" he blurted out.

"Is 'dat what you think?" I asked. "Why, you jealous?"

"Nah, it's not a jealous thing. I'm just curious. I like

how you talk, how you carry yourself. But some people might think it's slick and arrogant, almost like a dude."

"Well, fuck what people think and the boat they rode in on." I rolled my eyes, 'cause the nigga was actin' all funny all of a sudden. "And if you think 'dat 'bout me, fuck you too. I gotta get mine."

"Nah slim, I'm just saying, it's how you talk and present yourself. I know I've only talked to you a hand full of times, but you always on some rah rah, get money scamming tip." He laughed like he was making fun of me. "First it was the sex tape, then you told me about the drug deals, and the stripping on occasions. What don't you do?"

"I don't do you."

His expression changed. It didn't seem like he was used to my kind. The kind 'dat wouldn't take his shit. As far as I was concerned, 'dis date was over. I needed his contacts, so he could be kicked to the curb.

I moved closer, proppin' myself up on my knees, then took my forefinger, twirled it in the air, and landed the tip of my fire engine red fingernail on the bottom of his chin.

"Now, let's get down to business. What's the name of yo' best distributor? And how many units can they move in a month?"

Adrian had a blank look on his face. I sorta thought the nigga was deranged. "Tell me you're not serious."

"Look, I know yo' dick might be gettin' hard, but baby boy, I need information. Business before pleasure," I said seductively, then leaned in to kiss his forehead.

I made sure my Double D's smashed him all in the face; so much he could barely breathe. My tactics appeared to be workin', 'cause the nigga couldn't speak. However, the game soon switched.

Grabbin' the back of my head, Adrian quickly shoved his thick tongue into my mouth without an invitation. He then cupped one of my breasts and squeezed it like he was inspectin' a fuckin' tangerine inside the grocery store. It took a few seconds for me to pull away.

"Yo-Yo-Yo, you violatin'!" I shouted. I wondered where the hell he was tryin' to go wit' 'dis.

"What the fuck do you expect? You shouldn't be sticking your shit all up in my face!"

I didn't care for his tone, and at 'dis point didn't care 'bout the distribution. I would just have to find another way to get my sex tape out there, 'cause 'dis nigga had lost his mind. I jumped off the couch and stood a few feet away. "You need to get the fuck out. 'Dis shit is ova!"

Adrian looked at me wit' a crooked grin then stood as well. "Bitch, I ain't going anywhere until I get what I came for."

"Get what you came for? Nigga, ain't nobody checkin' for no sex tape shit after 'dat lil' stunt you just pulled." I pointed toward the door. "Now get out!"

"I'm not talking about the sex tape," he replied, wit' the same deranged look from before. Only this time, he seemed more disturbed. Something was definitely wrong.

"Adrian, get the fuck out!" I repeated.

He took a step toward me, ignorin' my constant demands. "Make me."

Wit'out even a second thought, my first instinct was to run. Turnin' around, I shot toward the kitchen to grab the steak knife 'dat was still on the table. I needed a weapon, fast. But I only managed to make it to the doorway before I felt Adrian's big masculine hands on my shoulder.

"Get off me!" I screamed.

If it was one time where I wished my neighbors were listenin', it was now. I tried my best to wiggle my way out of his tight grip, but it wasn't workin'.

"Shut up, bitch!" he yelled, pinnin' me up against the

wall. He placed his heavy forearm against the back of my neck and pressed hard.

"What are you doin'?" I asked, with the side of my face pushed against the eggshell colored paint.

"I'm about to show you what a real man feel's like." I could hear him fumbling with his belt buckle.

"Oh, no…please don't do 'dis," I pleaded.

"Didn't I tell you to shut up?" He grabbed me and tossed my body like a rag doll onto the cold linoleum floor.

Landin' on my back, I quickly sat up and used my elbows to try and crawl backwards, but Adrian grabbed my legs. I screamed at the top of my lungs, and tried to land several wild kicks, but every one of them missed or just merely grazed him.

Whether he was angry at my disobedience or unwillingness to give up, whatever the reason, it only took about three seconds for Adrian to place his three hundred and fifty pound body on top on mine. He slapped me across my face twice, completely catchin' me off guard. The stingin' sensation and the ringin' in my ear was overwhelmin'. He then placed his hands tightly around my neck and began to squeeze.

"I bet you'll shut up now," he stated, while applyin' even more pressure.

Starin' up at him, I knew I was lookin' into the eyes of a man who was tryin' to kill me. I had to break free…but how?

At 'dat moment I was convinced 'dat somethin' bad was 'bout to happen to me. Adrian was gonna do whatever he wanted, and until I could reach the knife, there was nothin' I could do to stop him.

A rush of fear ran through me as I began to lay motionless. A signal 'dat I was givin' up. Besides, I didn't want to fight back anymore. I was ready to get it over wit'.

As if he sensed my submission, Adrian removed one of his hands and began to fumble wit' his pants once again. Seconds later, I could feel him placin' his hand under my dress and tuggin' at my panties. When he was finally able to rip them off, he looked at me and frowned.

"Scream again, and I'll kill you." He tightened the one hand around my neck just to let me know he was serious.

After gettin' himself into position, it only took seconds to lunge his huge dick inside my pussy. At first he called me a bitch, told me I was dry, but 'dat didn't last long. After a few long and deep strokes, he was into it. He began to fuck me wildly, drivin' his manhood deeper inside until my coochie felt like it was on fire. The more he pushed the more pressure he placed around my neck. I could barely breathe.

Hearin' him moan, made me sick to my stomach. He even went as far as tryin' to kiss me again, but I turned my head. Tears began to well up in my eyes, and made their way down my cheeks soon after. *He didn't even wear a condom*, I thought. My body felt numb as he pounded away at my pussy like a jackhammer against concrete. I wanted to scream as beads of his sweat began to fall in my face. For the first time in my life, I felt helpless.

"Ahhh…shit!" Adrian yelled out. His body began to jerk like he was havin' a seizure. I could tell he was 'bout to cum.

Even though the awful grumblin' was like music to my ears, the thought of a complete stranger releasin' his nut inside my body made the tears roll even faster. I wasn't in a position to have a baby. I couldn't believe 'dis was happenin' to me. It was like a nightmare.

Adrian slowly removed his dick from inside of me along wit' the hand around my neck, and propped himself up on his knees. "Turn over," he said, still out of breath.

I was shocked. I wanted him to go. "What?"

"Turn over!" he yelled.

"No, Adrian please…you got what you wanted."

He displayed a wicked grin. "Who said I was done."

"Please don't do…"

Before I could even say another word, Adrian hit me in the face again. 'Dis time using his fist. I could taste the blood in my mouth immediately.

"I said turn the fuck over!" He grabbed my legs and flipped me over like a damn pancake.

However, what came next was devastatin'. It felt like my anal walls were 'bout to rip apart as Adrian rammed his dick inside my ass and began to pump back and forth. The pain was excruciatin'…unbearable.

"Oh God no, please stop!" I cried out, thinkin' he would have some type of sympathy on me. But it didn't work. The more I yelled out, the faster his balls slapped against my ass cheeks. He wasn't goin' to stop. He was enjoyin' 'dis shit.

Ten minutes later, I was still layin' on the floor when Adrian finally stood up and placed his dick back inside his pants. He had the nerve to be talkin' shit 'bout how good my ass felt, but I was barely listenin'. All I wanted to do was lay there and play dead, hopin' he would leave. Besides, I was afraid if I said somethin' else he would take his pants back off and start all over. I wanted to stay as quiet as possible. 'Dat was until I heard Adrian fumblin' around on my kitchen table. I sat up immediately.

"I'ma have a real good time with this shit." I watched as he grabbed two of the sugar bags. "Hustling has definitely paid off for you, baby."

Wit' everythin' happenin' so fast, I had completely forgotten that I'd left my money out on the table. I stood up and lunged toward him. "What the fuck are you doin'? Put my shit down!" I yelled reachin' out for one of the bags. I had a pretty good grip on the plastic until Adrian was able to snatch my hand away.

"I'm getting what I came for."

I was sick of him sayin' 'dat. "Why would you do 'dis. You supposed to be a football player. You got yo' own damn money." I tried to reach for the bag again, but he pushed me away.

Adrian again flashed a crazy grin. "I wouldn't be too sure about that. The closet thing I get to football is T.V. I hustled your ass at the party just like you tried to hustle me."

I was in complete shock. "What?"

Makin' sure he had a good hold on all four bags, Adrian sprinted out of the kitchen like Carl Lewis, knockin' me over in the process. By the time I got back on my feet, he was already halfway out the front door. I ran behind him at top speed, but couldn't seem to catch up.

"Stop!" I yelled, running through the parking lot. "Somebody help me!"

Unfortunately, nobody came to my rescue. It was painful watchin' Adrian gettin' further and further away and my hard earned money disappearin' in front of my own eyes. Stoppin' in the middle of the street, I dropped down on my knees and cried like a newborn baby.

13

Jewell

"Oh my God, Jewell, wake up! I can't believe you're still in the bed," Nadia nagged.

"Yeah, you were supposed to be dressed and ready to go by now," Tori added in a solemn tone. For some reason, she just didn't seem like herself.

Little did they know I was already wide awake, but just couldn't move. Plus Julia, and even Devin, had tried to get me up just minutes before, but I'd sent them both away.

I watched as Nadia walked over and opened the custom made curtains, allowing an overwhelming amount of bright sunlight to come through. I wanted so badly to tell them to get out, to leave me alone in the coffin like room, but I knew it wouldn't work. Regardless of what I said, I knew they weren't going anywhere. They were here for a reason. They were here to take me to my father's funeral.

Tori walked over to my bed and pulled off the duvet comforter. "C'mon girl. We gonna be late. It's 11:20. The service starts at noon."

"I still can't believe your mother didn't get a family car for y'all. This is crazy," Nadia added.

"Why not? She a straight bitch," Tori replied.

I still hadn't spoken a word while the two went back and forth. Nadia seemed outraged, yet Tori just behaved strangely. She was angry at my mother, yet calm.

The last seven days had been the worst days of my life, but this day proved to be the hardest. Every night since my father's death, I found myself balled up in a fetal position, crying until my eyes stung. I remember asking God why He would do something like this. Why He would leave me without a father? My emotions went back and forth and would quickly turn from sadness to anger. I was angry at God. I was angry at Him for allowing this to happen…but then it hit me. Regardless of how I felt, my father was dead. Dead… and there was nothing I could do to bring him back. Love was something I didn't even fully realize until I lost him, and the emotional impact of his death could only be proportionate to dropping a bomb on my heart. A heart that ached with sorrow.

Nadia reached over and gently touched my arm. "Jewell, I know this is hard, but we gotta go." Placing her hand under my back, she lifted my body then sat me up.

I finally gave my friend eye contact, then shook my head in disagreement. "I don't think I can do this." My voice was groggy.

"Yes you can. You'll be mad at yourself if you don't say goodbye," Nadia replied.

"Dats right, baby girl, you gotta try and be strong. Your dad wouldn't want to see you like 'dis," Tori said, with a soft tone. This was the first time I'd ever seen her so sincere. "I know I've always picked on you 'bout your pops, but to be honest, I was just jealous. Y'all had the best relationship, and that's somethin' I wish me and my pops coulda had. Shit…sometimes watchin' yo' ass made me wanna break down and call 'dat nigga. Well, 'dats if I could find him. He probably back in jail."

Nadia agreed. "Yeah, I just told myself the other day that I needed to try and work things out with my dad."

Tori rolled her eyes. "Shit, good luck. Uncle Earl is tough."

"Shut up, Tori," Nadia responded, before looking at her watch. "Please come on, Jewell, it's 11:30."

Despite my hesitation, I finally decided to give in. "Okay," I said, in the same groggy voice. My head immediately started going in circles as I slowly got out of bed, and placed my feet on the plush carpet. Recently, I couldn't remember the last time I woke up without a hangover. "Grab my black Roberto Cavalli dress and the ankle wrap Manolo's out the closet. Everything should be in the classy section."

As Nadia scurried away, I looked at Tori, who had a comforting smile. "Dats crazy how yo' closet got categories," she mentioned.

Even she looked professional in her Nicole Miller pencil skirt and cream shirt that actually covered her breasts. I tried to return the smile, but couldn't. Besides, I wasn't the same person that I was a week ago. Oddly, Tori didn't seem the same either.

When Nadia returned with the items, I noticed how good she looked in her grey Diane von Furstenberg jersey dress. She had definitely been stepping her wardrobe up lately. I stood up and immediately began taking off my Juicy tank top and shorts. Luckily, I still had on my bra from the night before.

"Thanks," I said. As I placed the dress over my head, I could see Tori and Nadia looking at me like I was crazy. "What?" I asked.

It looked as if Nadia was about to speak, but Tori beat her to the punch. "So, you ain't gon' take no shower? Not even a bird bath?"

So much for the sincere Tori. I shook my head no. "We're late, right?"

The hell with a bath or even applying concealer to my face. Not that I had bad skin, but it was the dark circles under my eyes that I wanted to hide. After putting on my shoes, I walked a few steps over to my nightstand, and reached for my new best friend, a bottle of Courvoisier. Now more than ever,

I'd turned to liquor to numb the pain that had proven to be too much for me to handle.

I picked up the shot glass that was conveniently placed beside the bottle, and filled it with the $260.00 cognac. Taking the shot to the head, I could immediately feel the warm liquid traveling through my body. A feeling that I desired several times throughout the day. Staying sober offered no relief from the agony.

"That was good," I said, licking my dry coated lips to give them a little bit of moisture. After placing the glass back on the table, I looked at my two friends, who appeared to be studying me. "Y'all ready?"

Not really caring what their response would be, I picked up my Gucci sunglasses that were also on the nightstand and headed for the door.

$$$

Fifteen minutes later, we were pulling up to Hope Valley Baptist Church. A church where my father wasn't necessarily a member, but had given so many donations that he should've been an honorary member. Even though I was surprised that we'd gotten there so fast, I shouldn't have been because Tori was known for driving like Mario Andretti. If Nadia had driven, we probably wouldn't have arrived until the following week.

Scanning the large crowd that was already forming into the church, I began to become uncertain about going inside all over again. Not only did I not want to see my father laid up in some coffin, but I wasn't prepared to be phony. I didn't want to smile or pretend to connect with the multiple hands that would reach out. I really just wanted to be left alone.

"You ready?" Nadia asked.

I let out a huge sigh. "Yeah, ready to get this over

with."

"So, you gotta walk in with the family, don't you?" Nadia questioned. She looked out of the window. "Has anybody even called you to see where you were?"

"Don't you see this ain't the average funeral?" Tori chimed in. "Her mother probably don't even care if she show up. And the rest of the family either."

"What family? The only family I had is about to be buried," I replied, in a low tone. "My phone is off anyway."

Nadia seemed curious. "What about your Uncle Louis?"

"He's not my real uncle. He was my father's best friend and attorney, who's obviously so busy trying to kiss my mother's ass, he doesn't have time to be consoling."

"'Dats why you got us," Tori assured.

Despite the pain I was in, I looked at my friend with concern. I didn't understand why she wasn't cursing somebody out by now. "Are you okay, Tori?"

"I'm fine," she said, even though her response wasn't too convincing.

I tried to force another smile while popping a mint into my mouth. "Well, let's go." I opened up the car door and hopped out, then waited for my two friends. Seconds later, we made our way to the front doors of the church with Nadia holding my arm for support the entire way. I hadn't even made it ten feet before people were coming up to me left and right with their condolences. However, the only response they received was a head nod. Call me a bitch, but I wasn't here to make friends. Even Kenny's bitch-ass had the nerve to walk up to me. My response to him was my middle finger going up in the air. He had a lot of nerve showing up uninvited.

As soon as we walked into the church, my emotions hit me like ton of bricks. Seeing the two huge photos of my late father displayed on each side of his platinum colored casket, was too much to bear. I had to cover my mouth to keep from screaming to the top of my lungs. My knees felt weak…my body once again numb. Now more than ever, the loss had finally struck me. How was I going to get through this service without trying to climb into the casket with him? In a way, I was glad that the casket was closed, because regardless of how peaceful he might've looked, I would've been devastated to see him like that. I needed to hold on to the good memories.

Seeing that I was about to lose it, Tori instantly grabbed one of my arms, while Nadia held onto the other one. We could see Rosa standing at the front of the church waving her hand the further we walked inside. Obviously, she'd saved me a seat, and it was a good thing she did, because now looking around, the place was wall to wall packed.

Making our way to the front, I could finally see my mother, who'd taken her position on the front row along with my father's financial planner, Howard, a few other men in business suits, and Uncle Louis, who was rubbing her back way too sensual. I still couldn't believe that I hadn't seen or talked to my mother since the first day I found out about my father's death. She was obviously taking the whole restraining order thing very seriously. What kind of mother would do such a thing? Why couldn't we pretend to love each other just for today? For a split second, grief turned to anger and it took all of my willpower to control my rage. What else could I have done anyway? If I'd allowed my anger to get the best of me, I would've ended up disrupting my father's funeral, and that was simply unthinkable.Once we made it to the front, I walked up to Rosa and gave her a huge hug.

"Oh, baby. It's good to see you," Rosa said, kissing my cheek. "Here, I have seats for you and your friends." She directed us to the second row, behind my mother, of course.

"Thanks for everything you've ever done," I responded.

Rosa was teary eyed. "You're like my daughter, Jewell. I'm gonna always be there for you regardless of..." She was instantly cut off by my mother, who called out her name.

"Rosa, sit down," she demanded, in a low but stern voice. It was at that point when we finally made eye contact. And just like I thought, she turned away. It was like I never even existed. It was like I was more of a spectator than family.

"Come on, baby, sit down," Rosa instructed. She was and had always been good at ignoring the tension between the two of us.

As soon as we took our seats, the choir, along with my father's favorite R&B artist from his label, softly began to sing, which quickly prompted my tears to make an appearance. The more the songstress wailed, *Amazing Grace*, the faster the tears rushed down my cheeks. But I wasn't alone. Rosa, Nadia, Tori and even my mother had all began to become overwhelmed with emotion. It was hard not to.

When the song was finally over, the singer received several heartwarming hand claps before the pastor took his place at the podium. Everything that he said was pretty much a blur until I heard the words, "If anyone wants to come up and share something about Joseph, you may do so at this time." I stood up so quickly, it was as if someone had pushed me.

"Jewell, are you sure," I could hear Nadia whisper as I made my way toward the podium.

Even though I was nowhere near prepared, there was no doubt in my mind that I wanted to be the first one to speak. When I approached the microphone, the first person I looked at was my mother, who once again looked away. The tears never stopped rolling as I scanned the rest of the large crowd and then finally spoke.

"To those of you who don't know who I am, my name is Jewell Givens. Joseph Givens was my father. I wasn't prepared to say anything, so I'm going to be brief." I wiped a few tears away before continuing. "I'm sure everyone here today knows that Joseph Mckinley Givens was a good man, but what most of you probably didn't know is that he was an even better father. There's really an absence of proper words to describe the love that I have for my father, but it's not due to a lack of a vocabulary. They just don't exist. I'm gonna miss him sooo much, but most of all I'm gonna miss his unconditional support. I could always rely on him for reassurance, despite what was going on or who was at fault. And although I will not have him by my side anymore, I'll always have the lessons that he imparted on my life. I'll remember the times with him as vividly as the great music he made, where I'll know every word, every note, every solo. And it is my belief that if we all carry a little piece of Mr. Joseph Givens with us, he will never truly die." Again I wiped away my tears. "You know…I have no idea how I'm supposed to return back to my normal life. A life without a dad, without his laughter, or even his disapproving looks, but Daddy I'm gonna try."

When I looked out into the crowd, there wasn't a dry eye in sight. Again, even my mother had managed to show some type of sentiment. I then looked down at the podium and saw for the first time my father's charming smile on front of the funeral program. "Just remember everyone. You will always find my father wherever you find a path of love, kindness, and a grace that lingers. I love you, Daddy."

Holding up the program, I kissed the picture before stepping off the podium and heading back to my seat. Throughout the rest of the service, tears came and went, but never for too long as there were steady arms around my shoulder or laughter spilling over from a pleasant memory.

Overall, the service turned out to be nice, and I'm glad I got a chance to say goodbye.

As the huge crowd spilled out forty minutes later, everyone kept coming up to me. letting me know how much they enjoyed my speech. This time, I thanked each and every person, because for some reason I was in a much better mood. That is until Howard walked up to me. For some reason, I had a feeling his little visit wouldn't be pleasant from the smirk on his face. I couldn't wait for Tori and Nadia to pull up with the car.

"Nice speech, Jewell. I'm sure Joe was listening to you," he said, placing his massive arm around my shoulder.

"Thanks, Howard. I'm really gonna miss him."

"Yeah, me too. I don't know who I'm going to argue with now. That man was such a pistol when it came to his finances."

"Well, I'm sure my mother won't have a problem filling those shoes."

He smiled. "I guess you're right about that. Oh, speaking of affairs, I'm so sorry to hear that your father didn't get a chance to finalize his will. There were so many good plans for his estate."

My heart almost skipped a beat. "What do you mean he didn't get a chance to finalize his will? What the hell does finalize mean?" I guess from my reaction he could tell that I was concerned.

"Oh, I'm sorry, Jewell. I thought Joyce might've told you already."

"She never tells me anything!" I yelled. "Now, what are you talking about?" A few people turned and looked in my direction.

Howard seemed hesitant, but knew he wasn't going to get away from me until he told me everything.

"Joseph never got a chance to sign his Last Will &

Testament before he got sick. And I'm so mad because I've been pushing for him to get one for years, but he was always so busy."

"So, what does that mean for me?"

"Well, the entire estate will be going to your mother, so now she's in charge of everything."

I stood in shock for what seemed like an eternity. *Everything...going to my mother? How can that be? Why didn't my father leave me anything? What does this mean for me? Am I broke?*

14

Nadia

I popped two extra-strength Advils when Monae and I left Bank of America on W. Sahara Avenue, after opening up a new bank account. As we walked to the car, I felt light-headed unsure about how things were gonna go down. I was officially a scam artist. My mind flashed to how things had gone down so far.

We'd gotten up early after spending an uninteresting night together and met up with Big Jake, Monae's connect with the fake ID's. He already had the information ready when we got there. I remember staggering in nervously like we were walking into an ambush. Immediately, Big Jake clowned me, asking Monae where she got my scared-ass from. I didn't care; being like Monae wasn't anything to be proud of.

He handed me my name for the day- Lolita Williams. All I had to do was take the picture, and out came an authentic ID twenty minutes later. Monae had pre-chosen at least twenty-five names, letting me know she'd planned on doing this for the long haul. I thought *damn, on the real, this is some Thelma and Louise type shit.*

Big Jake boasted about how much money he pulled in for the week by creating the best fake ID's in the state of Nevada. Three hundred per ID was the charge. Of course Monae got gangsta, reminding him how many people she'd sent his way. So after a lil' more slick negotiating, she peeled off six hundred dollars for us both and headed out to complete the next task.

It was wild how I'd let Monae use me to her advantage. Our relationship was so foul now. I didn't even wanna look at her half the time. We rode down Tropicana Avenue in silence on our way to the Treasure Island Hotel and Casino. Getting approved for a casino credit account was the last step in making sure we could pull off the scam. I'd caught a serious case of the jitters. But the ride over in the car gave me a chance to reflect on my life. *What am I thinking*? I asked myself. I knew better. I had big dreams. Dreams that could become a reality. Just like my parents, hard work would pay off, if I stuck to it. Instead, I opted to chase fast money with Monae.

We arrived at the front of the hotel faster than I expected. When the Escalade pulled to the curb, a valet guy ran over to us like we were royalty and popped open my door. I shuffled to get my off-brand slip-ons back onto my feet.

"Checking in?" he asked.

Monae nodded, hopped out, and shuffled her way into the hotel, never even looking back. I followed behind as if I really didn't want to be involved. I knew she was irritated by my demeanor, but shit, I was scared. Within seconds, my ears rung from the loud sounds of slot machines going off, and high-rollers hollering from the crap tables. I tried to walk a little faster to catch up with Monae, but she was on a mission.

"Come the fuck on, Nadia!" she shouted, standing in front of a door that read Credit Office.

As soon as we hit the other side of the door, an attractive wealthy looking white woman pulled her glasses down slightly toward her nose. "May I help you?" she asked, like we didn't belong.

"Sure can," Monae boasted. Instantly, she had her hands moving with all sorts of assertive hand gestures. She looked the woman up and down, like there was an instant at-here."

She smiled.

Monae moved toward the plush seats where potential clients sit and pulled out a chair. Although uninvited, she sat making herself at home before we got started.My eyes darted toward the lavish carpet and the expensive looking décor.

"Can we get this show on the road?" Monae asked arrogantly. "I know the procedures already. So check my info. I'm ready to get my gamble on," she said convincingly, then rubbed the insides of her hands together rapidly. "Sit down, Lolita," she said to me.

A stupid look appeared on my face for a moment. I had already forgotten my new name. I brushed past the woman who was finally introducing herself to Monae as Ms. Berelli. She moved a few yards to the opposite side of her desk, while Monae and I sat across from her waiting for instructions.

Ms. Berelli wasn't very friendly and her disposition was clear as she whipped out two sheets and grabbed two pens. She barely wanted to look at either of us. It was clear she was uncomfortable with the sexual looks she was getting. I wasn't even mad at the disrespect. My feelings for Monae were disappearing, quick. *I shoulda never fucked up with Day-Day*, I said to myself.

"I'm going to need to see some identification. And I'll need you both to fill out the highlighted section of the application," Ms. Berelli commented, and pushed the applications Monae's way.

"Anything for you, sweetie," Monae said.

Ms. Berelli looked away and opened a drawer, pretending to look for something. Her face became flushed, while my nerves were being irked.

I glanced at my application with butterflies in my stomach, while Monae filled in her details with ease. She traction. "We both wanna set up credit lines. I'm a big wheel over at the Wynn, but I heard the tables are pretty good over here."

She smiled.

Monae moved toward the plush seats where potential clients sit and pulled out a chair. Although uninvited, she sat making herself at home just before we got started.My eyes darted toward the lavish carpet and the expensive looking décor.

"Can we get this show on the road?" Monae said arrogantly. "I know the procedures already. So check my info. I'm ready to get my gamble on," she said convincingly, then rubbed the insides of her hands together rapidly. "Sit down Lolita," she said to me.

A stupid look appeared on my face for a moment. I had forgotten my new name. I brushed past the woman who was finally introducing herself to Monae as Ms. Berelli. She moved a few yards to the opposite side of her desk, while Monae and I sat across from her waiting for instructions.

Ms. Berelli wasn't very friendly and her disposition was clear as she whipped out two sheets and grabbed two pens. She barely wanted to look at either of us. It was clear she was uncomfortable with the sexual looks she was getting. I wasn't even mad at the disrespect. My feelings for Monae were disappearing, quick. I shoulda never fucked up with Day-Day, I said to myself.

"I'm going to need to see some identification. And I'll need you both to fill out the highlighted section of the application," Ms. Berelli commented, and pushed the applications Monae's way.

"Anything for you sweetie."

Ms. Berelli looked away and opened a drawer pretending to look for something. Her face became flushed, while my nerves were being irked.

I glanced at my application with butterflies in my stomach, while Monae filled in her details with ease. She never ceased to amaze me. I watched her as I copied the address from my license onto the application. Her legs were crossed in confidence and she hummed while writing as quickly as she could.

"I wanna shoot for a $10,000 line, beautiful," Monae announced. Her voice was crystal-clear. How could she talk so confident, knowing she was impersonating a non-existing person?

"Is that so?" Ms. Berelli asked with crinkled brows. "I'll have to see how much we can extend," she said, typing into the computer with speed.

The sound of her fingernails hitting the keys swiftly kicked up my nervousness a notch. Instantly, I knocked over a large blue binder that sat on the end of the desk. Monae's eyes swayed my way with a look of death.

"I'm sorry about that," I said.

Ms. Berelli peered over her glasses and shot me an irritated look, followed by a switch in her focus to Monae. "Ms. Conley, we can only approve you for a $6,000 line for now. You've got a decent amount in your bank account to cover any funds you may lose. However, there's not a lot of other information popping up about you."

"No problem." Monae banged on the desk with enthusiasm. "But we cannnnnnnnn get to know each other." She winked. "If you know what I mean."

"That won't be necessary," Ms. Berelli quickly responded, after shaking her head in disgust.

"I'll play here a few times, and you'll call to upgrade me," Monae laughed.

Ms. Berelli never commented. She grabbed my sheet, reviewed my info, and within ten minutes, she quoted me a credit line of $8,000. Monae was pissed. I could see it in her eyes. I guess we were both wondering what was typed into the computer to come up with a fair credit amount. We knew the names were fake, and other than reviewing our bank accounts, what did they have to draw on for decision-making purposes? But it didn't matter, we were in.

"Okay, ladies, give us about thirty minutes to finalize everything and you'll both have your names updated in all the systems." Ms. Berelli spoke to us like a kindergarten teacher would speak to her students. She rose from her desk, letting us know the process was over. "If you want cash to play with, go to our cash booth. If you want chips, you may go right to the tables and ask for your markers there."

"Bet. We got it," Monae said quickly, as if she wanted her to shut the hell up. She grabbed my elbow and pulled me along toward the door.

"Oh, and ladies…you do know you're supposed to pay your markers back before you leave the casino with any winnings, right?"

"Of course. You think we're rookies," Monae snapped.

Ms. Berelli shrugged her shoulders. "Just a part of my job to let you know. If you don't pay it back, the money will be taken directly from the checking account you listed.

"We're winning tonight," Monae responded, then blew Ms. Berelli a kiss. "You'll be seeing me again beautiful. We'll do dinner."

$$$

Four drinks later, I found myself sitting at a blackjack table with Monae, a skinny, middle-aged looking man, and an eighty year old woman who couldn't play to save her life. She kept taking hits when she wasn't supposed to, and not taking a card when it was time. I knew a little about blackjack, so I was able to sustain myself even with her bad moves. I was still trying to figure out why two hours later we were still at a blackjack table that was taking our money. Besides, we vowed not to stay long.

When Monae initially told me we were gonna get money from our markers at the table, I was totally against it. But she said it would be good to change things up a bit. Her philosophy was that if we got chips at the table instead of cash at the booth, we could play a bit, just to make things look legit. I thought bullshit, but of course had no say in the matter.

I looked over at Monae's stack of chips, which had gotten lower and lower by the hour, thinking she should've listened to me. I was furious, and about three hundred down. But Monae had already lost nearly a 'g'. I shot her a hand movement and uttered a few annoying throat sounds, letting her know it was time to go. She just wouldn't listen.

"Is something fuckin' wrong with your throat!" she snapped, and downed another free drink.

"I'm ready to go," I announced.

She rolled her eyes at me, and at the little old lady who asked for a hit. "Sit yo' five dollar ass down before I make change," she told me. Then laughed at her cheesy *New Jack City* movie quote.

The liquor obviously had Monae's thought process twisted. Getting approved for the credit was already a gamble, but now we were actually gambling at the table instead of leaving with a profit.

"Ahhhh…twenty one," the dealer said sarcastically, as he turned over his last card. "Miss, that was all your fault," he said to the old lady.

"You damn right it was her fault!" Monae belted. "Old ass self. Who the fuck comes to the casino with an oxygen tank?" She snatched my drink and downed it too. "You need to take your ass to another table!"

"That's it," I announced and got up. "I'm cashing in my chips and I'll meet you at the truck."

I stormed off with several people watching. Most seemed interested in what seemed like a spat between two lovers. I even heard one woman say, "I think that's her girlfriend." I turned to give up a nasty look, but said, "Fuck it." It came with the territory.

Before long, I'd cashed in my chips and made my way curbside in front of the hotel. Monae had the valet ticket, so I sat on the bench, hoping she would come out soon. My first thought was to cut out with the $7,300 in my purse. I'd lost seven hundred at the blackjack table. Still, it was the most money I'd ever had in my hand at one time. I had big plans for that cheese. My mind switched back and forth from a new car, to paying off my credit card debt, and even paying upfront for school next semester. But my dreams were shattered when I saw Monae walking toward me with her hands in the air. She was fussing, but I made myself tune her out. My buzz had my head hurting even more, so Monae's bickering wasn't gonna make it any better.

"What was that all about, Nadia? You think you doing somethin' slick!" Her head moved like she was beefing with a nigga on the streets.

"Monae, I don't wanna argue. Can you just get the truck pulled around?"

"I call the shots! Now where is the cash?"

"What cash?" I threw my neck back.

"Whoaaaaa...what do you mean?"

"You know the rule. I told you already and I made it clear. It's an even split. Always an even split," she repeated.

She pulled her cash from her pocket and held out her hand, waiting to add mine to her stash. I wasn't sure what she was trying to pull cuz I had a marker for $8,000 originally, and hers, $6,000. But she'd lost. How much? I wasn't sure.

I pulled the cash from my purse slowly and handed it to her. Monae counted it right out in the open, which surprised me. She was normally low key and very secretive when it came to counting money. But the liquor from her breath confirmed she was bent.

I listened to her count. Then listened to her re-count. Then listened to her shoot off a number. I thought that was how much I was getting until she placed half of that in my hand.

"What the fuck!" I jumped up to say. "Your ass said an even split!"

We got $8,400 all together. I lost the rest," she said without a care. "So you got $4,200."

"Is that my fault? I told you not to sit there and gamble."

"Quit crying. You make people hate you." She rolled her eyes, then handed off the valet ticket to the worker passing by. "We gotta hit another spot tomorrow."

"I'm not." I folded my arms.

"What you need to do is find us two or three more people. We can take this town," she bragged. "Get it while the gettin' is good," Monae continued.

I walked away. I wanted no more parts of Monae; even though the thought of more money sounded good. If I could save at least ten or twenty thousand I would be satisfied.

"Umm..." I said as the Escalade pulled up. I'd changed my mind that fast. "One more time, Monae. Just one more time."

"Bitch, get in the car. I gotta date."

15

Tori

"Can I get another Courvoisier on the rocks, please?" Jewell asked loudly.

She lifted up her glass and shook the ice back and forth. We hadn't even been at the bar fifteen minutes, and the girl was already on her third drink. Jewell was known to be a heavy drinker, but since her father died, she seemed to be tossin' 'em back even more.

"Why don't you slow down after 'dis one?" I suggested. Even though I was on the second Jack and Coke myself.

"That's right, Jewell, slow down. I'm a little worried about you," Nadia chimed in. She placed her hand on Jewell's shoulder.

"Well, you need to be worried because I probably don't even have enough money to pay for this shit," Jewell responded.

Me and Nadia looked at each other then shook our heads as the waiter sat the drink down in front of her. Her ass always said crazy shit whenever she got drunk. Normally when we sat at the bar, Jewell always seemed to fall off the damn stool, so it was a good thing she was sittin' between us. This way we could keep a close eye on her.

"You really need to stop drinkin' now. 'Dat shit got you trippin'," I said.

Jewell took the six ounce glass to the head. "Who the hell said I was tripping? Shit, I'm serious."

Again me and Nadia flashed each other dumb-ass

looks. "What are you talking about, girl?" Nadia asked.

"I'm broke!" Jewell yelled out.

I laughed. "Yeah right! Yo' pops had plenty of money. How you gon' be broke?"

Shit, what they didn't know was 'dat I was the mufucka wit' only a hundred dollars left to my name. I hadn't been 'dis broke since I was thirteen. Jewell looked like she could use yet another drink.

"You're right, Tori. My father did have a lot of money, hell he was a millionaire. But it's too bad he didn't leave me any of that shit."

She lifted up her hand and tried to get the bartender's attention again, but Nadia pulled it back down. "You can't be serious."

"Have you ever known me to play around about my fucking money, Nadia?" Jewell asked. She seemed irritated.

Nadia was caught off guard by Jewell's reaction. "I…I guess not."

"Then I'm serious. I found out at the funeral that my father didn't have a will. So, you know what that means?" she looked back and forth at both of us. "It means that bitch gets everything."

I don't know 'bout Nadia, but I couldn't say shit. Normally, I always had a quick come back, but not 'dis time. All types of thoughts ran through my mind until my cousin finally spoke up.

"Well, Jewell, I'm sure your mother wouldn't do nothing foul like not give you anything. She knows how much your father adored you."

Jewell rolled her eyes, then sighed. "Always the confident one, huh Nadia? My mother is not gonna give me a fucking dime."

"But how do you know that?" Nadia asked, in an annoyin' tone.

"You wanna know how, Nadia? You wanna know?" Jewell quickly went in her purse, pulled out her American Express Black card then yelled out, "Bartender, bartender!" When the young white guy came over, she handed him the card. "Charge the bill to this."

After the guy walked off, Jewell quickly tapped her nails against the walnut colored wood like she was typin' something. Hell, it wasn't even my card and the shit was nerve rackin' waitin' on his ass to come back. It felt like we was hangin' around for some fuckin' test results.

A few seconds later, the bartender returned. "I'm sorry Miss, but your credit card was declined."

He handed the card back to Jewell then stood in front of us. Waitin' to get paid, I guess. I just hoped he wasn't waitin' on me. Shit, as broke as I was, I hoped Jewell would pay my portion of the bill anyway. But now it looked like we might be bustin' some fuckin' suds, especially at 'dis expensive-ass seafood spot. The average plate was at least a hundred dollars per person. Or maybe Nadia could hold us down since she had her new lil' bun 'dat she still hadn't confessed to us about yet.

"Just keep the tab open then, sir. We'll pay later," Nadia instructed. He seemed a lil' hesitant at first, but finally made his way to the other end of the bar.

"Now, do you believe me? My credit card has never been declined. That bitch probably closed the account," Jewell said, tossing the plastic back in her purse. "This shit is the worst."

"What about your other cards?" Nadia inquired.

Jewell looked defeated. "Same thing."

Nadia scratched her head. "But how can she do that?"

"Because I'm just an additional card holder on my father's credit card accounts. Everything was in his name," Jewell replied.

When I started thinkin' 'bout the bill again, I quickly got frustrated. "Nadia, I can't believe you called an emergency get money meetin' and chose 'dis spot. Why we ain't at Cravings or some shit. We go to 'dat buffet sometimes." I knew my odd penny-pinchin' attitude would raise a red flag, but fuck it. They would have to find out what happened to me sooner or later.

Nadia looked at me wit' a strange expression. Even Jewell turned around. "Since when you care about prices, Tori?" she inquired.

"Since when you start choosin' five star restaurants to eat at? I thought you was a McDonalds type of chick. Since when did yo' ass upgrade?" I hated talkin' shit to my own family, but I guess being wit' out money was startin' to affect me. "When we gon' start 'dis meetin' anyway?"

"Damn, Tori, calm down. I'm normally the impatient one," Jewell replied. "You know you've been acting a little weird lately."

"A bitch is more like it," Nadia added.

I looked at my cousin, ready to give her a piece of my mind, when a tall, light skinned broad walked up behind Nadia and smiled.

"What's up, baby girl?" the stranger asked Nadia.

When Nadia turned around, she returned the smile. Only her shit seemed bigger. "Hey girl. I'm glad you finally made it. My cousin, Tori, here was starting to get a little antsy." She pointed her finger at me.

Who the fuck is 'dis bitch, I thought, as the stranger nodded her head in my direction. I wondered if this was the get money bitch I'd heard about.

"My bad. I had some deals to make," the stranger said to me.

Huh, 'dat sounded like some shit I used to do. Ever since the drama went down wit' me and Adrian, I wasn't in the mood to do anythin' or even be around anybody for 'dat matter. However, I did have plans to fuckin' execute Adrian's ass whenever I saw him again. I'd already called up a nigga I knew from Reno, and asked him to hook me up wit' some heat, a 9mm to be exact.

If Adrian really lived in LA, I knew it would only be a matter of time before he came back. If he lived in Vegas, I knew he would eventually show his bitch-ass somewhere. And when he did, I would most certainly be ready. Yeah, I had it all planned out.

"Hey, Tori…Jewell, this is my friend, Monae," Nadia said, taking me away from my thoughts.

"Yo' friend?" I asked wit' a slight attitude. "Why ain't I ever heard of 'dis *friend* before?"

Jewell stepped in. "Nice to meet you, Monae."

Nadia had a crazy look on her face like I was embarassin' her, but I didn't care. I had an even better reason not to fuck wit' strangers anymore.

"What up Jewell, Tori?" Monae said, wit' another head nod.

I eyed her baggy fittin' True Religion jeans and Ed Hardy skull t-shirt, then threw the head nod right back. "What up?" She was dressed like a straight dude.

"Monae is the reason why I called an emergency meeting today," Nadia announced. "She's also the person who picked this place, Tori."

"Yeah, I wanted us to have a nice dinner while we go over some business," Monae included. "And if y'all ready, I told the hostess on my way in to seat us. Sitting at the bar ain't gonna work."

"I agree," Nadia joined in.

Who the fuck did 'dis girl think she was. And apparantly Nadia was all up her ass. A part of me wanted to say somethin', but the constant looks Nadia kept givin' me told me not to go there.

"Well, as long as I can order some drinks, and you paying, I don't give a shit where we sit," Jewell said.

From the look Monae gave Jewell, the gay suspicions were confirmed. "Sure sweetie. You can order whatever you want. The bill is on me."

"Oh, Monae we got a bill at the bar too," Nadia stated. "How much was it Jewell, about sixty dollars?"

When Jewell nodded her head, Monae went in her pocket and peeled off one of the many hundred dollar bills she had in her pocket. "He can keep the change."

Shit, 'dat was all I needed to see. Obviously the girl had money or was 'bout it, so after drinkin' my last bit of Jack and Coke I hopped off the bar stool, ready for whatever. "Y'all ready?"I inquired.

Wit' Monae leading the way, all three of us followed her like lil' kids who were in trouble. However, Nadia was the worst one of us all. She was damn near breakin' her neck to be the first one behind Monae, which to me looked like some ole stalker type shit. My cousin was definitely changin', and I didn't know if it was for the better either.

$$$

Minutes after we sat down, several waiters were already bringin' us a few drinks and several appetizers 'dat consisted of lobster bisque, seared scallops and jumbo lump crab cakes. I wasn't sure if Monae was on some type of VIP status in the restaurant, but whatever the case was, it felt good being around money. Over the past few days, I'd been eating bologna and cheese sandwiches damn near every day, so 'dis meal definitely had me feelin' like a rich girl again.

As soon as we ordered our entrees and a few more drinks, Monae didn't waste anytime speakin' up. I could tell she liked to take the leadership roll.

"Listen, ladies, I have a few things lined up that I gotta go handle in about a hour, so I don't have time to beat around the bush." She looked around before continuin' then spoke in a lower tone. "Basically, I don't know if Nadia told y'all or not, but we got a good lil' thang going on and want to see if y'all wanna get down."

Jewell's face frowned. "Well that depends on what you're talking about Monae. I'm really not into some of that freaky shit."

"Damn, I wish you were beautiful," Monae replied.

Oh yeah 'dis bitch a raunchy type of dyke, I thought. When I looked over at Nadia, she didn't seem too pleased wit' Monae's comment.

"Can we move on?" Nadia asked.

Monae smiled. "Sure, baby girl. Anyway, like I was saying, me and Nadia got a lil' thang going on involving some serious money, and we wanna know if y'all down. The more people, the more money."

It didn't even take long for me and Jewell to sit straight up in our seats. "What type of money you talkin' 'bout and what we gotta do?" I asked. I wasn't a virgin when it came to scams, so pretty much whatever Monae had going on, I automatically knew she had my vote.

After Monae broke it down to us, I had to keep myself from droolin'. I couldn't believe it. Here I was down to my last bit of paper, and a new hustle had already fallen right in my lap. "Oh, hell yeah! Where the fuck do I sign up?" I could barely control my excitement.

"Dats what's up. What about you gorgeous? You in?" Monae looked over at Jewell.

"I guess," Jewell replied.

Monae held up her index finger and waved it back and forth. "Nah…nah…nah. This ain't nothing you need to be guessing about. Either you sure or not. We ain't got time for that undecided type shit."

I loved her cockiness. It sorta reminded me of myself.

"Yeah, it's a lot of risk involved, so you gotta be sure," Nadia added.

As Jewell continued to contemplate, I tried to break it down. "See, Monae, Jewell ain't never had to work in her life. Her pops had money, so she ain't used to 'dis hustlin' and shit. She a silver spoon type of girl."

"I know a little bit about her already," Monae said, wit' a smirk. I turned to Nadia and wondered what else Monae might know.

"I'm in," Jewell stated out of the blue.

We all looked at her at the same time. "Are you sure 'cause this shit is serious. We can't have mistakes," Monae demanded.

"No mistakes," Nadia mimicked.

"Nadia, can you stop fuckin' co-signin'?" I yelled. I was sick of her actin' like a damn tape recorder. She rolled her eyes while Monae laughed.

"Yes, I'm sure," Jewell answered.

"Good, well I'll make sure Nadia gives y'all the rest of the details." Monae looked at her watch. "I gotta bounce."

"You're leaving. But the food hasn't even come yet." Nadia's strange behavior toward Monae was startin' to piss me off.

"Y'all go head and enjoy everything." Monae reached in her pocket again and quickly peeled off eight one hundred dollars bills from her stack and then threw them on the table. "Dat should be more than enough. Whateva left ova, y'all can split 'dat shit. I gotta run. I got this honey waitin' on me ova at the Ghostbar."

I knew her ass was gay, I thought, lookin' at my cousin who picked up her Apple Martini and downed it.

Monae stood up and gave each one of us a pound like a straight up dude, then threw up the peace sign before walkin' out. She wasn't even gone a hot second before I immediately started drillin' Nadia. "So, what's up between y'all two?" I asked. "I heard some shit 'bout you, but said to myself...nah, not my cuz."

She took the cherry 'dat was in her drink and placed it in her mouth. "What do you mean?" she answered nonchalantly.

"Why the fuck you hangin' out wit' a dyke, 'dats what I mean. Yo' ass ain't never told me and Jewell 'bout her before. Where you meet her at? How y'all come up wit' 'dis scam?" My questions could go on for days.

"Don't trip, Tori. She's Day-Day's cousin who I met weeks ago. She's the one who turned me on to the scam," Nadia replied.

"Is Day-Day in on it too?" Jewell asked.

Nadia shook her head no.

"So, 'dis how you been able to rock all 'dat new shit lately," I mentioned. "I can't believe you been holdin' out on us like 'dat."

As soon as those words came out of my mouth, I instantly felt guilty. Shit, who was I to talk. I still hadn't told them 'bout my secret.

"Look, I was tired of being broke so I had to find a way to get mine," Nadia responded. "I couldn't keep being around y'all with outfits that I would take back to the store the next day." Me and Jewell looked at her wit' a confused expression. "Yeah, that's right. I used to keep the tags on all my clothes so I could return them, but not anymore."Nadia started on her other Martini, and then looked at me. "And you better not clown cuz I don't have money like you, but I'm on my way."

As soon as Nadia said 'dat, something inside me said to just let everything out. Especially since 'dis meetin' seemed more like a fuckin' counselin' session. I held my head down then shook it back and forth.

"I was raped. He took all my money," I blurted out.

Both Nadia and Jewell held their mouths open and looked at me wit' wide eyes. They seemed lost for words.

"His name is Adrian. I met him at the Jay-Z party. He was supposed to help me get my sex tape out there, but shit didn't work out 'dat way." A single tear ran down my cheek and rested under my chin, which was a sure sign to them 'dat I wasn't jokin'. If it was one thing I didn't show very much, it was emotion.

Jewell reached across the table and grabbed my hand. "Oh my God. Are you okay?"

"Did you file a police report?" Nadia asked.

"No, I didn't do shit but lay in my bed, and ball my fuckin' eyes out. All 'dat money I worked so hard for is gone, like 'dat." I snapped my fingers. "I still can't believe he robbed my ass, but you mark my words. I'ma see 'dat mu-fucka again, and when I do, it's a rap."

"Why didn't you tell us, Tori? Why would you go through that alone?" Jewell questioned.

"I don't know. I just had to get through it by myself I guess. I was out of it for a minute, like at yo' pops funeral, but I'm cool now. I put 'dat shit behind me little by little every-day," I assured.

Again silence fell over the table. "Look, don't worry 'bout me. I'ma be alright. Have y'all bitches ever known me not to bounce back?" I picked up my glass and raised it in the air before looking at each of them. "And I'ma start by gettin' 'dis paper. Now, y'all raise them mufuckin' glasses up so we can say our shit." The girls seemed hesitant. "Come on y'all broke bitches, get 'em up!"

Jewell and Nadia both smiled before finally raising their glasses.

On the count of three, we all yelled out, "Rich girls for life," before bringin' our glasses together. It felt good to know 'dat I was on my way back to the top, and 'dis time I was determined not to let anybody stop me.

16

Jewell

It was confirmed. After trying countless times to use my credit cards for my weekly spa appointment, a payment to my personal trainer, and hell, even the dry cleaners, each transaction was declined. It couldn't be a coincidence that each credit card wasn't working. Now, reality was really starting to set in that my mother had definitely shut me out. I couldn't believe this was happening to me. It was like I was in a nightmare, and couldn't wait to wake up. To make matters worse, I knew the credit cards were just the beginning. It was only a matter of time before my health insurance would be cut off and the locks were changed on my brand new home; a home that still held my father's name on the deed. But now it obviously belonged to her.

I hated myself for never listening to one of my father's long lectures about saving money, because after checking my bank account, I only had about twenty-five hundred dollars left. I'd blown the rest on gambling, traveling and tons of other unnecessary shit. Twenty-five hundred versus the six digit figure I was used to. What was I supposed to do with that? My lifestyle required a lot more, and even if I sold everything I owned, which only amounted to clothes and two cars, it still didn't put a dent in my father's bankroll. There was no doubt in my mind that I was completely on my own. I was going down. Fast.

Someone beeping their annoying car horn quickly snapped me out of my trance. It was at that point when I realized I'd been daydreaming at a stop light, and before I could even take my foot off the break, they pressed the horn again. When I looked in my rearview mirror and saw a lady pointing her index finger and mouthing something, I went off like she could hear me. "Bitch, you better stop beeping your fucking horn! Damn, can I step on the gas first?" Making my way through the light, I looked in the passenger seat and glanced at the bottle of Courvoisier XO and contemplated about rolling down my window and throwing it at her car when she passed by, but decided against it. Not only did I not feel like kicking her ass, but there was at least two swallows of alcohol left. I couldn't afford to waste my shit on nonsense.

Every drop counts, I thought to myself. Especially when it came to controlling the depression that had been fluctuating ever since my father died. Mood swings, crying spells, feeling worthless, you name it, I'd met everything head on. I'd even gone as far as seeing a doctor, who subscribed me some tranquilizers for the tension. Whatever I had to do to numb the pain or get the feeling of relaxation again, I was willing to do it. Whatever allowed me to function without constantly thinking about how much I missed my father, I was ready to take on the challenge.

I pulled over on the side of the road, and whipped out my cell phone before dialing my mother's number. Even though I knew she didn't want to talk to me, I had to know what her response would be when I asked about my father's will.

Shit, who knows, maybe she'll have a change of heart, I thought as a funny talking machine started speaking. "We're sorry, the number you're trying to reach 704-555-0982 has been changed to an unlisted number."

Each time my mother did something to basically push me out of my life was even more hurtful than before. I knew that I wasn't the best daughter growing up, and probably had done or said some disrespectful things in the past, but that was just it. The past. Now, I was willing to go the extra mile for the two of us to have a better relationship, even if it was just for my father's sake. I just hoped that one day she would feel the same.

A part of me wanted to go to my mother's house and demand that we try and have a decent conversation, but I knew if she'd changed the phone number, I'm sure the gate code was changed as well. Shit, she'd probably fired Rosa and gotten a new housekeeper, so they wouldn't let me in anyway. I had to come up with a new plan.

Looking in my side view mirror, I waited for two trucks to past by before I made a sharp u-turn and headed straight for my father's office on Howard Hughes Parkway. Maybe I could convince someone there to give me her new number or at least call her for me.

When I entered the parking lot at GMG twenty minutes later, visions of my father pulling up in his midnight blue Phantom with the word 'MUSIC' on the license plate filled my head. I smiled, thinking about how his motto, 'fill your life with music' was something he definitely took to , and how much he cherished the company. I never heard him complain about having to go to work, about overtime, or the twelve hour, seven day work week he would labor through most of the time.

Remembering the amount of effort he put into his job, along with the hard work and his numerous sacrifices, made me stop and think about whether I should finally take a position at the company. In my mind, it was only right to be a part of my father's legacy, to carry on his persistence, his determination and his constant dedication. To finally make him proud.

Even though I'd agreed to do the scam with my girls, I was still a bit hesitant about it, because in reality, doing something illegal to get money just wasn't me. All my life I never had to result to shit like that, so why start now. *I'll make sure I call and talk to Nadia tonight*, I thought, putting my car in park. *I would rather run my father's company*. After turning off the ignition, I looked into the rearview and adjusted the brim on my BCBG baseball cap then grabbed my purse.

Once I got out of the car, I knew I looked a bit unusual with my baggy Abercrombie sweat pants on, but fuck it. I was here to take care of some important business, not compete in a fashion show. Besides, until I really found out if I was broke or not, I could care less how I looked.

Making my way inside the building, I spoke with several of my father's employees who ran up and offered their condolences and told me how much he was missed already. After exchanging plenty of heartwarming hugs and handshakes, I finally made my way up to my father's office located on the fifth floor. As soon as I stepped off the elevator and walked up to his secretary's desk, she seemed more than surprised to see me.

"Jewell, honey, is that you?" Corrine asked. I guess she wasn't used to seeing me dressed like this. When I shook my head yes, she instantly jumped up from behind the huge wood desk and walked over toward me. "It's so good to see you, baby. I've been worried about you," she said, giving me a huge hug.

"I'm doing okay…I guess."

She gave me a sincere expression. "I didn't get a chance to tell you at the funeral, how nice your speech was about Joseph. You had me in tears."

"Thanks. It was from my heart."

"I'm sure it was. I'm gonna miss that man. You know I've been with him since he started this company."

I glanced at a few pictures of successful artists that were displayed behind her desk and smiled. Corrine was a sweet woman, who'd been my father's secretary for years, and never took a higher position in the company regardless of how many times he offered.

"What brings you here anyway?" Corrine asked.

"Umm…actually I'm here for two reasons. One, I need my…" Before I could even continue, I heard a woman's voice coming from inside my father's office. Then she started to giggle like someone was tickling her. I turned my head and stared at the closed door before looking back at Corrine.

"Who's in there?"

Corinne looked at me like she knew I wasn't going to like her response. "It's your mother."

I scrunched up my eyebrows. "My mother? What is she doing here? She never comes here." I instantly got an attitude. "Is she cleaning out his office already? She can't do that!" Not even having the patience to wait for an answer, I looked at the door again, then walked straight toward it.

"No, Jewell wait a minute. That's not a good…" I heard Corrine say before I swung the door open.

It was too late. Nothing in the world could've ever prepared me for what I saw. I felt the hairs on the back of my neck instantly stand at attention as I closed my eyes and hoped like hell that this was a bad dream. However, I wasn't so lucky. When I opened them, they were both behind my father's desk scrambling to put on some clothes, eyes wide, mouths hanging open. I couldn't believe it. My own mother fucking Uncle Louis in my father's office.

"What the hell are you doing in here!" my mother screamed. "Corinne, why would you let her in here?"

"Maybe you should lock the fucking door next time," I answered, while Corinne seemed lost for words. I then shot Louis a cold look. I refused to put the word Uncle in front of his name now.

"Get out!" my mother yelled again.

"Oh my Lord," Corrine said, quickly turning around to

walk back to her desk. I guess she thought my mother was just talking to her, but I'm sure the request was for both of us. But I wasn't going anywhere.

"Couldn't you have picked somewhere else to fuck this man? Why here?" I asked, looking around.

However, when I surveyed the office, I noticed that all of my father's possessions were gone. His favorite golf clubs, old record collections, the pictures of us on vacation…everything...completely gone. The more I looked around the room, the more upset I became. But once I looked on my father's desk, I felt like I wanted to pass out. His gold trimmed name plate had been replaced with *Louis Cobb-CEO*.

"Don't bring your ass in here talking to me like that. You're not even supposed to be anywhere near me," my mother informed. By this time she and Louis had managed to put on a decent amount of clothing.

I pointed to the name plate. "So, my father has already been replaced? You're gonna let Louis run the company now?"

"Listen, Jewell, I know things seem a bit odd," Louis finally spoke up before my mother cut him off.

"Louis, you don't have to explain anything to her. That's the shit Joe used to do." She turned to me. "Whatever my fiancé and I do with this company is none of your damn business. You understand that?"

As Louis took a seat behind my father's desk, I looked at her like she was insane, and hoped that I hadn't heard the last comment correctly. "Yeah, that's right, I said it. My fiance." She lifted up her left hand and flashed the huge rock that sat on her ring finger. The canary yellow diamond was decent, but didn't stand a chance up against what my father had given her.

"I can't believe this," I said, shaking my head. I wanted to call her a hoe, but knew it would only make matters worse.

"Well believe it because it's true. Louis and I are in love and are getting married in a few months," she proudly stated then looked at him and smiled.

My head began to throb. As I attempted to rub my temples, my mother looked at me with a bit of disgust then displayed a wicked grin. "I guess being broke has already taken its toll on you, huh? I've never seen you like that. What happened to all your Gucci?"

I'd had enough. "You think this shit is a fucking game! You know I don't have any money, and you wanna make a joke about it. My father would've never done this to me!"

"Well, you see, that's just it. Your father isn't here anymore, so everything belongs to me," she replied.

"How am I supposed to live? How am I supposed to pay my mortgage?" I asked.

She frowned. "I don't give a damn how you live. Besides, I thought Joe paid off your mortgage."

I put my head down briefly then stared back at her. I didn't have enough guts to tell my mother that I'd blown the mortgage money a while ago. She'd get a kick out of that.

"Well it doesn't matter. Your house is in Joe's name anyway, so I'll just have you kicked out then sell it, so don't worry about the mortgage," my mother stated.

"So, I guess you're the one who canceled all my credit cards?" I asked.

"Of course. I hope you didn't think I was going to pay your bills every month," she replied. "As a matter of fact, anything that Joe put in his name for you, I'm going to destroy."

I was beyond hurt, and never knew she hated me this much. "What kind of mother are you?" I knew that question would get under her skin.

"The kind that's going to call security if you don't get

the hell out." From the look on her face, I knew she was serious.

"Jewell, baby, please go ahead and leave before things get out of hand!" Corrine yelled out from her desk.

"You better listen to the lady. Normally, I would be pissed that Corinne is all in my business, but in this case she's right," my mother replied, with an evil smile. "Now, for the last time. Get out!"

I wanted to cry, but didn't want to give her ass the satisfaction of knowing she'd hurt me. It was bad enough I was leaving without a fight. Instead, I turned around and made my way out of my father's office, never looking back. I didn't even give Corinne eye contact as I passed by her desk and headed straight for the elevators. All I wanted to do was get out of there so I could call Nadia and confirm what time we were meeting up for the scam. Now I had no other choice but to do it.

17

Nadia

"Wait! Hold that door!" I shouted, running to get clocked in. I was already ten minutes late fooling with Tori, Monae and Jewell. I grabbed my purse and pulled out two Advils before locking it up to enter the cash booth. My head thumped from frustration. Two days of nonsense was beginning to wear on me. I was starting to think it was a bad idea to bring Tori and Jewell aboard. It had taken us five hours yesterday to get ID's from Big Jake, and open up the bank accounts at Bank of America on Charleston Boulevard.

What irked me most, was the way Tori flirted with Big Jake and made him lose sight of the reason we were there. It shouldn't have taken him two hours to do four ID's, but between Tori throwing her legs all over the place, and rolling blunts for herself, Big Jake, Monae, and I thought we'd never make it out of there.

And now today, they took another hour just to go inside the bank to deposit additional cash. Monae claimed it was cuz they wanted to get higher credit lines. It was all her idea. She didn't care if she made me late for work or got me fired today.

"Bitch, I gotta go close the account at the other bank before I forget," she'd said to me. "If they take my cash in a few days when they realize I didn't pay back that marker, you gon' give me the money?"

I shook my head like I was shaking Monae off my brain. I kept thinking about what she said to me before I hopped out of her truck to run inside. "You shoulda told'em you wasn't workin' today!" she shouted in an evil tone. "Yous a slave! You only on the schedule for four hours? Stupid-ass," she added.

"Okay, that's it," I mumbled under my breath. No more thinking about Monae or her comments. "Hello…hello," I spoke to the two people working on my shift as I entered the cash booth.

They watched me clap my hands, and shake them up side down to show the cameras that they were empty.

"What's up, Nadia?" they both chimed in.

I kinda put them both off, not really wanting to make small talk. I wanted to focus on my short shift, cuz I was sure my girls would waltz through the casino shortly, ready to make moves. The plan was for them to go to the credit office one by one and set up credit accounts. Afterward, they would follow the plan that had been working so well. I just prayed they wouldn't come to my line to retrieve their markers. I was nervous enough. I asked Monae to choose another casino, but she told me to shut the fuck up.

I wanted to scream inside. The visions of my life flashed before me. I wanted something more. I needed something better. Where was my big break?

One by one, customers showed up and cashed in chips. Every time I did a marker, my skin crawled, wondering where the girls were. They'd taken much longer than I anticipated. The plan was for them to start opening the accounts as soon as I got to work. After a quick glance at the clock, it was confirmed. An hour had already passed. *Where were they*, I wondered, getting worried.

I bit my nails for another fifteen minutes, thinking about my dysfunctional-ass life. I wondered why I hadn't met some wealthy man who wanted to marry me so I could raise his kids. In between customers, I even glared onto the casino floor looking for anyone who seemed decent enough to date. *Where are all the good men*? Then finally, the sight of Tori positioned third in my line threw me for a loop. She stood smacking hard on some gum and twitching her body from side to side. I would've thought she had enough common sense not to wear a skanky mini-jean skirt that would attract unnecessary attention. Wrong!

I watched her from the corner of my eye while waiting on my customer. She continued to pop gum and wave at every available man that passed. She had a nerve to wink when our eyes met. I almost got whiplash the way I jerked my head in the other direction. She intentionally kept giving me eye contact. A risk taker she was, a braniac she wasn't.

Things were really moving quickly, cuz all of a sudden Jewell appeared outta nowhere. She walked past the cashier's booth, contemplating on which line to enter. I prayed it wouldn't be mine. We'd discussed the details all morning and I made it very clear, only one of them in my line.

Many thoughts flooded my mind while I waited on my next customer. For one, whatever my split was for the night, I was gonna pay for my fall tuition. The whole part-time thing was setting me back. I also decided to take my parents to dinner next week, to let them know how my life would be different from here on out. No more childish behavior. No more hanging out with the wrong crowd. No more Monae. No more Jewell. Unfortunately, Tori was a different story. She was family. I had been taught long ago family is everything. It's all we really have in life.

I'd seen the way my father and Tori's father drifted apart. And as much as my dad didn't want to admit it, the hurt could be seen deep in his eyes. He treated Tori just as he did his brother, always justifying his actions by saying they wanted nothing outta life. Drugs, jail time, and a bunch of children would be the extent of their legacy. He even went as far to say that his brother betrayed him, so Tori needed to keep her distance, too.

When Tori's voice snapped me from my daze, I couldn't do anything, but greet her. After all, she had always been my role model no matter what my father thought about her. She was my road dog for life! "How can I help you?"

Her lips smacked. "Ummm…I need to get a marker, please."

"How much?" I asked professionally, scanning the license she handed me.

"Ten thousand for now."

Oh shit. I couldn't wear what I was thinking on my face. But they had gone crazy. Ten thousand was too much. Somebody in security would figure out the coincidence of two black chicks all getting high-dollar markers at the same time. *Correction, three black chicks*, I thought to myself as Monae got into my line behind Tori.

No...no...no…I cried inside. This was all wrong. I shook my head slightly, while processing Tori's marker. The supervisor on duty was an older white guy named Kyle that I had never worked for before. He seemed stern and hadn't cracked a smile since my shift started. He breezed by, but didn't seem too interested in me or Tori. His focus landed on an Asian man speaking Vietnamese, and asking for a $20,000 marker.

It was normal for their race to roll like that, but three black chicks in the same hour, I wasn't so sure. Maybe it was just my nerves.

"Okay Miss…here you go," I said to Tori as I counted out her funds in all hundreds.

My eyes glanced over at Jewell who was being serviced by Oscar, my Indian co-worker. Unlike Tori, she wasn't showing any emotion, nor did she seem like herself. Of course she hadn't gotten over her father's death, but the look she was giving up said mental ward. I tried to listen in to see how much Jewell had requested, but the marker slip seemed blurry from where I stood.

"Thank you, Missy," Tori spat, after picking up her cash from the counter. "You have very good customer service."

I wanted to smack the shit outta Tori. She was such a dare devil. That was her way of getting me roused up. You would think the rape incident woulda changed her a bit. Maybe even calmed her down, but it didn't.

Nervously, I looked to my left, then checked my right, making sure no one watched our interaction. It was clear I didn't want to do any small talk. When I moved my head slightly to the right to ask the next customer if they needed any help, she slowly strutted away still smiling. Unfortunately, my next customer was Monae.

"Well, well, well…my favorite employee." She grinned, showing her full set of braces. "I need a marker please," Monae bellowed, like she was enjoying making me uncomfortable.

Just then, my supervisor, Kyle, walked by and reached over me. He placed a memo before me, and made his words very clear. "This is important, so read it carefully," he announced. "This affects us directly."

I thought my eyes were deceiving me. The words - **Fraudulent Accounts** were written in bold letters. Instantly, I started hyperventilating. Small beads of sweat swept across my forehead fast like lightening. But I had to maintain my composure. I glanced down at Monae's slip where she had written $15,000 as the marker request on the sheet. I thought, *we're all going to jail*. $15,000 was no big deal for a marker limit at the MGM, but we agreed to keep the credit lines low to stay under the radar.

My heart raced even more and I couldn't stay focused. Each step Kyle took made me move slower with printing Monae's slip for her to sign. The memo sat in front of me, but

I could never stay focused long enough to read the details. All of a sudden another supervisor, a female, walked in the cage and whispered into Kyle's ear.

Before I knew it, they'd inched toward me. It wasn't unusual for them to scrutinize ID's when processing markers, but I guess because I knew the one that Monae had was fake, I nearly pissed on myself.

I pulled the fifteen thousand from the drawer and started counting out her money. I figured if I stopped in the middle of the transaction, they would know I was in the wrong. Jail wasn't for me, so I stuttered, sweated in my panties and counted directly in front of both supervisors. Seeing Monae stand strong at the cashier window like their presence didn't even bother her, amazed me.

I guess they were waiting to bring the cops in cuz the moment I finished counting, Kyle stepped closer to me, while the female supervisor stood to the left of him. They had me surrounded.

"Nadia," Kyle spoke in an awkward tone. "Did you read the memo, I just placed in front of you?"

I stuttered. "A-a-a-s-s-s much as I could. I had a customer," I said a little defensively, while watching Monae slip away.

"Well, be careful, be smart and pay close attention to details. There have been several fraudulent accounts opened in different casinos on the strip over the last two weeks. So, MGM wants us to be extra cautious." Kyle pointed to the other supervisor, using his index finger. "Anything suspicious, let one of us know. Each shift supervisor is well aware of what's happening."

"Got it." I'd been nodding my head like a zombie the entire time he was talking. I felt sick. My eyes felt glossy, I guess from my internal break down, but managed to glance at the clock thinking, *two more hours to go.*

$$$

By the end of my shift, no one couldn't convince me that I hadn't had a massive stroke. My hair had sweated every tiny curl that was once so close to my scalp. It was crazy how I paced back and forth in front of our meeting spot. The girls were already ten minutes late. They knew my shift had ended at midnight, so keeping me waiting was torture. Then it dawned on me, had they been caught?

I continued to pace outside the walkway leading to the monorail, when suddenly I heard familiar voices. Laughing voices. I thought, *what the fuck is so funny*? I stood scared to death, while other people were enjoying themselves.

Out of the blue, Monae and Tori appeared three yards away. Their over-eccentric laughter irritated the hell outta me. I watched them walk toward me having a good time. Tori ambled along, close to Monae, with her hand on her shoulder. They hadn't been friends long enough for all of that. Instantly, my feelings erupted.

I almost forgot Jewell was even in our presence. She stood off to the side as if she wasn't a part of the group.

"I've been waiting," I said softly and crossed my arms.

"So," Monae snapped. Then laughed uncontrollably with Tori.

It was apparent they were all bent. How many drinks I wasn't sure. But their behavior proved my thoughts. They acted as if I wasn't even there, laughing at jokes, quoting famous movie lines, and falling all over one another.

"Can I get my cut so I can go?" I made sure my question was directed at Monae.

"You can never trust a bitch with hazel eyes," Monae said, in a more serious tone. She looked at Tori like she was schooling her on some serious shit. It sounded dumb to me. What the fuck did my eye color have to do with anything?

Monae then stopped her individual conversation with Tori like she was offended. She quickly dug into her pockets quick. "Here you go. Merry Christmas. It's three thousand."

"Merry Christmas! What's that supposed to mean? This is not a gift. I earned my money just like the three of you." I looked down at the hundreds to get a quick scan. "And three thousand can't be the right amount."

"It's your amount," Monae taunted in a matter of fact tone. She grabbed Tori's hand and placed it on her torso.

I was shocked. *What the fuck*? She always had a way of getting under my skin.

"Look, Nadia, I just left the bar. We feeling good, and 'bout to hit another spot." She winked at Tori. "Here's a few more dollars," she said, peeling off a twenty from her stack. "Catch yourself a cab."

"And you might need to take Jewell's depressed-ass wit' you," Tori suggested, peeking over at Jewell who was still in a daze near the railing.

My skin cringed at the sight of them. That was Monae's MO...she would definitely try her hand with my cousin. I knew that in my heart. But little did she know, Tori wasn't her style. She was too outspoken. Monae went after the timid kind. My kind. Even still, I saw the connection. It was almost like they were made for each other.

I started ranting. "That's all I get?"

Monae just shot me a look that said, hell yeah! Then brushed me off, and looked the other way.

"You're serious, aren't you?" I shouted in anger. I looked around to see the expression on Jewell and Tori's face. I knew Jewell was in no position to take up for me. But I expected Tori to say something. She was the more outspoken one anyway.

"Tori, you gonna let her do this shit to me? It was supposed to be an even split! Tori took $10,000, you $15,000, and Jewell, I'm not sure. At least $5,000, if not more." I turned to look at Jewell who wasn't even looking in our direction. "How much, Jewell?"

She said nothing.

"I'll tell you how much," Monae roared.

For the first time she marched in my direction. Her tone seemed stronger than before. "I'm tired of your lil' whiney-ass. You shoulda called out from work, and put in some real work like the rest of us." Her head bobbed, signaling this was a real beef. "We collected $30,000 all together. Ten percent is your cut!" she shouted. "Next time, do more than ten percent of the work!"

"Fuck you, Monae!" I yelled.

But before I could even say anything else, Monae rushed me like a defensive lineman. She held me by the neck tightly, causing me to gasp for air. I figured if I remained quiet, she would eventually let go. Then out of the blue, her next attack had tears streaming from my eyes. A knife. Monae pulled a fuckin' knife on me.

I cried as I listened to Tori finally say, "Let her go."

Monae turned, looked at Tori, and backed away from me. My eyes burned as I watched Tori calm Monae with a few rubs to the back.

"Just for you," she mumbled to Tori, in a sexy-like tone.

Tori didn't respond. She just gave off a phony laugh and turned away to keep from looking me in the face. I pressed my hand up against my mouth, trying to force my nasty words inside. Jewell remained silent and seemed to be two steps away from cutting her wrist. The fact that she had been spending days couped up in the house, not answering my calls, and acting like a zombie worried me.

I rushed over to Jewell and asked her did she get her cut. She nodded and looked away again. With all the patience left inside I said my goodbyes to Monae and Tori. I quickly convinced Jewell to leave with me so that I could make sure she got home safely. As we walked away, my mind slipped into deep thought.

"My own fuckin' cousin," I chanted inside. I learned early that bitches couldn't be trusted. But a backstabbing cousin, damn…life was a bitch. "On the real, my father was right about Tori. The bitch was like Hitler. The question was how to overthrow the hoe.

18

Tori

I didn't waste anytime twirlin' my tongue up and down his stiff dick then over the tip of the head before placin' every inch of his tool in my mouth. Deep throat style. I wanted to show 'dis nigga how much of a pro I really was, not to mention better skills meant better money. So I made sure to grip his manhood tightly and gently jerked it simultaneously. From the way his head rotated back and forth, I could tell he was enjoyin' the softness of my lips and the warmth of my mouth. Pickin' up the pace, I quickly began to bob my head up and down and listened as his breathin' got heavier by the minute. Suckin' his dick wit' extreme passion, I made sure to make loud and nasty slurpin' sounds every time I brought my head up.

"Damn, girl…suck that shit," Day-Day said, fuckin' my face by 'dis point.

When I started bobbin' my head even faster, I could feel his shaft gettin' harder by the minute. I knew it was only a matter of time before he exploded, which also meant it was time to pull out. Using my hand to finish the job, I jerked him off wit' fast rapid strokes and within seconds his body began to jerk out of control.

"Aaahhh!" he yelled out.

I began to slow down my pace as the thick sticky cum shot out and landed all over his stomach. Luckily, he was laying on his back 'cause if not, he probably woulda put my eye out wit' 'dat shit. *Another satisfied customer*, I thought, removin' my hand from his dick, 'dat surprisingly wasn't soft. *Damn, I wonder if 'dis nigga take Cialis.* Thinking 'bout his stamina, I glanced over on the nightstand and eyed the picture of him and Nadia at some club. Lookin' at how happy my cousin was, for the first time since I'd gotten to his apartment, I felt bad. *What the hell am I doing*, I thought. The longer I stared at the picture, the worse I began to feel. Suddenly, I was havin' second thoughts. Sittin' up on my knees, I was 'bout to get off the bed when Day-Day stopped me.

"Where you going?" he asked, grabbin' my hand. "How you gonna leave me with a stiff dick. We ain't done yet." His voice was deep and mesmerizin'.

Quickly switchin' positions, Day-Day sat up, then laid me on my back before removin' my black lace thongs. He didn't even give me a chance to say anythin' before he began spreadin' my legs apart, then brushed his hand against my neatly trimmed pussy.

Using his fingers, he parted my lips then began to tease my clit wit' his index finger. Instantly, my nipples became swollen and my eyes rolled into the back of my head. I couldn't believe how good 'dis nigga was wit' his hands, and began to wonder why the hell Nadia had let him go. I swallowed hard, trying to wet my suddenly dry throat.

Slowly, he slid one of his fingers into my treasure then decided to insert another one until I was soakin' wet. As good as it felt, I couldn't help but moan. Movin' his long fingers in and out, it didn't take long for him to find my spot, and by 'dat time, my moans had already turned into slight screams. I hadn't had sex since Adrian raped me, and didn't even want a man to touch me after 'dat, but as good as 'dis shit felt, I'm glad I'd reconsidered.

"You like it?" Day-Day asked.

All I could do was shake my head up and down. Removin' his fingers, I was damn near blown away when Day-Day began to lower his head until his mouth reached my drippin' wet pussy. Never in a million years had I expected him to perform ‘dat task. He slipped his tongue into my openin’, then brushed it up against my clit several times makin’ short circles before suckin’ on it like a straw. He had to grab my thighs to keep’em from shakin’.

“Oh, shiiiiiit!” I yelled out archin’ my back.

At ‘dat point, he started flickin’ his tongue rapidly like a snake, and my body began to quiver. I needed him inside of me. Bad.

“Fuck me,” I moaned wit’ pleasure.

He stopped tastin’ me so he could respond. “You sure?”

“Yesssss.” I didn’t want to wait another minute.

Drippin’ wit’ anticipation as he brought his face back up, Day-Day positioned his body between my legs then entered me nice and slow wit’ his rock hard dick. A big dick might I add. Again, I thought Nadia was stupid for lettin’ ‘dis stallion get away. Seconds later, it was on. Wit’ each stroke his pace began to speed up and eventually got stronger and harder. Before I knew it, he was rammin’ his dick so hard it felt like my shit was ‘bout to explode.

A part of me wish we’d started off in my favorite doggy style position ‘cause at least ‘dat way I could throw my pussy back wit’ each thrust. I wanted him to know ‘dat I could fuck as well as give good head.

I could feel myself ‘bout to cum as his shaft continued to dive and pound on my treasure like I’d stole somethin’ from his ass. Suddenly, I let out a loud moan, ‘dis time knowin’ ‘dat I was ‘bout to have an orgasm.

“I’m cummin’,” I called out, as my walls began to contract, and body shook. No sooner than I said ‘dat I could feel Day-Day’s body began to tremble just like mine.

“Aaahh, I’m cummin’ too…shit!” he yelled out.

It felt weird cummin’ at the same time ‘cause I’d never experienced ‘dat shit wit’ anybody else. It wasn’t long before he finally pulled out and collapsed his body beside mine. Moments later, we were both on our backs starin' up at his ceiling.

"You on something?" he asked, slightly out of breath.

"What do you mean like birth control?"

"Yeah, you see I ain't strap up."

Damn, he was fuckin' my ass so good, I forgot all 'bout 'dat shit, I thought to myself, before answering. "No, not at all. Normally I do condoms."

"Yeah me too." He reached over on the nightstand and picked up the Magnum wrapper before tossing it back down. "And my shit was right here, too." Never making eye contact wit' one another, he continued. "So, we on the same page if anything happens, right?"

I knew exactly what he was talkin' 'bout and felt the same way. Me and children didn't mix. "Hell yeah, we on the same page. You think I'ma let some baby fuck up my figure. I don't think so."

"Good." He reached over on the nightstand again and grabbed a small stack of money 'dat I'd obviously overlooked when I first saw the picture. Being a professional money counter, when he lifted the stack and peeled off a few bills, it looked like it was no more than a thousand dollars.

"Here," he said, handing me five, one hundred dollars bills. "You were worth it."

Under normal circumstances, I wouldn't even have fucked a dude for 'dat lil' bit of money, but unfortunately my plans had changed. Until I stacked my paper back up, I had to take it back to the old school. Placin' the money tightly in my hand, I finally looked over at him. "So, let me ask you somethin'. What is 'dis really all about? I mean, have you been checkin' for me even when you was wit' my cousin or…"

I was suddenly interrupted by what sounded like a door closin. Not knowin' what it was, I looked over at Day-

Day for answers, but for some reason he didn't seem the least bit concerned. Even though my female's intuition told me otherwise, I shoved it off like it was nothin' and was gettin' ready to ask him the question again until I heard a female's voice.

"Day-Day…you in here?"

'Dis time I quickly sat up and began to look around for my clothes, while his ass just laid there like he wanted to get caught. "What the fuck are you doin'?" I asked in a low tone.

By the way he was actin', thoughts of Day-Day possibly settin' me up ran through my mind. I scrambled to put on my thong until I looked toward the doorway and saw Nadia standin' there wit' her hands coverin' her mouth. She looked devastated. Who could blame her? She'd just caught me and *her ex-boyfriend* layin' butt-ass naked on top of his bed. There was no gettin' out of 'dis shit.

It was so quiet you could hear an ant piss. No one said a word. After placin' one of Day-Day's pillows over my naked body, I began lookin' around the room to see what objects Nadia would throw, and how I was going to take cover. Seconds later, the silence was finally broken.

"How the fuck you get in my house?" he asked.

Nadia uncovered her mouth as tears welled up in her eyes. "I have a key, remember."

Day-Day finally sat up, but never even attempted to cover his limp dick. "Then you need to give my shit back. Besides, who told you to let yourself in anyway? I didn't invite your ass over here."

"I…I came over here to talk to you. I wanted to see if we could work things out. I still love you," Nadia replied.

Day-Day started clappin' his hands. "Will somebody give this actress a fucking reward? Stop lying. You don't love me. Shit I know that for a fact."

"How could you? How could y'all do this to me?"

Nadia asked, lookin' at both of us. All I could do was lower my head.

He let out a strange laugh. "Bitch, are you serious? How the fuck you gonna ask a question like that when you know what you did. How could you fuck my cousin, Monae?"

I quickly lifted my head, then looked in my cousin's direction, not sure if I'd heard wrong.

"Yeah, oh sweet Nadia decided to fuck another woman, and for what? Money probably," Day-Day announced. "I guess this makes you a dyke now, huh?"

By 'dis time, Nadia's tears where streamin' down her face. "So, is this your way of getting back at me? Fucking my cousin is your way of getting even?"

Being 'dat Nadia didn't dispute his accusation, I guess it was true. She did fuck Monae after all. They were more than just friends. My own cousin, into coochie lickers. Who woulda ever guessed 'dat shit.

"You damn right I did it to get back at your ass. How the fuck do you think I feel losing my girl to another chick," Day-Day admitted. He'd answered the question I wanted to know all along.

Nadia wiped her face then pointed at me. "She probably fucked Monae too."

"I wouldn't be surprised. Monae seems to have her way with the ladies," Day-Day responded.

"I didn't do shit wit' Monae," I said, in my defense. "Don't put me in the same category. She turned you out, not me."

"Did you give this bitch any money for her services, Day-Day?" Nadia asked.

He shot her a quick smirk. "Now come on Nadia. Do you think Tori would give me any pussy without me paying her? How do you think I got her over here?"

I couldn't believe they were talkin' like I wasn't even in the room. Nadia stared at me wit' the coldest pair of eyes I'd ever seen. I couldn't believe she was still standin' in the doorway, and still hadn't made her way further inside the room. Shit, 'dat couldn't have been me. If the roles were switched, I woulda been waxin' the floor wit' both they asses.

"Are you on money that fucking hard, Tori," she asked. "Was it worth it?"

I was definitely at a loss for words, but felt as though lying would only make things worse. "When it comes to money everythin' is worth it," I replied, with only a touch of shame.

Nadia shook her head wit' disgust. "See, this is why don't nobody in the family fuck with you now. You don't give a shit about anybody but yourself, Tori." She took the key 'dat was in her hand and threw it in Day-Day's direction. "Fuck both of y'all!" She then turned around and stormed out.

"Make sure your dyke-ass close my door on the way out!" Day-Day yelled out.

When we heard the front door slam, I stared at Day-Day for a few seconds, and wondered if his lil' act was all a front. I knew he loved Nadia. He was just hurt. I knew how pain could have you sayin' and doin' some stupid shit. But then again what the fuck was my excuse?

19

Tori

My strut outta Big Jakes's spot read ruthless! Monae thought her connects were solid, but Big Jake was now my friend for life. I smiled inside thinkin' 'bout what I had just done. Monae was always on top of her game and always in control, but the power of a lil' pussy shut her shit down. She'd ran game too many times ova the last few weeks, rattlin' on 'bout how we had a special connection. A bond 'dat was rare between her and any otha chicks. Ha! I laughed inside thinkin', *don't try to run game on an original playa*.

I knew it smelled like bullshit, but I played along while beggin' for a few thousand of her money in the process. She wanted to lick my clit and have my brain all fucked up like Nadia's. *But hell no*, I thought, after lookin' down at my two fake license's Big Jake had just created for me on such short notice. He came up real good by the time I left. He got six hundred for creatin' the ID's, and another three hundred just to keep his mouth shut. Monae didn't need to know my biz, 'cause her slick-ass would figure out, I was up to no good.

My plan was to work her marker scheme by myself, the exact same way we all worked the system together. The whole splittin' the money idea had gotten old. My solo move would put me back where I needed to be financially. I smiled while pressin' the unlock button on my car key remote. I hopped inside my ride, surprised 'dat Monae hadn't blown my phone up yet wit' her numerous, demandin' phone calls.

Today's plan to meet at the Monte Carlo Hotel had thrown me off completely. She sent us all a text, me, Nadia, and Jewell at 7 a.m., sayin'…

URGENT deal going down. Monte Carlo front lobby- 2 p.m. Don't be late BITCHES!!!

I couldn't figure out what was goin' down, or why it was so urgent. We hadn't put money into any new bank accounts ova the last week, and hadn't discussed openin' a credit account at the Monte Carlo. So why 'dis trick was stalkin' us, I wasn't sure.

Part of the reason I even showed up was so I could see Nadia. I'd rang her phone consistently over the last week, but she was obviously done wit' me. Finished. Finito. I needed to get shit right between me and my cuz. She was all I had left as far as family. A part of me felt like she wasn't gonna show up though. I just crossed my fingers, hopin' 'dat she would.

Fifteen minutes later, I found myself alone, pacin' the marble floors of the lavish Monte Carlo, and absorbin' the awkward stares. I guess my mostly spandex one piece cat suit had people in awe, especially the men. The fact 'dat people gloated on my appearance had me wavin' the haters off, and ignorin' the comments from the male admirers.

"Where the fuck they at?" I mumbled under my breath. I flicked my wrist for a time check. 2:15 p.m. Had me thinkin' 'bout leavin'. I shook my head a few times, disgusted at myself for waitin'. My body itched to be at another hotel workin' my own scam. All of a sudden, the time didn't matter anymore, and my mind filled wit' uncertainty.

When I saw Nadia prance toward me, my heart thumped. For the first time in my life, I felt guilty. Guilty-like a whore...a tramp. When Nadia saw me we made eye contact. I waved her ova to me, while searchin' her eyes for any sign of hope or forgiveness. It wasn't my style to beg, but I needed her to remain in my life. She seemed irritated, yet composed. Maybe she'd decided to forgive my triflin'-ass.

"Nadia, look, I wanna…"

"No need," she interrupted, wit' the palm of her hand planted firmly near my face. "I'm not here to bring up your shit again. I'm done with that. You got some life issues you need to deal with." She turned away, as if she was lookin' for Monae or Jewell.

"We still cousins, right?" I knew 'dat shit sounded lame, but 'dats all I could come up wit'. My voice sounded as if I was beggin' for my life.

"Yep."

"I want us to sit down and talk about 'dis, okay."

"No need," she said crisply.

"C'mon, Nadie," I begged, "maybe over lunch or dinner. My treat."

"Nah, and don't fucking call me Nadie." I couldn't stand her new snobbish attitude. She was playin' me.

"Why won't you talk to me, Nadia?" I moved forward to get closer.

She quickly took two steps backwards, like I had the plague. "I already told you. I'm not here to discuss anything or patch things up. I'm here to make some money to leave this town." Her voice was firm, and sounded as if she knew more than I did.

"Oh, so we makin' money today?"

"That's what Monae told me. I talked to her for a while this morning."

At the same time, both of our eyes shot toward the left side of the lobby entrance. Our conversation was cut short when Monae walked in typin' on her phone. Her eyes shot beyond where me and Nadia were standin', then to each of our sides. She looked like she was high. Weed, cocaine, ecstasy, I wasn't sure, but she acted sorta out of it, and didn't want us to look at her in the face. I discretely sniffed her ass like a misbehaved dog, tryna see if it was weed. She looked like the normal Monae we were used to, wearin' a pair of fresh, crisp

Air Force One's and a white baseball cap wit' rhinestone stitchin'.

"Where the fuck is Jewell?" she asked.

"How would I know?" I countered. My smirk showed my sarcasm while Nadia said nothin'. "Why we here anyway?" I questioned.

"We here to make money, right, Nadia, baby?" Monae blew a loud sounding kiss in Nadia's direction.

"But we didn't plan for 'dis. Nothin' is set up," I told her.

"Lemme spit this fact to you. I gotta friend." Monae grinned widely. "We just go to the booth, fill out the marker form, and get the cash," she explained.

I wasn't down at all. "Dis shit tonight sounds a lil' suspect if you ask me."

"That's just it," Monae snapped, "I never fuckin' asked you. I'm telling you."

"Isn't that a bit risky," Nadia finally chimed in. "That's not what you told me on the phone." Her eyes widened and looked Monae directly in the face. "I told you the casinos seem to be onto this shit. They talk you know…so we gotta be extra careful on this last go 'round."

Monae blew through her tightened lips. She seemed to be sick of us. It was obvious she had told Nadia 'dis would be the last time, but I wasn't buyin' it. Lil' did she know 'dis was just the beginnin' for me.

"Think about the memo I got at work last week, Monae." Nadia was in convincing mode. I just watched her work on Monae quietly. I didn't wanna put my two cents in and have her even more pissed off at me. "They've probably hired investigators by now and got everybody on close watch," she pointed out wit', fear in her voice as usual.

"Everywhere! Not just at the MGM!"

Nadia grabbed her forearms and looked around makin' sure none of the bystanders had gotten close enough to listen in.

"Shut your scared-ass the fuck up!" Monae barked. "Why did you come, Nadia! Huh? Why?" Monae turned in two miniature circles, unsure 'bout her next move. "You fuckin' up my high! If you really think this is a problem, go home!"

Nadia got teary eyed. I remained frozen, wantin' to fight for my cousin, but the situation between us was too weird right now.

"Nadia, don't stay if you feel funny 'bout 'dis. Maybe Jewell will show up," I told her. "The three of us will do it, and I'll share my cut with you. It's the least I can do."

"Ahhhh....Isn't that so fuckin' sweet. Fuck you Tori," Monae told me to my face. She pointed at me like I was her child. "And fuck your cousin right here too. We know if something goes down, her scared-ass will snitch on the spot."

Nadia stood silent while shakin' her head wit' speed. Her confusion showed all over her face. "I need the money," she finally blurted out. "It's my last time, so I'm down. I'm leaving Vegas after that."

My mouth opened wide and my jaw bone dropped low. We needed to talk immediately, but Monae took control of the conversation.

"Check this, Tori," Monae said, gropin' the side of my hip. She then turned all her attention to me, as if Nadia didn't even exist. I thought, *damn, maybe Nadia had some stale pussy or somethin'*. She just didn't seem to be able to keep a man. Day-Day, the many others before him, and now Monae.

"I'm gonna be straight up," Monae continued. "I met this chick the other day who's really feelin' me. She works in the cash booth over here." Monae purposefully stopped to move her body in between me and Nadia, wit' her back facin' Nadia. I guess she figured turnin' her back on her would make it clear the decision to go inside wasn't in her hands.

"C'mon hurry…let me hear it," I edged. My quick hand motions confirmed the urgency.

"Check it. We don't need an account when we roll up in there. Just use the other fake ID and she'll process the marker, and give us the cash. We just gotta cut her in evenly on the split. She'll probably get fired, so the take gotta be good."

"Umh," I responded, runnin' everythin' she'd just said through my mind.

"What the fuck is that supposed to mean? This will work," she pressed. "Believe me, the broad is on me." She grinned.

"I should've known," Nadia blurted out, then turned the other away.

We all stood silent, lookin' at each other for a few minutes. The lobby seemed to be gettin' more packed by the minute. We looked suspect in my eyes, but I guess nobody knew our silence meant we were up to no good.

Finally Monae clapped her hands together. "Let's do this," she cheered, as if we all agreed. Before I knew it, Nadia was followin' Monae toward the casino, and I was two steps behind.

$$$

By the time we made it to the casino, I'd gotten excited. The slot machines were going off, and a group of niggas on the crap table roared like they were makin' paper. I started calculatin' in my head how I would make a few moves, without Monae or Nadia. I even had my eyes set on a chocolate lookin' nigga on the crap table 'dat I wanted to brush up against wit' my tits. All 'dat got side-tracked when we stepped within two yards of the cash cage. When Monae pointed out the cashier to us, she seemed like the type she would go after. A petite naïve lookin' red-bone who wore her hair in a tight ponytail, sat behind the booth starin' nervously in our direction. Monae pointed to me and Nadia, lettin' her know who was all good for the markers. She watched us closely and simply nodded. Monae rushed us over into a corner off to the side for a few seconds, and plotted out who was goin' first and how much. The amounts were set pretty quickly. Between the three of us, we would all walk away from the cash window wit' $30,000. I thought 'dat was steep, but I was down.

Before long, Nadia and Monae had gotten their markers done wit' ease. I was up next. I marched up to our girl like I belonged there. "Hi, I need to get a marker?" I told her. I used my white girl voice. She looked at me funny, then proceeded.

I thought, *hater-ass bitch*. She didn't give Monae or Nadia 'dat kinda energy. Suddenly, outta nowhere, two men in black suits entered the cash cage and stood behind our co-conspirator. *Supervisors always want to watch closely when I was around*, I complained to myself.

Monae's girl never flinched, so I remained calm and watched the actions of everyone in the booth. Both supervisors talked to one another casually, yet the bald-headed, dark-skinned brother walked over to look at my signature and identification. I figured it was routine, but the taller supervisor made me feel a bit uneasy. Before I knew it, they clapped their hands under the cameras and left the booth. My sigh of relief was probably the biggest I'd heard in weeks.

By the time our connection cashed out the twelve thousand that I was supposed to get, I was all smiles. She returned a slight smile toward the end when she counted out the cash. I thought, *okay maybe she's coo*l.

Monae was supposed to meet up wit' her later after her shift to give up her share of the money. I knew what 'dat was all about. The pickin' her up after work was more of a booty call than a business meetin'.

I met up wit' Nadia and Monae a few minutes later, and we all headed for drinks. We sat at the bar inside the Pub havin' back to back Mojito's along wit' Monae's Hennessy straight up. Monae claimed we needed to wait around the hotel to see if Jewell would show up, or return any of the numerous text messages we'd sent her. Soon, I knew it was time for me to break away. I stretched my arms out toward the ceiling and yawned. "Ladies, I gotta call it a night," I finally said.

Nadia behaved like she was ready to roll too. She was just waitin' for her cut of the money.

"You callin' it a night, Tori?" Monae questioned. "You tryna go fuck some nigga aren't you?" She laughed loudly. "I ain't mad at ya. Me and Nadia 'bout to take a ride anyway."

Nadia looked at her as if to say, no the hell we not.

"Here's your cut."

Monae counted out $7,000 and handed it to me, before downin' the rest of her Hennessy. She handed Nadia the same amount, which made her beam instantly. It was the first time I'd seen her smile or seem happy the entire night.

She hopped up said her goodbyes like she would never see us again. It was kinda strange. "Nadia, hold up. I gotta talk to you," Monae announced and jetted behind her.

"Nadia, don't go anywhere until we talk, okay?" I called out. "I'ma come by later tonight."

Nadia kept walkin' so I left the bar and headed toward the garage like I was leavin' too. Monae needed to be called out for cheatin' me out my loot. But I let it ride. $30,000 dollars split four ways wasn't $7,000 a person. "Fuck it! She got me." I shook my head thinkin', I woulda done the same damn thing. Besides, 'dat was change compared to what I was 'bout to do.

I double-backed after a few minutes, makin' sure the coast was clear. There was no sign of Nadia or Monae, so I walked back toward the cashier's booth again. I pulled out one of the extra ID's I had grabbed from Big Jake and held it tightly in my hand. I tried to get Monae's girl's attention. I didn't know her name, or anything else 'bout her. I just hoped she would be down when I made it to the front of her line. The casino was pretty busy which was good for me. I searched for the supervisors on duty, but only saw one. It was the bald-headed guy who had his back turned, talkin' on the phone.

When Monae's girl saw me in her line, she gave me the impression 'dat it was okay. At 'dat moment, it dawned on me 'dat 'dis shit could be addictive. But if I had to be an addict, bein' hooked on gettin' money was alright in my book. I started dancin' slightly, movin' my body to an imaginary beat. *Rich Girl* by Gwen Stefani rang in my head and the beat sounded so clear. The song was perfect 'cause I was 'bout to be a rich bitch.

Na na na na na, na na na na na
Na na na na na na na na na na
If I was a rich girl, na na na na na na na na
See, I'd have all the money in the world,
If I was a wealthy girllllllllllllllllll

The rhythm got too good. When I started hummin', people started gazin' at me. I put my hand ova my mouth and made myself think of somethin' else. While I waited to be next, Nadia crossed my mind again. I couldn't get her cheerless face outta my mind. She seemed so pitiful. Although she was my right hand, I felt like I was outgrowin' her for some reason. She wasn't a go-getter anymore. She was weak. No fight in her at all. I needed to be around somebody who had similar game, interest, goals, and all 'dat bullshit. Jewell was two steps from the mental ward, and Nadia was just plain stupid. She was my cousin, but real is real.

I stepped up next as soon as the guy in front of me turned to walk away. "Hello," I said, like 'dis was my first time seeing 'dis chick. "What do I do to access my marker? It's my first time." I played dumb.

"ID please," my new associate answered.

For the first time I noticed her name tag. Destiny it read. I thought, *funny. My destiny is to be paid*. I laughed inside.

Destiny pushed the blank marker form my way and gave me the evil eye. 'Dis bitch was bi-polar. She started typin' into the system real fast. It seemed like she was typin' forever. She would look at the screen strangely, then start typin' again. I loved her game. She was playin' it off real good. I mouthed to her thirty percent 'cause she had a confused expression on her face. I guess she wondered why I was back again. After all, it's not what she and Monae agreed on.

Several minutes past, and Destiny still had me waitin'. I got antsy for a sec, 'cause I was used to signin' for the marker on a paper lookin' check 'dat the cashier would print out. None of 'dat was goin' down. Destiny started fumblin' wit' the cash, and actin' nervous. I cleared my throat, tryna get her attention, when her bald-headed supervisor left from behind the booth. I wasn't sure how long he would be off the cage floor 'cause 'dats how the supervisors rolled.

I kept glancin' at my watch, givin' Destiny a sign 'dat 'dis was takin' way too long. I wanted to flick her ass my middle finger. She seemed slow, mentally slow. Finally, she pulled a stack of hundreds from her drawer ready to count it out to me. I breathed a heavy sigh that meant, finally. My adrenaline pumped at the sight of all 'dat green. She counted the money quickly. Quicker than she had moved the entire time. In three seconds flat, I had eight thousand in my hand. My next step was to stick it down in my purse before movin' away from the counter.

Suddenly, outta no where came three men dressed in dark blue security uniforms. They surrounded me closely wit' stern faces, and hands on their sides, grippin' weapons. I hung onto my motto, never let'em see you sweat.

"What's going on?" I asked, puttin' on my best voice on.

I searched for an exit in between their miniature circle. There was none. Out of the blue, the same bald-headed supervisor emerged onto the casino floor. He shot me a disapprovin' stare that said 'gotcha.' Then he nodded toward the officers a secret code. Like clockwork, the two officers grabbed me by the arm on each side and tugged me along the casino floor.

"Where the fuck you takin' me!" I shouted.

"We're trying not to cause a scene, Miss. Just come with us to see the proper authorities."

"Proper authorities? What do you need wit' me! Lemme go!" I shouted while squirmin' to get free. I felt my Giuseppe heels slidin' across the floor, thinkin' *'dis shit ain't too good.*

Suddenly, from the corner of my eye, I felt some relief. Help had arrived. I saw Monae and Nadia standin' near a Wheel of Fortune slot machine. Monae shook her head and instantly developed a smirk, while Nadia crossed her arms and watched closely. She didn't seemed surprised at all, almost like she'd seen the whole thing go down.

Whatever the case, at least they could call me a lawyer, or talk some sense into these toy cops. "Nadia!" I shouted, resistin' being pulled along. "Help me, Nadia. I don't know where they're takin' me."

Nadia turned slightly, like she didn't know me. I figured she didn't want anyone to know we were together, so she wouldn't be questioned. Not to mention, she might've been slightly embarrassed since so many people had gathered around to be nosey. Somehow watchin' four Las Vegas police officers enter the casino abruptly as my toy cops pulled me to the front was exciting to most of the bystanders. They watched like my fate was entertainin'.

I saw Nadia followin' along toward the front, so I yelled over to her again. "Nadia, find out where they takin' me!" I shouted over my shoulder as I saw flashin' police lights out front of the hotel.

I prayed I was hearin' things. It seemed like she said, "What goes around comes around." *Nah...she family* I told myself, even though she looked like she didn't give a shit 'bout what was happenin' to me.

"Dis is all a mistake!" I shouted.

"Sure it is," a uniformed Vegas officer said as he approached and took hold of me from the Monte Carlo security officers.

When I felt another policeman slap the handcuffs tightly onto my wrist, I knew 'dis was serious. I had to keep my composure and trust 'dat I would get out.

As I was being led to the police car, Nadia developed a victorious smirk. Our eyes met instantly. I quickly thought, *Monae was right, never trust a bitch wit' hazel eyes.*

Then, like somethin' out of a movie, Q appeared, wearin' a crisp linen pant suit. He had a drink in his hand wit' a matchin' smirk just like Nadia's. He stood near the entrance way watchin' just like all the other nosey folks. "What comes around goes around, bitch," he mouthed.

20

Jewell

"Why can't I talk to her!" I yelled into the phone. "Who the fuck are you anyway? Where's Corinne? Put her on the phone!"

"Miss, you need to calm down," the women replied.

"Whhhooo the fuck aaarrre you? Where's Corriiine?" I repeated, this time slurring a few of my words. I took another sip of my drink that was in my hand and waited for the bitch to reply. I was done with Courvoisier. Now Remy Martin was my new alcohol of choice. Straight…no chaser.

"Corinne no longer works here Miss. I'm the new executive secretary now."

I couldn't believe it. After twenty-six years on the job, Corrine was no longer at GMG. I wondered if she'd quit or if my mother had fired her. Either way, it was fucked up.

"What? Corrine noooo longer works theeerre. Put my bitch-ass mother ooon the phooonne. Do you know whooo I am? My father owns GMG!" I looked like a crazy woman sitting on top of my kitchen counter with blood shot eyes, hair all over my head and a two day old maxidress on. Lately, I didn't give a shit how I looked.

"Yes, I know who you are. Jewell, right? I've been instructed not to let any of your calls through to Mrs. Cobb."

"Mrs. Cobb? What the fuck did you just say?"

"Goodbye."

I continued to yell into the phone, but it was no use. She had already hung up. I downed the rest of the Remy, then started refilling the glass before it even touched the counter. I downed that one as well. As thoughts of my mother intentionally trying to ruin my life danced around in my head, I suddenly became enraged. Not to mention I felt betrayed. I was on an emotional rollercoaster, a ride that wouldn't seem to stop.

Tossing my phone down, I fixed myself another drink then hopped off the counter before walking over to the side of my refrigerator; a place where I kept my Valium. Picking up the prescription bottle, I opened it with the palm of my hand then popped two of the small white tablets into my mouth, washing it down with Remy of course. As the warm liquid made its way down my throat, I knew it was only a matter of time before I felt good again. I needed that feeling to get through the day most of the time.

"Please don't tell me you're taking another tranquilizer?"

When I turned around, I saw Devin standing a few feet behind me. "What the hell are you doing herrrre, Devin? Ain't shit to cook. Besides, didn't I already firrreee your asssss?" My voice was the least bit enthused.

"I'm not here to cook anything. I'm here because I was worried about you."

"Well don't be. I'm fine. As a matter of fact, geeettt outttt! Leave me alone!"

He took a few steps toward me. "Jewell, you don't need to be by yourself like this."

I threw the prescription bottle, hitting him in the chest. "Didn't you just hear what I said? Give meeee my damn keys back. You can't just cooome to my house like that. You better stayyy in your place."

"I'm not going anywhere until you calm down."

I was heated. "Oh yeah…well I'll leave then. And when I get back, your ass better be gone." I knew it didn't make sense for me to leave my own house, but I had to get out.

Maybe I'll go back over to GMG and see if my mother is there fucking Louis again. That way I can kick her ass this time, I thought.

"No, you can't leave. Haven't you been drinking?" Devin asked.

"Watch meeee." When I attempted to walk past him, Devin grabbed my arm. "Get your damn hands off me! Don't fuck with me, Devin, because I'll call the police on your ass!"

"Come on, Jewell. I'm not gonna hurt you. I'm just trying to help," he assured.

I gave him an evil glare. "Well, start by taking your fucking hands off me!"

Reluctantly, Devin removed his hand and watched as I stormed toward the foyer. Grabbing my purse and the car keys off the marble table, I realized that I'd left my phone in the kitchen, but didn't even think twice about going back to get it. I knew the only phone calls I'd get anyway would be from Nadia or Tori, calling to see what happened to me. Shit, they'd texted me a few times already. I felt bad for standing everybody up at the Monte Carlo, but the more I thought about it, I realized that I just couldn't go through with the scams anymore. I wasn't a hustler, I was a rich daddy's girl, and that's the way I wanted to stay. Fuck working hard for money. That was never going to happen.

Grabbing the door knob, I could hear Devin telling me to wait, but he could save his breath. No matter what he said or tried to do, I was leaving. As a matter of fact, I wanted to give my mother a piece of my mind now anyway, so my intentions were to go and find her ass.

Happy that I'd parked my car right out front, I pressed the button to disable the alarm, and then opened the door. I never looked back as I hopped inside, shut the door and started the ignition. When I went to throw my purse in the passenger seat, I noticed a half empty bottle of Remy laying there like an unclaimed lottery ticket. A smile made its way across my face. Picking it up, I quickly removed the cap and took a huge swig before placing it between my legs for easy access. Now, I was ready to go. I pulled out of my driveway like I was competing for first place at the Daytona Speedway.

In less than three minutes, I'd made it out of my neighborhood and onto Boulder Highway, which was normally a ten minute drive. At ninety mph, I was on a serious mission to get to my mother as quickly as possible. I didn't care how many times she put me out or even refused to see me. I wasn't gonna stop fucking with her until she gave me what I deserved. MONEY.

Glancing in my rearview mirror, I noticed a dark colored sedan right on my tail. I panicked thinking it was an undercover officer preparing to pull me over. Knowing I had way too many DUI charges, I knew the officer would probably lock my ass up as soon as he ran my license and smelt alcohol on my breath. There was no way I would get out of this one, especially now that my father wasn't around to protect me. I slowed down my pace just a bit waiting for the flashing blue lights to appear, but to my surprise nothing happened.

"What the fuck is taking so long? Let's get this over with," I said to myself.

Hoping to piss the officer off, I increased my speed back to ninety mph then did a quick, unsafe lane change. However, the sedan switched lanes right along with me, but there was still no sign of the annoying siren.

What the hell? Fuck it, if it's a cop, then I'll just have to get a ticket, I thought, jumping into another lane. Again, the car was right behind me. *That can't be a damn cop. Maybe it's just some asshole trying to play games.*

I tapped on my brakes to demonstrate my agitation,

but it didn't stop the car from staying right on my ass. I had to get rid of this fool. With the gas pedal now pressed to the floor, I weaved in and out of traffic until I reached the Flamingo Road exit. Quickly hopping off the highway, I knew if the sedan followed me I would have some serious problems. So, I waited until I got caught at a stop light to see if the car was still behind me. It was.

At that point all types of questions ran through my mind. *Did the Feds find out about Monae's little scam? Are they out to get everybody involved? Were they watching us at dinner that night? Did she bring us in just to set us up*? "Damn!" I said out loud.

Tapping the steering wheel with nails that desperately needed a manicure, I looked in the rearview again, and tried my best to make out the driver. Staring into the small mirror by this point, the more I looked, the wider my eyes became. Not unless I was hallucinating, the guy in the driver's seat looked a lot like Kenny. I quickly turned my head so I could get a good look on the passenger's side, and when I did there was a dark skinned girl sitting there with a smile bigger than Texas.

Oh hell no, it couldn't be. Kenny and Alyssa? *Why in the hell would they be following me*? As questions continued to invade my thoughts, I wiped both of my eyes with the back of my hand, then placed the Remy bottle to my lips. I needed a taste. *Are those muthafuckas insane*? I thought, when the light finally changed.

Not wasting any time, I shot down the street like a speeding bullet, trying my best to get away from the sedan. I had no idea what was going on. All I knew was that I had to get away. Driving down Flamingo at an unbelievable speed, I tried to keep my eyes focused on the road and watch the sedan at the same time, when all of a sudden someone on a motorcycle jumped right into my lane.

Not wanting to slam on brakes, I quickly jerked the steering wheel to the left, straining my muscles, I became frantic when the car didn't respond the way I wanted it to. As it began to swerve back and forth, I yanked the wheel back to the right, only to make things worse. Goose bumps prickled on the back of my neck when I realized that I'd lost complete control of the car, and was headed to the opposite side of the street. I was going way too fast.

I panicked even more. With my fingers locked around the steering wheel, I tried once again to keep my car straight and to avoid the oncoming vehicle headed in my direction, but I couldn't. I gasped the closer the car approached me. My eyes widened. I finally hit the brakes, but it was too late. Just before impact, I could see the other driver's expression, which mirrored my own look of horror. Somewhere I could hear a woman screaming just before everything went black. I recognized it. It was my own.

21

Nadia

When Monae's Escalade pulled up in front of my apartment, I grabbed my overnight bag and stood for a minute taking a long pause. A new beginning was needed. I couldn't believe I was right back in Monae's presence again after last week's craziness with Tori getting locked up. The white truck sparkled from the distance and seemed extra clean with a fresh coat of wax. The closer I got, her music blasted my ears with the sounds of Anthony Hamilton's, *Struggle No More. How appropriate*? I thought, opening the passenger door. Every song lately had me relating the lyrics to my life. When he sang, "And they say when it rains it pours…Well, it's raining at my door." I almost cried.

"Put your shit in the back," Monae ordered when I opened the door. Immediately, my eyes caught a glimpse of the black duffle bag sitting on the floor.

Every time I thought she could change, I got disappointed. She was the same nasty, deceitful Monae she was a week ago.

I hopped in and shut the door. "What's up?" I said softly, trying to be polite.

I threw my bag to the back. I really didn't wanna speak, but had to in order to get what I wanted. We were on our way to the MGM. I had to work, and had agreed to let Monae come to my booth even though shit was hot. Life meant nothing to me anymore. My parents weren't even speaking to me, my cousin had betrayed me, and my girl, Jewell, was dead.

I took in the music and glared out the window, wondering how all my plans would be pulled off successfully. Monae was supposed to score big this time. $20,000 to be exact.

Monae turned down the music abruptly, spoiling my peace. “What’s got your ass in shitty mood? she asked turning the corner slowly. “Cheer up. We ‘bout to score, big!”

“Forgive me if I can’t be happy right now,” I blurted with sarcasm. “I keep thinking about Jewell.”

Monae got silent for a minute. Maybe she did have a tiny bit of morals. I thought back to the funeral the day before. I expected Monae to show up, but she didn’t. I remember when I’d first heard about the accident on T.V, my stomach churned. I shoulda sensed weeks ago that Jewell needed help. She hadn’t acted like herself, or appeared to be the same since her dad died. *I shoulda checked on her more.*

The crazy part was when I walked into her funeral, I expected to see a fancy coffin and tons of flowers. Her funeral shoulda reeked money. Instead, there was a vase sitting on top of a wobbly iron stand, and a sign that said ‘In Lieu of Flowers, donate to Jewell’s favorite charity.’ I got angry thinking about it. That bitch-ass mother of hers had her cremated, and had a 5x7 picture of her posted off to the side. Her father was probably rolling over in his grave.

Jewell woulda never gone for that, I told myself. Her mom barely spoke to any of her friends, and gave a dry, brief speech during the funeral services. I breathed a deep depressing sigh as Monae picked up speed, pulling onto the freeway.

I couldn’t get Jewell’s mother’s face outta my mind. She didn’t seem like she cared in the least; especially once she told me her ashes would be spread over the Vegas strip. Hell, I was still tripping over the fact that she was already married to another man.

The crazy part of it all was when Day-Day showed up to the church to pay his respects, I barely looked him in the eye. He spilled his guts to me toward the back of the church about how sorry he was for all that he'd done. I wasn't interested in why he decided to fuck Tori. But I was all ears when he confessed the ultimate.

Monae paid him to allow her to move in on me. He knew all along she wanted to use me for her casino scams since I was a cashier at the MGM. He claimed he thought it would be simple. He took the $5,000 she offered him the day after I met Monae. He thought I would help her do a few scams and make a little cash. That was it, so he claimed. His plea was that I got outta hand when I started messing with her. "Money is evil, Nadia," he told me. "I'm sooooo sorry," he kept apologizing.

"What the fuck you over there thinking about?" Monae shouted, interrupting my thoughts.

She placed her hand on my knee which caused me to wanna throw up. I felt sick inside thinking about how she had used me; used me like an old garbage bag. When she turned the corner going into the lot on the north side, I panicked. I wanted to tell her that I knew. I knew everything. But instead, I focused on the road. I had to be sure I made her park where I wanted her to.

"No, not here," I said, with more energy than before.

"Why?"

"I got another place to park. It's free for me. And my boy can keep the truck in the front where he can watch it."

Monae grinned. I knew she would say yes to that. She liked feeling special, even though she was a piece of shit. I gave her ass a nasty look behind her back. When we pulled into the lot where I had directed her, I saw my buddy, Reggie, working hard for his tips. I rolled down the window and stuck my head out. "Hey, Reggie, where can I park so you can look out for me?"

"Oh, what's up, Nadia?" he grinned extra hard. "Right

here…right here," he said like he had clout.

We pulled over to the side where all the high-dollar vehicles were parked. They probably paid big money, but we were good. It felt good inside, finally being the one with a hook up.

Monae reached over and grabbed the black duffel bag from the floor. When I realized she was gonna take that big bag with her inside the casino, I stopped her instantly.

"What are you doing? Leave your bag. It's safe right here with Reggie," I assured her.

She looked at me crazily and unzipped the bag. Shockingly, it was filled with cash.

"Damn, Monae, what the fuck?" I watched her with amazement. I never knew what she was up to.

"I gotta make a move when I leave here. But I guess it will be okay," Monae commented, after noticing Bentleys and Benzes among the other cars being closely looked after. She grabbed the bag and stuffed it behind the seat. "You know where your boy lives, right? Just in case I gotta put a bullet in his head."

I shook my head, knowing she was serious. "Let's go. I gotta get to work. The truck is more than safe."

Monae handed off the keys to Reggie with a shifty stare. "Watch my shit."

"I sure will." Reggie tore off a valet ticket and handed it to Monae.

We rushed inside so I could get to work. I told Monae not to take more than thirty minutes to come over to my line. When I told her about this overly nosey new supervisor who would be coming in shortly, she understood. My mind raced, hoping everything would go okay, as I rushed toward the employee check point. Monae had gone the other way pimping like a nigga on a mission. My heart pounded…"This has to work out," I repeated to myself.

By the time I settled in at work, I felt better. Much better. I wasn't as depressed, yet still a little nervous. My supervisor, Lisa, and I had talked for the first five minutes of my shift. She was so cool. That's what I really like about her. She even patted me on my back for support when she asked about Jewell's funeral. The day Jewell died, I called out, and I remember Lisa not asking anything other than, how many days I needed.

"I'll be back to check on you," Lisa said, before leaving the front of the cage.

I stood out front feeling lonely for what seemed like days. I kept my sign up that said closed for a few minutes, pretending to get my cash drawer situated. It took about five more minutes before I saw Monae gliding her way toward me. Instantly, I removed my 'closed sign', and gave her the eye signal to come on over.

I had about fifteen thousand in my drawer, and knew I would have to call back for more. When Monae approached the window, the marker form was already out and pushed her way. She filled it out like a pro, and handed it back within minutes.

"Okay, Miss…I've gotta get some more cash out here," I said soothingly, like I wanted to win employee of the month.

Monae looked at me crazily. "Just give me what you have. I'll change the amount on the paperwork," she snapped; then smiled.

I had already pushed the button for a supervisor. Lisa came out smiling. "Yes, Nadia."

"I need more cash to process this marker."

"Sure," she said, before glancing down at Monae's ID and marker form. She gave Monae no eye contact at all.

I could tell Monae wasn't feeling how all this was going down. She wore a suspicious look on her face as she turned to look behind her. I assured her with my eyes that everything was okay. In return, she started a rhythmic beat with her hands on the counter while she waited. I had to get her to stay.

"Here we go," I said, before Lisa even came back. I counted out five hundreds then stopped to type into the computer. I got caught up for a second trying to read the response. I squinted, then breathed inside deeply.

Lisa all of a sudden appeared with more cash for my drawer. I looked up at the camera above making sure they could see all the money.

Within minutes, I'd finished counting out the entire twenty thousand. Lisa remained behind me with a poised expression. She didn't make me nervous, but the uniformed officers did. They had been in the back since I first got to work, but it felt like my first time seeing them. They had assured me, I wouldn't go down; only Monae. Of course, they had no proof that I'd ever done anything.

I saw them on the outside of the booth headed toward Monae. I wanted them to hurry, cuz I knew she would make a run for it. I had already called Reggie down in the parking lot when I first signed in, so she wasn't gonna get the keys to that Escalade. Quite frankly, there was no escape.

The first officer who grabbed Monae had extra hairy facial features. That's what Monae deserved, a monster who would take her away. After all, she was a monster in disguise. The second officer was short, but his words were long. When he started reading Monae her rights right there on the floor, I knew they had solid evidence.

Monae's face reddened. I had never seen her defeated. Lisa had already instructed me to step back away from the window. All customers had been re-directed to another cash booth, so my view was perfect. I heard Monae speaking in a muffled voice, trying to charm her way out of the cuffs. She pointed my way, I guess tryna take me down with her.

I nodded, *no, no. I got you baby*!

She gazed at me like the shit was unbelievable to her. A devilish grin eased across my face. Shortly after, her face twisted into an evil scowl. It was almost as if she had just realized I set her up. My mind flashed back to all the demeaning things Monae had done to me. She went from being my lottery ticket, to being the person who would take me down in life.

"Bitch, you gon' pay!" she shouted to me.

I chuckled and pressed my back into the wall even more.

"You can't protect her," I heard her boast to the uglier officer. "She's done."

"That's enough," the officer warned. "Where you're going, she'll be far way from you."

Although she was five yards across the casino floor, her words pierced me still. I knew she was on her way to jail, but Monae had connections.

"You know you were involved!" she yelled back over her shoulder. "It'll all come out! Hopefully for you, you'll be locked up before I make bail! 'Cause I will," she laughed with confidence.

Lisa rubbed my shoulder blade in hopes of calming my nerves. Little did she know I was scared to death. But even in my fearful moment, I felt proud. Finally, I wasn't the one getting tricked.

22

Nadia

The next day seemed like the longest day of my life. With only two bags in the back of Monae's Escalade, I hit the road balling. My rims shone brightly all the way down Interstate 15. When I rolled down the window to toss out all Monae's personal shit in the glove compartment and around the cup holder, I laughed out loud. She was done.

I'd heard through the grapevine, she'd spent her first night in jail plotting on sending somebody to take me out. She'd called everybody she knew, trying to get next to me. Little did she know my bout with Vegas was done. L.A. bound was where I was headed. Somewhere in the Hollywood Hills where rich girls belonged.

Lisa assured me before I left work last night that Monae was done. She had collected over $25,000 from the MGM illegally, and another $ 45,000 from the other hotels. The bitch was on camera in the MGM, so there was no wiggling outta that one. For me, I knew leaving town as soon as possible was best for me, before they started probing and then telling me not to leave town. I was one up on their asses.

It's funny, cuz all my crew pegged me to be the naive one. Jewell, Tori, Day-Day, Monae, and even my parents. They all felt sorry for me in a strange kinda way. I was thought of as the one unable to get fast money, the one unable to think quick on my feet; the scared one. The naïve one. I started pressing the different CD tracks in the truck while shaking my head. They had me wrong. All wrong. I looked young and innocent, but now I'd become ruthless, vindictive, and no-nonsense.

I knew I would set Monae up the day we were all at the Monte Carlo Hotel. Surely, they'd all underestimated me. They were the stupid ones, thinking that I showed up cuz I wanted to make more money with them. Ha! I was just tryna stay in good with Monae to lure her back to the MGM, where I'd already informed my supervisors that Monae threatened me with a gun on numerous occasions. I told them she said she would kill me and my family if I didn't give her the cash when she presented her marker. They just needed the proof.

The best part of it all was when Monae picked me up with all that cash in the truck. That was one piece of the puzzle I never expected. On the real, it was a gift, a perk. Reggie had already been hipped to what was going down. So he knew not to give Monae the keys to her truck once we pulled into the parking lot. Instead, I waltzed into the parking lot after work and retrieved the keys from Reggie myself. He got a hefty tip, and thought a date with me was coming down the pipe soon. Wrong! I still wasn't doing blue collar workers.

My stock had just gone up tremendously. When I pulled out of the lot, and pulled over to count up the loot in Monae's black duffel bag, I nearly fainted. Just over a hundred grand sat neatly bundled inside. Monae's money plus what I'd managed to save from the marker scams had me sitting pretty.

It's what I always dreamed of. I vowed I would slow my roll a bit though. Being a rich girl didn't mean as much to me as it did before. Just think, Jewell was paid, spent most of her life chasing money, and now she's dead. Tori, got paid by any means necessary, now she's locked down. Monae, was a story in itself. She had multiple illegal dealings going on, and kept crazy cash. But look where it got her. Instead of spending my money, I would pay for college as a full time student. My degree was important. When my parents saw me again, I would finally be a college graduate. Hell maybe even a CPA.

The ringing phone startled me. But there was nobody I really needed to talk to. I even rolled down the window, ready to throw the shit out onto highway 15, just as I'd done with Monae's. I didn't even recognize the number. It said unknown, but I decided to take a shot anyway.

"Yeah," I answered apprehensively.

"Bitch I'm locked up and you not even tryna get me out!" Tori blasted loudly into my phone.

For the first second, I moved the phone away from my ear, contemplating whether or not to throw it out the window. The breeze from the evening air felt good. The temperature was about seventy-eight and the wind calmed my nerves.

"You 'posed to have my back! You my cousin! Fuck all 'dis other bullshit!" Tori shouted. "You gon' 'dis me, all 'cause I fucked yo' man!"

I remained silent and allowed her to rant and rave. Her voice was filled with anger, and mine stayed soundless. I really had nothing to say. Thoughts of her fucking Day-Day flashed through my mind, followed by her cascading around with Monae like I didn't exist.

"You gon' get me out, Nadia?"

"How can I?" I finally said.

"You would know if you had at least showed up at my arraignment or bond hearin'. You had me in here like some nobody!" She paused, I guessed waiting to see if I would say anything. "My bond is only $50,000. Go see a bail bondsman, pleaseeeeeeee, Nadia?" she begged. "I think you only gotta put up ten percent. I promise I'll make everythin' up to you. You all I got. Nobody else is comin' to get me."

"I'm broke," I announced, as bluntly as I could. "I'm moving out my place. Probably moving into a shelter."

"What the fuck!"

"Yep. That's what this life brings us, I guess. You made your bed. Now lie in it," I said, as hurtful as I could say it.

"Nadia, I swear. I'ma give yo' ass two days. You better be here to get me out 'dis mufucka! Call Jewell, she got some money left."

Her words hurt me to my heart. Jewell? I guess the news about her death didn't travel to the jail like everything else does. "Tori, Jewell is dead," I confessed sadly. "She was in a bad accident and didn't make it."

"What are you sayin'?"

"I just said it." I used a matter of fact tone with Tori cuz I still wasn't feeling her. However, I felt the appropriate thing to do was answer her questions about Jewell. After all, they were friends. I spent the next two minutes filling her in on the details. She listened intently. I didn't hear any crying, yet there was silence the entire time I talked.

"Did you get any money from her place?" she finally stated.

The nerve of Tori's unsympathetic-ass. That was it for me. "Tori, let's just say Jewell's mother has all her money. Hopefully, she has made peace with God. I know Jewell is in Heaven where she belongs, and doesn't care about her money anymore. What about you?" I questioned. "Have you asked for forgiveness for all you've done?"

"I already made peace wit' God, Nadia. 'Cause I swear if you don't get me out, I'ma have you killed. Cousin or not!"

For the first time in my life I wasn't even scared, knowing what her conniving-ass was capable of. "Tori, all I can say is every good hustler has his or her time. I guess your time is up. Jewell is dead, now consider me dead too."

She screamed so loud her voice went hoarse and started crackling. "Fuck…"

I pushed the end button and tossed the phone out the window, then pressed the gas pedal, increasing my speed to eighty mph. It felt good being in control, and being in the fast lane.

As the track switched on the CD changer, I finally came across a song that was perfect. When Tori originally mentioned the song to me, it meant nothing. Now I understood perfectly. I turned up on volume to ten and sang along.

Na na na na na, na na na na na
Na na na na na na na na na na na
If I was a rich girl, na na na na na na na na
See, I'd have all the money in the world,
If I was a wealthy girllllllllllllllllll

Meet Mirror Carter, a hood chick from Shady Grove Trailer Park who would die to forget her past, and bask in a more sophisticated lifestyle. Although Mirror gets a small taste of the glamorous life, her appetite for wealth continues to grow as she constantly searches for the next big money-maker. That is until she meets, Brice Tower, the handsome, and filthy rich owner of the Houston Rockets, and her meal ticket to the millionaire s club. Soon, chaos erupts and Mirror's fairy-tale life turns into a nightmare when she finds out Brice's best kept secret. As Mirror vows to hold on to her spot at the top, Brice struggles to keep her away. When the game of fatal attraction turns hood, Mirror's past is exposed and all hell breaks lose.

In Stores November '08

The Brooklyn Streets Have Never Been Hotter!!!

COMING DECEMBER '08

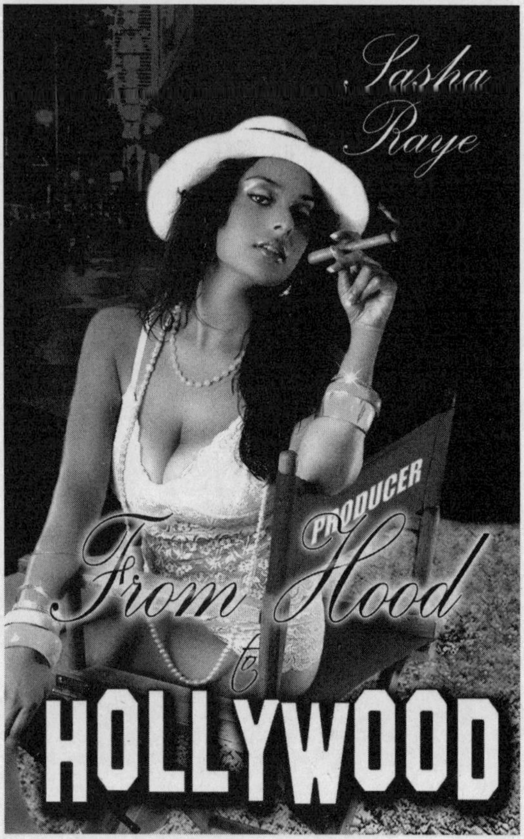

Every female raised in Harlem, develops glamorous goals and big dreams, but Demi Anderson tops the cake. Her dreams of becoming an A-list actress sets her above the rest, and opens the door for a fruitful future. Will she make it to the top, or lose everything?

Find Out February '09

Have you ever wondered how truthful your mate really is? Chanel Martinez, a five foot nine bombshell with a devastating secret will trick the average playa on the spot. Between credit card scams, wild nights on the town, and her over the top lifestyle, no ordinary man can handle a real relationship with her. In comes Samuel, a Jamaican baller destined to sweep Chanel off her feet. Their short-term romance turns into a love affair that Chanel all of a sudden can't resist. Unfortunately for her, Samuel has something to hide of his own. Imagine...two lovers, two mysterious secrets, and the law...all wrapped up into one novel. Makes you stop and think- be careful who you share your bed with.

IN STORES NOW!!

ORDER FORM

MAIL TO:
PO Box 423
Brandywine, MD 20613
301-362-6508

FAX TO:
301-579-9913

Ship to:	
Address:	
City & State:	Zip:
Attention:	

Date:	
Phone:	
E-mail:	

Make all checks and money orders payable to: **Life Changing Books**

Qty.	ISBN	Title	Release Date	Price
	0-9741394-0-8	A Life To Remember by Azarel	Aug-03	$ 15.00
	0-9741394-1-6	Double Life by Tyrone Wallace	Nov-04	$ 15.00
	0-9741394-5-9	Nothin Personal by Tyrone Wallace	Jul-06	$ 15.00
	0-9741394-2-4	Bruised by Azarel	Jul-05	$ 15.00
	0-9741394-7-5	Bruised 2: The Ultimate Revenge by Azarel	Oct-06	$ 15.00
	0-9741394-3-2	Secrets of a Housewife by J. Tremble	Feb-06	$ 15.00
	0-9724003-5-4	I Shoulda Seen It Comin by Danette Majette	Jan-06	$ 15.00
	0-9741394-4-0	The Take Over by Tonya Ridley	Apr-06	$ 15.00
	0-9741394-6-7	The Millionaire Mistress by Tiphani	Nov-06	$ 15.00
	1-934230-99-5	More Secrets More Lies by J. Tremble	Feb-07	$ 15.00
	1-934230-98-7	Young Assassin by Mike G.	Mar-07	$ 15.00
	1-934230-95-2	A Private Affair by Mike Warren	May-07	$ 15.00
	1-934230-94-4	All That Glitters by Ericka M. Williams	Jul-07	$ 15.00
	1-934230-93-6	Deep by Danette Majette	Jul-07	$ 15.00
	1-934230-96-0	Flexin & Sexin by K'wan, Anna J. & Others	Jun-07	$ 15.00
	1-934230-92-8	Talk of the Town by Tonya Ridley	Jul-07	$ 15.00
	1-934230-89-8	Still a Mistress by Tiphani	Nov-07	$ 15.00
	1-934230-91-X	Daddy's House by Azarel	Nov-07	$ 15.00
	1-934230-87-1-	Reign of a Hustler by Nissa A. Showell	Jan-08	$ 15.00
	1-934230-86-3	Something He Can Feel by Marissa Montelih	Feb-08	$ 15.00
	1-934230-88-X	Naughty Little Angel by J. Tremble	Feb-08	$ 15.00
	1-93423084-8	In Those Jeans by Chantel Jolie	Jun-08	$15.00
	1-93423088-5	Marked by Capone	Jul-08	$15.00
			Total for Books	$

*** Prison Orders- Please allow up to three (3) weeks for delivery.**

Shipping Charges (add $4.25 for 1-4 books*) $

Total Enclosed (add lines) $

For credit card orders and orders over 25 books, please contact us at orders@lifechaningbooks.net (Cheaper rates for COD orders)

***Shipping and Handling of 5-10 books is $6.25, please contact us if your order is more than 10 books. (301)362-6508**